ANTONIO TABUCCHI

Message from the Shadows

Stories

Translated from the Italian by Anne Milano Appel, Martha Cooley,

Frances Frenaye, Elizabeth Harris, Tim Parks,

Antonio Romani, and Janice M. Thresher

First Archipelago Books Edition, 2019

Archipelago Books
232 3rd Street #A111
Brooklyn, NY 11215
www.archipelagobooks.org

Library of Congress Cataloging-in-Publication Data available upon request

Distributed by Penguin Random House
www.penguinrandomhouse.com

Cover art: Mário Cesariny de Vasconcelos

This book was made possible by the New York State Council on the Arts with the support of
Governor Andrew M. Cuomo and the New York State Legislature.

Archipelago Books also gratefully acknowledges the generous support of
the New York City Department of Cultural Affairs, Lannan Foundation, the
Nimick Forbesway Foundation, and the Carl Lesnor Family Foundation.

PRINTED IN THE USA

Message from
the Shadows

Contents

The Reversal Game

Le puéril revers des choses.
– Lautréamont

When Maria do Carmo Meneses de Sequeira died, I was looking at
Velásquez's *Las Meninas* in the Prado Museum. It was noon, July, and I
didn't know she was dying. I stood looking at that painting until a quarter
past twelve, then I left slowly, trying to carry away in my memory the expression of the figure in the background, and I remember recalling Maria do
Carmo's words: the key to the painting is in that figure in the background
– it's a reversal game. I crossed the garden and took a bus to Puerta del Sol,
had lunch at the hotel, a nice cold gazpacho and some fruit, and to escape
the midday heat I went to lie down in the shadows of my room. The telephone woke me around five, or maybe it didn't wake me, I found myself in
a strange half-sleep, the city traffic humming outside, the air conditioner

humming in my room, though in my consciousness this was a little blue tugboat chugging through the mouth of the Tagus at twilight, while Maria do Carmo and I watched. You have a call from Lisbon, the telephone operator said on the line, then I heard the electric crackling of the switch and a man's voice, low and neutral, asking me my name, saying: this is Nuno Meneses de Sequeira, Maria do Carmo died at noon, the funeral will be tomorrow evening at five, I'm calling at her direct request. There was a click and I said: hello hello. They've hung up, sir, the operator said, you've been disconnected. I took the midnight Lusitania Express. I had only a small suitcase with the barest necessities, and I asked the concierge to hold my room for two days. The station was almost deserted at that hour. I hadn't reserved a berth and the conductor sent me to the back of the train, to a compartment with only one other passenger, a snoring, fat gentleman. I resigned myself to a sleepless night, but to my surprise, slept soundly until the outskirts of Talevera de la Raina. Then I lay motionless, awake, staring out the dark window at the empty darkness of Estremadura. I had many hours to think about Maria do Carmo.

2

Saudade isn't a word, Maria do Carmo used to say, it's a category of the spirit, that only the Portuguese are able to feel, because they have this word in order to say they have it. A great poet said this. And then she'd start talking about Fernando Pessoa. I'd come to pick her up at her home on Rua das Chagas around six in the evening. She would be waiting for me behind a window. When she saw me turn onto Largo de Camões, she'd open the heavy front door and we would go down toward the port, wandering along Rua dos Fanqueiros and Rua dos Douradores. Let's follow a Fernandian itinerary, she'd say, these were the haunts of Bernardo Soares, assistant bookkeeper for the city of Lisbon, semi-heteronomous by definition, this was where he practiced his metaphysics, right here in these barbershops. At that hour, Baixa was crowded with hurrying, shouting people, the navigation companies and commercial businesses were closing up their offices, and long lines formed at the tram stops, you could hear the cries of the shoeshine boys and newspaper vendors. We'd slip into the confusion of Rua da Prata, cross Rua da Conceição, and walk down toward the Terreiro do Paço, white and melancholic, where the first ferries crowded with commuters were sailing for the opposite bank of the Tagus. We're already in an Álvaro de Campos zone, Maria do Carmo would say, in just a few streets we've passed from one heteronym to another.

At that hour, the Lisbon light was white by the river and pink on the hills, the eighteenth-century buildings looked like an oleograph, and the Tagus was furrowed with boats. We'd walk on toward the first piers, those piers where Alvaro de Campos went to wait for no one, Maria do Carmo would say, and she'd recite some lines from the *Ode Marítima*, the passage where the outline of a small steamer shows on the horizon and Campos feels a flywheel begin to revolve in his chest. Dusk was falling on the city, the first lights were going on, the Tagus shone with iridescent reflections. There was a great sadness in Maria do Carmo's eyes. Maybe you're too young to understand, I wouldn't have at your age, I wouldn't have imagined that life was like a childhood game I once played in Buenos Aires. Pessoa's a genius because he understood the flipping of things, of the real and the imagined, his poetry is a *juego del revés*.

<h2 style="text-align:center">3</h2>

The train had stopped, you could see the lights of the border town from the window, my travel companion had the surprised, uneasy expression of someone who'd been jarred awake by the light, the policeman carefully thumbed through my passport, you come to our country quite a bit, he said, what's so interesting here? Baroque poetry, I answered. What'd you say? he murmured. A lady, I said, a lady with a strange name, Violante do Céu. A pretty lady? he asked slyly. Could be, I said, she's been dead three centuries and always lived in a convent — a nun. He shook his head and smoothed his mustache in a knowing manner, stamped my visa, and handed me my passport. You Italians always love to kid, he said, you like Totò? A lot, I said, how about you? I've seen all his movies, he said, I like him more than Alberto Sordi.

Our compartment was the last to be checked. The door closed with a thud. A few seconds later someone on the platform waved a lantern and the train started off. The lights went out again, only a pale-blue lamp remained, it was the middle of the night, I was entering Portugal as I had so many times before in my life. Maria do Carmo was dead, I felt an odd sensation, as though I were looking down from above at another me who, one July night, inside a compartment of a semi-dark train, was entering a foreign country to go and see a woman that he knew well and who was dead. I'd never felt this sensation before and it occurred to me that this had something to do with its reverse.

4

The game went like this, Maria do Carmo would say, we formed a circle, four or five children, we counted off, and the one whose turn it was went into the middle, he'd pick anyone he pleased and throw out a word, any word, *mariposa*, for instance, and the one chosen had to immediately say its reverse – not thinking it over – because the other was counting – one two three four five – and at five he won, but if you managed to say *asopiram* in time, then you were king of the game, and you went into the middle and threw your word out at whomever you pleased.

As we walked up to the city, Maria do Carmo would tell me about her childhood in Buenos Aires as a daughter of exiles, and I'd imagine a court-yard outside the city, full of children, sad, impoverished holidays, it was full of Italians, she'd say, my father had an old gramophone with a horn, and he'd brought some *fado* records from Portugal, it was 1939, the radio was telling us Franco's forces had taken Madrid, and my father cried and played records, that's how I remember his last months, him in his pajamas, sitting in his armchair, silently crying, listening to the *fados* of Hilário and Tomás Alcaide, and I would escape to the courtyard and play the *juego del revés*.

Night had fallen. The Terreiro do Paço was almost deserted, the bronze horseman, green from the salty air, seemed absurd, let's get something to eat in Alfama, Maria do Carmo would say, *arroz de cabidela*, maybe, a Sephardic dish, the Jews don't wring a chicken's neck, they lop its head off and use the blood for the rice, I know a dive that makes it like no place else, it's five minutes from here. And a yellow tram would go by, slow, rattling, full of tired faces. I know what you're thinking, she'd say, why did I marry my husband, why do I live in that absurd mansion, why am I here playing the countess, when he arrived in Buenos Aires he was a polite, elegant officer, and I was just a girl, poor and melancholic, I couldn't bear it anymore, staring out the window at that courtyard, and he took me away from all that grayness, from that house with its dim lights and the radio on at dinner – I can't leave him – in spite of everything, I can't forget.

5

My travel companion asked if he might have the pleasure of inviting me for a coffee. He was an overly polite, jovial Spaniard who often traveled on that line. In the dining car we chatted pleasantly, exchanged formal impressions, riddled with clichés. The Portuguese have good coffee, he said, but this doesn't help them much, or so it would seem, they're so melancholic, they lack *salero*, wouldn't you say? I said that perhaps they'd replaced it with *saudade*, and he agreed, though he preferred *salero*. We only have one life to live, he said, one must know how to live it, dear sir. I didn't ask him how he managed this himself, and we moved to something else – sports, I think – he adored skiing, the mountains, from this perspective, Portugal was truly impossible to stay in for too long. I objected that there were mountains here, too, oh, the Serra da Estrela! he answered, imitation mountains, to reach two thousand meters, you need to put up an antenna. It's a maritime country, I said, a country of people who plunge into the ocean, they've given the world dignified, urbane madmen, slave-traders, and homesick poets. By the way, he said, what's the name of that poet you mentioned tonight? Soror Vilente do Céu, I said, her name would be splendid in Spanish too, Madre Violante del Cielo, a great Baroque poetess, she spent her life exalting her desire for a world she renounced. She can't be better than Góngora, right? he asked, worried. Different, I said, with less *salero* and more *saudade*, of course.

6

While the *arroz de cabidela* tasted refined, it looked revolting. It was served on a large terracotta tray with a wooden spoon, the boiled blood and wine forming a thick, brownish sauce; marble tables stood between a row of barrels and a zinc bar dominated by portly Mr. Tavares, at midnight a gaunt *fado* singer arrived, along with an old man carrying a viola and a distinguished gentleman carrying a guitar, the singer sang ancient *fados*, faintly, languidly, and Mrs. Tavares turned out the lights and lit candles on shelves, the customers there for dinner had already left, and only the regulars remained, the place filled up with smoke; after every finale came subdued, solemn applause, some voices called out *Amor é agua que corre, Travessa da Palma*, Maria do Carmo was pale, or maybe it was the candlelight, or maybe she was drunk, she had a fixed stare and enlarged pupils, and the candlelight danced in her eyes, she seemed more beautiful than usual, she lit a cigarette with a dreamy expression, all right, enough now, she'd say, let's go. *Saudade*, yes, but in small doses, or it'll give you indigestion. The Alfama district was half-empty, we stopped there at the Miradouro de Santa Luzia, by a pergola thick with bougainvillea, and leaned over the rail looking at the lights on the Tagus. Maria do Carmo recited "Lisbon Revisited" by Álvaro de Campos, a poem with a person standing at the same window from his childhood, but he's no longer the same person and it's no longer the same window, because men and things are changed by time; we started down toward my hotel, she took my hand and said: listen, who knows what we are or where we are or why we are, listen, let's live life like a *revés* – take tonight – you must think that you're me holding you tight and I'll think I'm you holding me tight.

7

Anyway, my travel companion said, it's not like I love Góngora, I don't understand him – you need the right vocabulary – besides, I'm not cut out for poetry, I prefer *el cuento*, Blasco Ibàñez, for instance, do you like Blasco Ibàñez? A bit, I said, maybe the short story's not my genre. Who, then – how about Pérez Galdós? Yes, I said, now we're getting somewhere. The waiter, with a sleepy expression, brought us coffee on a shining tray, I'm making an exception for you gentlemen because the dining car is closed, that'll be twenty escudos. In spite of everything, said my travel companion, the Portuguese are kind. Why in spite of everything, I said, they *are* kind – let's be fair.

We were going past construction sites and factories, it wasn't full daylight yet. They wanted to be on Greenwich time, but in reality, according to the sun, it's an hour earlier – say, have you ever seen a Portuguese bullfight? – they don't kill the bull, you know, the toreador dances around it for half an hour, then makes a symbolic sword thrust, then in walks a herd of cows wearing cowbells, the bull joins the herd and everyone goes home, olé, now does that sound like a bullfight to you? Maybe a more elegant version of one, I said, killing doesn't always mean slaughter, sometimes it only takes a gesture. Come on, he said, the battle between man and bull has to be mortal, otherwise it's just silly playacting. But all ceremonies are a stylization, I objected, this one preserves only the shell, the gesture, which seems more noble, more abstract. My travel companion seemed to be contemplating. Well, perhaps, he said, sounding skeptical, ah, look, we're outside Lisbon, we should go back to the compartment and get our luggage ready.

8

It's rather delicate, we've been afraid to ask you, we've discussed it, you might find it somewhat inconvenient, I mean, the worst that might happen is they'll refuse your entrance visa at the border, listen, we don't want to keep anything back, Jorge was going to be the courier, he's the only one with a UN passport, you know he's in Winnipeg now, he teaches at a Canadian university, we still haven't figured out how to replace him. Nine at night, Piazza Navona, on a bench. I looked at him, maybe I seemed confused, I didn't know what to think. I felt slightly embarrassed, ill at ease, like talking with someone you've known a long time who suddenly reveals something unexpected.

We don't want to involve you, it would have to be something exceptional, believe me, we feel terrible about having to ask, and listen, even if you say no, it won't affect our friendship, so, just think about it, we don't need an answer right away, just know you'd really be helping us out. We went for a gelato at a café on the piazza, we chose a small, outdoor table, at a distance from others. Francisco looked tense, maybe he was embarrassed, too: he knew this was something that even if I refused, I wouldn't be able to forget about either, no, maybe he was afraid I might regret it. We ordered two coffee granitas. We were quiet a long while, slowly sipping our frozen drinks. There are five letters, Francisco said, and a sum of money for the families of the two writers arrested last month. He told me their names and waited for me to say something. I stayed quiet and sipped my water. I don't think I need to tell you that the money's clean, it's from three democratic parties in Italy we contacted, who want to demonstrate their solidarity, if you think it's fitting, I can arrange a meeting for you with representatives of the parties in question, they'll confirm things. I said I didn't think it was fitting, we paid, and walked around the piazza. All right, I said, I'll leave in three days. He shook my hand briskly and thanked me, now remember what you have to do, it's simple, he wrote a number on a ticket, when you arrive in Lisbon, telephone this number, and if a man answers, hang up, and keep trying until you get a woman on the phone, then you have to say: a new translation of Fernando Pessoa has come out. She will tell you how to meet, she's the one who keeps the exiles in Rome in touch with their families back home.

9

It was very easy, just like Francisco predicted. At the border, they didn't even make me open my suitcase. In Lisbon, I stayed at a place behind the Trindade Theater and a few steps from the national library, a small hotel with a chatty, cordial concierge from the Algarve. On my first try, a woman answered the phone and I said: good evening, I'm Italian, I wanted to inform you of a new translation of Fernando Pessoa that might interest you. Let's meet in half an hour at Bertrand's Bookstore, she answered, in the periodical room, I'm in my forties, my hair's dark, and I'll be wearing a yellow dress.

10

Nuno Meneses de Sequeira received me at two o'clock in the afternoon. When I telephoned that morning, a male servant answered, the count is resting, he cannot receive you this morning, come by at two this afternoon. But where does the lady lie? I couldn't say, sir, my apologies, please come at two this afternoon. I got a room at my usual little hotel behind the Trindade Theater, took a shower, and changed clothes. We haven't seen you for a while, said the friendly concierge from the Algarve. Five months since the end of February, I said. And do you still work for libraries? he asked. That would seem to be my fate, I answered.

Largo de Camões was flooded with sunlight, in the small square, there were pigeons perched on the poet's head, retirees on benches, old men, dignified and sad, a soldier and a serving girl, a melancholy Sunday. Rua das Chagas was deserted, now and then, an empty taxi drove past, there wasn't enough of a sea breeze to cut the thick, damp heat. I stopped in a café to try and cool off a little, it was secluded and dirty, the blades of an enormous ceiling fan whirred uselessly, the owner was nodding off behind the counter, I asked for a *sumo* with ice, and he waved the flies away with a rag and wearily opened the refrigerator. I hadn't eaten and wasn't hungry. I sat down at a table, lit a cigarette, and waited for the time to approach.

11

Nuno Meneses de Sequeira received me in a Baroque salon with stuccos all over the ceiling and two enormous, chewed-up tapestries on the walls. He was dressed in black, his face shiny, his bald skull glistening, and he sat in a crimson velvet armchair; when I came in, he rose, bowed his head slightly, and invited me to sit on a small couch beneath the window. The shutters were closed and the room was filled with the oppressive, stagnant odor of old upholstery. How did she die? I asked. She had a terrible disease, he said, didn't I know? I shook my head. What sort of disease? Nuno Meneses de Sequeira clasped his hands in his lap. A terrible disease, he said. She called me in Madrid two weeks ago, and she didn't say anything about it, not even a hint, did she already know? She was already terribly ill, and was well aware. Why didn't she say anything? Perhaps she didn't think it was fitting, said Nuno Meneses de Sequeira, I'd be grateful if you didn't come to the funeral, it's strictly private. I didn't intend to, I reassured him. I am grateful, he said faintly.

The silence in the room grew tangible, uncomfortable. May I see her, I asked. Nuno Meneses de Sequeira stared at me a while, ironically, I thought. That's not possible, he said, she's at the Cuf Clinic, that's where she died, and then the doctor ordered a closed casket, it couldn't be left open, given her condition.

I thought about leaving, and wondered why he'd called me, even if Maria do Carmo had wanted it, what the point was of having me come to Lisbon, I was missing something, or maybe there was nothing strange here, just a painful situation that was pointless to prolong. But Nuno Meneses de Sequeira hadn't finished talking, he gripped the arms of his chair like he was about to stand, his eyes were wet, his expression strained, ugly, or perhaps it was the nervous tension he had to be feeling. You never understood her, sir, he said, you're too young, far too young to understand Maria do Carmo. And you were far too old, I wanted to say but didn't. You work in philology, hah! he snorted, your life is libraries, you couldn't possibly understand a woman like that. Tell me what you mean, I told him. Nuno Meneses de Sequeira stood up, went to the window, opened the shutters slightly. I would like to dispel any illusion, he said, that you actually knew Maria do Carmo. You only knew a fictional Maria do Carmo. Tell me what you mean, I repeated. Nuno Meneses de Sequeira smiled, very well, I can just imagine what Maria do Carmo must have told you, a tear-jerker of a story, her unhappy childhood in New York, her republican father who died a hero in the Spanish Civil War, listen closely, dear sir, I've never been to New York in my life, Maria do Carmo's the daughter of great landowners, she had a gilded childhood, fifteen years ago, when I met her, she was twenty-seven and the most courted woman in Lisbon, I was just returning from a diplomatic mission in Spain, and what we had in common was our love of country. He paused, as though to add weight to his words. Our love of country, he said again, I'm not sure if I'm making myself clear. It depends how you're using the word. Nuno Meneses de Sequeira adjusted his tie, pulled a handkerchief from his pocket, and took on a look of bored impatience. Listen closely, Maria do Carmo very much liked playing a game and played it her entire life, we always played it by mutual consent. I held up my hand, as if to stop him, but he went on: she must have reached her reverse. In a distant room came the chime of a pendulum clock. Unless you reached the reverse of her reverse, I said.

Nuno Meneses de Sequeira smiled again, how beautiful, he said, a phrase that could easily come from Maria do Carmo herself, it's proper that you'd surmise this, though believe me, it is a presumption on your part. A vein of contempt ran through his quiet voice. I stayed silent, my eyes lowered, focused on the carpet, a deep blue Arraiolos carpet with gray peacocks. I'm very sorry that you're forcing me to be more frank, Nuno Meneses de Sequeira went on, I assume you like Pessoa. Very much, I admitted. Then perhaps you're aware of his translations from abroad. What do you mean? I asked. Oh, not much, he said, just this: that Maria do Carmo received many translations from abroad, do you understand me? No, I said, I don't understand you. Let's just say you don't want to understand me, Nuno Meneses de Sequeira corrected me, that you'd rather not understand me, and I understand that you'd rather not understand me: reality's an unpleasant thing – you prefer dreams – please don't force me to go into detail, details are always so vulgar, let's just stick to the concept.

From the window, a siren sounded, perhaps a ship entering the port, and I suddenly longed to be a passenger onboard that ship, to enter the port of an unknown city called Lisbon and to have to telephone an unknown woman and tell her that a new translation of Fernando Pessoa had come out, and that woman's name was Maria do Carmo, and she'd be at Bertrand's Bookstore in a yellow dress, and she loved the *fado* and Sephardic food, and I knew all this already, but that passenger who was me and staring at Lisbon from the deck of a ship didn't know this yet, and for him, everything would be new and identical. And this was *saudade*, Maria do Carmo was right: it wasn't a word, it was a category of the spirit. In a way, this, too, was its reverse.

Nuno Meneses de Sequeira observed me in silence, looking calm and satisfied. Today, I said, is the first day of Maria do Carmo's new life, let's at least call a truce. He gave an imperceptible nod as if in assent, as if to say, that's just want I wanted to propose myself, and then I said, I believe, then, we have nothing further to say, he rang a bell and a servant appeared in a loose striped jacket, Domingos, this gentleman is just leaving, the servant stepped aside from the door for me, ah, one moment, said Nuno Meneses de Sequeira, Maria do Carmo left this for you. He held out a letter that he'd taken from a silver tray on a table beside his chair, I slipped that letter into my pocket; when I'd reached the door he said, I feel sorry for you, and I answered, the feeling is mutual, though probably with a different nuance. I went down the stone stairs, into the afternoon light of Lisbon, and hailed a passing taxi.

12

I opened the letter at the hotel. On a sheet of white paper was written, all in capital letters and with no accents, the word, SEVER. I automatically reversed it in my mind and then below, also in capital letters with no accents, I wrote in pencil: REVES. I considered that ambiguous word a moment that could be Spanish or French, with two utterly different meanings. I realized I had no desire to return to Madrid, I'd send a check from Italy and write to the Madrid hotel to have my luggage delivered, I phoned the front desk and asked the concierge to find a travel agency, that I needed a plane ticket for tomorrow, it didn't matter which airline, the first available flight. What, you're leaving already? said the concierge, you've never stayed such a short while. What time is it? I asked. According to my watch, it's a quarter past four, sir. Well, then wake me for dinner, I said, around nine. I undressed calmly, pulled down the blinds, again, a distant siren sounded, muffled by the pillow beneath my cheek.

Perhaps Maria do Carmo had finally reached her reverse. I hoped it was as she wanted, and I thought that perhaps the Spanish word and the French word might coincide at a single point. Maybe the vanishing point of a perspective, like when you trace the perspective lines in a painting, and at that moment the siren sounded once more, the ship docked, and I slowly walked down the gangway and onto the piers, the port was completely deserted, the piers were perspective lines verging toward the vanishing point of a painting, and the painting was *Las Meninas* by Velásquez, and the pier lines converged on the background figure, and her enigmatic, melancholy expression was imprinted on my mind: and how funny, that figure was Maria do Carmo with her yellow dress, and I was telling her: I understand that expression of yours, because you see the reverse of the painting, what on earth do you see from that side? — tell me, wait for me, let me come, too, I'm coming now to see. And I set off for that point. And at that moment, I found myself in a different dream.

Translated by Janice M. Thresher

Clouds

– You stay here in the shade all day, said the young girl, don't you like going in the water?

The man gave a vague nod that could have meant yes or no, but said nothing.

– Can I use *tu* with you? asked the girl.

– If I'm not mistaken, you just did, the man said, and smiled.

– In my class we also use *tu* with adults, said the girl, some teachers allow it, but my parents won't let me, they say it's impolite, and *lei*, sir, what do you think?

– I think they're right, responded the man, but you can use *tu* with me, I won't tell anybody.

– Don't you like going in the water? she asked. I think it's special.

– Special? the man repeated.

– My teacher told us we can't use awesome for everything, that sometimes we might say special, I was about to say awesome, for me going in the water at this beach is special.

– Ah, said the man, I agree, it seems awesome to me too, even special.

– Sunbathing's awesome too, the young girl went on, in the first few days I had to use the SPF forty cream, then I went to twenty, and now I can use the golden bronzing cream, the one that makes your skin sparkle like it has little gold specks all over it, see? But, sir, why are you so white? You came here a week ago and you're always under the beach umbrella, don't you like the sun at all?

– I think it's awesome, said the man, I swear, to me sunbathing is awesome.

– Are you afraid of getting sunburned, sir? asked the young girl.

– And what do you think? answered the man.

– I think you're afraid of burning, sir, though if a person doesn't start out slowly, he'll never get tan.

– That's true, the man confirmed, it seems logical to me, though do you think it's mandatory to get tan?

The girl mulled this over.

– Not entirely mandatory, nothing is mandatory except for mandatory things, but if someone comes to the beach, doesn't go in the water, and doesn't get tan, then why is he coming to the beach?

– You know what? said the man, you're a logical girl, you have a gift for logic, and that's awesome, to me the world today has lost its logic, it's a real pleasure to meet a logical girl, may I have the pleasure of making your acquaintance? What's your name?

– My name is Isabella, though my close friends call me Isabèl, but with the accent on the e, not like the Italians who say Ìsabel, with the accent on the i.

– Why's that, you're not Italian? asked the man.

– Of course I'm Italian, she objected, totally Italian, but I care about the name my friends give me, because on television they always say Mànuel or Sebàstian, I am totally Italian like you and maybe even more than you, sir, but I like languages, and I also know the Mameli anthem by heart, this year the president of the republic came to visit our school and talked with us about the importance of the Mameli anthem, which is our Italian identity, it took so long to unify our country, for instance that political guy who wants to abolish the Mameli anthem, I don't like him.

The man didn't say anything, he was squinting, the light was intense and the blue of the sea and the sky merged, swallowing the horizon line.

– Perhaps, sir, you didn't get who I'm referring to, said the girl, breaking the silence.

The man didn't speak, he kept his eyelids half closed, the young girl seemed to hesitate, drawing squiggles in the sand with her finger.

– I hope you're not in his party, sir, she went on, as though encouraging herself, at home I was taught that one must always respect others' opinions, but that guy's opinion, I don't like it, am I being clear?

– Perfectly, said the man, one must respect others' opinions yet not disrespect one's own, above all not disrespect one's own, and why don't you like this guy?

– Oh, well . . . Isabella seemed to hesitate. Apart from the fact that when he talks on television, he gets some white foam at the corners of his mouth, but this I could forget, the main thing is he swears a lot, I heard him with my own ears, and if he swears, I wonder why they yell at me when I swear, but luckily the president of the republic is more important than him, otherwise he wouldn't be president of the republic, and he explained to us that we ought to respect the Mameli anthem and sing it like the national team does at the world championship, with our hands on our hearts, at school we sang it together with the president, we read the copies our teacher gave us, but he didn't read, he knew it by heart, I think that's awesome, don't you agree, sir?

– Pretty special, confirmed the man. He dug into the bag he kept next to his beach chair, took out a glass bottle, and put a white pill in his mouth.

– Am I talking too much? she asked, at home they say I talk too much and might annoy people, am I annoying you, sir?

– Not at all, answered the man, what you're saying is even special, please go on.

– And then the president gave us a history lesson, since as you know, sir, we don't study modern history at school, in the last year of junior high the really good teachers get us up to World War One, otherwise we don't make it past Garibaldi and the unification of Italy, but we learned a ton of modern things, because our teacher's been great, but the credit should go to the president, because he's the one who gave the input.

– Who gave the what? asked the man.

– That's what they say, explained Isabella, it's a new word, it means someone starts and drags the others along with him, if you want, sir, I'll repeat what I've learned, really a ton of things that not many people know, d'you want to know them?

The man didn't answer, kept his eyes closed, and was completely still.

– Did you fall asleep, sir? Isabella's tone was shy, as though disappointed.

– I'm sorry, sir, perhaps I chattered so much I made you fall asleep, it's also why my parents didn't want to buy me a cell phone, they claim they'd have to pay an astronomical bill because I talk so much, you know, in our house we can't afford anything extra, my father is an architect but he works for the municipality, and when you work for the municipality...

– Your father's a lucky man, said the man, his eyes still closed.

Now he spoke in a low voice, almost a whisper.

– Be that as it may, he continued, the profession of building houses is beautiful, much better than the profession of destroying them.

Isabella gave a little shriek of surprise.

– My god, she exclaimed, there's a profession of destroying houses? I didn't know that, they don't teach that at school.

– Well, said the man, it's not that it's really a profession, you can also learn it in theory, like at a military academy, but then moments arrive when a certain knowledge has to be put into practice, and when all's said and done that's the goal, to destroy buildings.

– And you, sir, how do you know this? asked Isabella.

– I know it because I'm a soldier, answered the man, or rather I was, now I'm retired, let's put it that way.

– So, *you* destroyed buildings, sir?

– What happened to *tu*? the man replied.

Isabella didn't answer right away.

– The thing is, I'm naturally shy even if I don't seem so because I talk too much, I asked you, sir, if you destroyed houses once too.

– Not personally, no, said the man, and neither did my soldiers, to be honest, mine was a war mission for peacekeeping, it's kind of complicated to explain, especially on a day like this, but, Isabèl, I'd like to tell you one thing that maybe they didn't tell you at school, in the end the story can be summed up like this: there are men like your father whose profession is to build houses, and men of my profession who destroy them, and things go on like this for centuries, some build houses and others destroy them, build, destroy, build, destroy, it's a little boring, don't you think?

– Very boring, answered Isabella, really very boring, imagine if there weren't ideals, fortunately there are ideals.

– Sure, confirmed the man, fortunately in history there are ideals, who told you this, the president or your teacher?

Isabella seemed to mull this over.

– Now I'm not sure who told me.

– Perhaps the president gave the input, said the man, and what can you tell me about ideals?

– They are all respectable if one believes in them, answered Isabella, for example the patriotic ideal, then maybe someone makes a mistake because he's young, but if his intentions are good, the ideal is valid.

– Ah, said the man, this is something I need to think about, but it doesn't seem the right day for it, today is so hot and the sea looks so inviting.

– Then get in the water, she prodded.

– I don't really feel like it, responded the man.

– That's because you aren't motivated, I think your problem is stress, you can't imagine the negative effect of stress on our spirit, I read it in a book my mother keeps on her bedside table, would you like me to get you something at the hotel bar, something for stress? As long as it's not a Coke, that I wouldn't get.

— This you'll have to explain, you really must, said the man.

— Because Coke and McDonald's are the ruin of mankind, said Isabella, everybody knows it, at my school even the janitors know it.

The man dug into his bag and took another pill.

— You sure take a lot of stuff, exclaimed Isabella.

— I have an hourly schedule, said the man, my prescription calls for it.

— All these pills can't be good for you, she stated with conviction, Italians take a ton of pills, they said that on television, what we should be doing instead is tuning our spirit to the positive forces in the universe, that's why we should avoid certain foods and drinks, because they carry negative energy, they aren't natural, am I being clear?

— Isabèl, can I tell you something in confidence?

The man wiped his forehead with a handkerchief. He was sweating.

— Coke and McDonald's never took anybody to Auschwitz, to those extermination camps you must have learned about at school, but ideals did, have you ever thought of that, Isabèl?

— But those were Nazis, objected Isabella, horrible people.

– I totally agree, said the man, the Nazis were truly horrible people, but they too had an ideal and went to war to impose it, from our point of view it was a perverted ideal, though for them it wasn't, they had great faith in that ideal, you have to be careful with ideals, isn't that true, Isabèl?

– I need to think about it, answered the girl, maybe I'll do it at lunch, it's twelve thirty, before long they'll serve lunch, you're not coming?

– Maybe not, said the man, today I don't have much of an appetite.

– Excuse me for repeating this, but in my opinion you take too much medicine, you're doing the same as all the Italians who take too many pills.

– So are you Italian or not? the man repeated.

– You already asked me that and I already answered, replied Isabella, irritated, I'm totally Italian, maybe even more than you, anyway if you don't come to lunch you'll be missing out, today there's a buffet lunch at the hotel and after that Croatian stuff they've been giving us, they're finally going to serve *fettuccine all'arrabbiata*, actually on the menu it says *fetucine all'arrabbiata*, anyway it should be ours, sometimes when you're abroad you have to forgive spelling mistakes, but sorry, why do you take so many pills, you aren't a deviant like those guys who go to discotheques, are you?

The man didn't answer.

– Come on, tell me, insisted Isabella, I won't tell anybody.

– I'll be sincere, said the man, I'm not a discotheque deviant, a doctor prescribed them to me, they are legal pills, they just make me less hungry, is all.

– They make you throw up too, said Isabella, I realized that, yesterday you came for lunch and at a certain point you got up and ran to the bathroom and when you came back you were white as a corpse, I bet you went to throw up.

– You're right on target, said the man, I really did go and throw up, that's the pills.

– So why take them? Don't take them, she concluded.

– That would be logical, the thing is, on the one hand they're good for me, but on the other they're bad, maybe pills are a bit like ideals, it depends who you force to swallow them, I don't push them on anyone else, I'm not hurting anybody.

The girl kept making squiggles in the sand.

– I don't understand, she said, sometimes it's hard to understand you adults.

– We adults are stupid, said the man, we're often stupid, however, sometimes you wind up having to take pills regardless of whether you're Italian or not, but you, Isabèl, since you say you're totally Italian, will you tell me where you were born? Look, it's not fundamental, I for instance was born in a country that's no longer on any maps since they call it something else now, but I'm Italian, to the point where I am, or rather I was, a captain in the

Italian army, and to be a captain in the Italian army you can't be a foreigner, does that seem logical to you?

Isabel nodded.

– And where were you born? she asked.

– In a district that was just invented now, have you heard of Walt Disney? Isabella's eyes shone.

– When I was little, I saw all the Disney movies.

– Right, it's a place like that, a wonder-world, all made of crystal, a crystal that's actually ordinary glass, from a realistic point of view it's in northern Italy, in the same way Tuscany is in central Italy and Sicily is in southern Italy, but at this point geography has become secondary and so has history, better not to talk about culture, what counts today is the fable, but since adults aren't just stupid, they're complicated, I don't want to complicate things any more, let's get to the point, the question I first asked you, where were you born?

– In a little town in Peru, said Isabella, but I became Italian really soon, as soon as my parents adopted me, that's why I feel Italian like you.

– Isabèl, said the man, to be perfectly honest, I did realize you weren't Aryan like me – anyway I'm white as a corpse, you said so yourself – whereas you're a little bit darker, you're not pure Aryan.

– Which means?

– It's a nonexistent race, answered the man, some fake scientists invented it, but you know, if the people with these kinds of ideals had won the war, you wouldn't be here now, or rather, maybe you wouldn't be at all.

– Why? asked Isabella.

– Because non-Aryan people wouldn't have had the right to exist, dear Isabèl, and people with skin that's a little dark, like yours, which actually has a very beautiful color, especially now with the bronzing cream, would've been . . .

– Would've been what? she asked.

– Never mind, said the man, it's a complicated matter and on a day like this it's not worth complicating our life, why don't you take a good swim before lunch?

– I can maybe take one later, answered Isabella, right now I don't feel like it, but then, sorry, when I saw you last week, always here reading under the beach umbrella, I thought you were someone who could explain things I didn't understand, I thought I would have an interesting conversation with you like it's hard to have with grown-ups, but now it's even worse, we've been talking for half an hour, and to be perfectly honest you seem a little out of it, all the nonexistent countries and people destroying houses and you making war that was really peace, in my view there's a lot of confusion in your head, and I don't get what your so-called profession was, either.

– It involved watching those who destroyed each other's houses, responded the man, this was the war mission for peacekeeping, and it was happening right here.

– On this beach? asked Isabella, excuse me, but that doesn't seem possible, no offense.

The man didn't answer. Isabella stood up, she had her hands on her hips and was looking at the sea, she was thin and her slender figure was outlined against the strong noon light.

– In my view you say these things because you don't eat, she said in a slightly altered voice, not eating makes you say strange things, you're not thinking straight, excuse me for saying this but we have a first-class hotel here, it's super expensive because I've seen the prices, you can't say these things just off the top of your head, you don't eat, don't sunbathe, don't go into the water, I think you have some problems, perhaps you need to get some food in you or drink a good fruit shake, would you like me to get you one?

– If you'd really like to be kind, I'd rather have a Coke, said the man, it quenches my thirst.

– I want to be kind, declared Isabella, but you're the one who isn't kind, first you have to explain to me why you came right here for vacation if there was a war and houses were destroyed and you stood here watching, can that be true?

– That's how it was, it's just that nobody wanted to know it, and even now, you know, people don't like to know that there was a war where they spend their vacation, because if they think about it, their vacation gets ruined, you follow the logic?

– So why'd you come here too? It's a logical question, if you don't mind my asking.

– Let's say it's for the rest of the warrior, said the man, even if the warrior wasn't fighting, in the end he was a warrior, and he must find rest where the war once was, that's classic.

Isabella seemed to be mulling this over. She was kneeling in the sand, half in the sun, half in the shade, she was wearing a bikini on her slender, childish body, but the top wasn't necessary, her thin shoulders began shaking as though she were weeping, but she wasn't, she seemed cold, she kept her hands buried deep in the sand and her head was bent over her knees.

– Don't worry, she murmured, when I get like this everyone worries, but it's only a little developmental crisis, the thing is, I have developmental problems, that's what the psychologist said, I don't know if you understand.

– Perhaps if you raise your head, I'll understand better, said the man, I can't hear you very well.

The girl looked up, her face was red and her eyes damp.

– Do you like war? she murmured.

– No, he said, I don't like it, do you?

– So then why'd you do it? asked Isabella.

– Like I told you, I didn't, I was there to watch, but I also asked you a question, do you like war?

– I hate it, exclaimed Isabella, I hate it but you talk like all grown-up people and you're making me have a developmental crisis, because last year I didn't have any developmental crises, then at school they taught us about the various kinds of war, the bad ones and the good ones, and we wrote three essays about it, and it was only after that when I started having these developmental crises.

– Take your time explaining yourself, said the man, tell me calmly, in any case the *fettuccine all'arrabbiata* is being kept warm under the halogen lamps, I didn't even ask you what grade you're in.

– I just finished seventh grade, but after ninth grade I'll go to *ginnasio* so I'll also be studying Greek.

– Wonderful, but what does that have to do with your crisis?

– Maybe nothing, said Isabella, the thing is that throughout the year we studied Caesar and also a bit of Herodotus, but most of all whether war can serve peace, that was the theme in history class, am I being clear?

– Not quite.

– In the sense that sometimes war is necessary, unfortunately, she said, war sometimes is useful for bringing justice to countries where there isn't any, but then one day two kids came from that country where they're bringing justice and the kids were hospitalized in our city, and it was my class that brought them candy and fruit, that is, me and Simone and Samantha, the best students, am I being clear?

– Go on, said the man.

– Mohamed is right around my age, and his little sister is younger, but her name I don't remember, though when we entered the little room in the hospital, the thing is that Mohamed didn't have any arms and his little sister . . .

Isabella broke off.

– His little sister's face . . . she murmured. I'm afraid if I tell you about it, I'll have another developmental crisis, their grandmother was with them, keeping them company because their mother and father died from the bomb that destroyed their house, and so I dropped the tray with the kiwis and tiramisu, I started crying and then I had a developmental crisis.

The man didn't say anything.

– Why aren't you saying anything? You're like the psychologist who keeps listening to me and never says anything, say something to me.

– In my opinion you don't really have to worry, said the man, we all have developmental crises, each person in his own way.

– You too?

– I can guarantee you, he said, despite what the doctors think, I believe I'm right in the middle of a developmental crisis.

Isabella looked at him. Sitting cross-legged now, she seemed calmer and no longer had her hands buried in the sand.

— You're kidding, she said.

— Not at all, he answered.

— Wait, how old are you?

— Forty-five, answered the man.

— Like my father, that's late for having a developmental crisis.

— Absolutely not, objected the man, the developmental period never ends, in life we don't do anything other than *evolutionize*.

— The verb *evolutionize* doesn't exist, said Isabella, we say *evolve*.

— Right, though in biology it exists, and it means each one of us *evolutionizing* has our own crisis, your parents have theirs too.

— And you, how do you know that?

— Yesterday, said the man, I heard your mother talking with your father on her cell phone, and it was easy to understand that they're right in the middle of a developmental crisis.

— You are such a spy, exclaimed Isabella, you shouldn't listen to other people's conversations.

— Sorry, said the man, your umbrella is three meters from mine and your mother was talking as if she were at home, what should I do, plug my ears?

Isabella's shoulders shivered again.

– The thing is they aren't together anymore, she said, and so I was left in my mom's custody and Francesco in my dad's, one for each is just, said the judge, Francesco was born after they'd stopped waiting, but I love him like I love no one else and at night I feel like crying, but my mom cries at night too, I've heard her, and you know why? Because she and my dad have existential disagreements, that's what they call them, does that mean anything to you?

– Sure, said the man, it's a normal thing, everybody has existential disagreements, there's no need to get worked up about it.

Isabella had her hands in the sand again, but now she seemed almost jaunty, and she giggled a little.

– You're clever, she said, you haven't told me yet why you spend your days under the umbrella, you know everything about me and you don't talk about yourself, but why did you come to the beach if you spend your days in a beach chair taking pills, what are you doing?

– Well, murmured the man, to put it simply, I'm waiting for the effects of the depleted uranium, but that takes patience.

– What do you mean?

– It's too long to explain, effects are effects and to understand the results there's nothing to do but wait for them.

– Do you have to wait for long?

– Not so long now, I think, about a month, maybe less.

– And meanwhile what do you do all day long, here under the umbrella, don't you get bored?

– Not at all, said the man, I practice the art of *nefelomanzia*.

The girl opened her eyes wide, made a face and then smiled. It was the first time she'd really smiled, showing little white teeth crossed by a metal thread.

– Is that a new invention?

– Oh no, he said, it's a very ancient thing, imagine, Strabo talks about it, it has to do with geography, but you won't study Strabo till *ginnasio*, in junior high you only study a bit of Herodotus as you did this year with your geography teacher, geography is a very ancient thing, dear Isabèl, it's existed forever.

Isabella was watching him, doubtful.

– And what would this stuff consist of, what's it called?

– *Nefelomanzia*, said the man, it's a Greek word, *nefele* means cloud and *manzia*, to foretell, *nefelomanzia* is the art of predicting the future by observing the clouds, or rather, the form of the clouds, because in this art, form is substance, and that's why I've come on vacation to this beach, because a friend from the air force who deals with meteorology assured me that in the Mediterranean there's no other coast like this one where clouds form on the horizon in an instant. And as quickly as they take shape they dissolve again, and it's right in that instant that a real *nefelomant* must practice his art, to understand what the shape of a certain cloud foretells before the formation dissolves in the wind, before it transforms into transparent air and turns to sky.

Isabella had gotten to her feet, mechanically shaking the sand from her thin legs. She combed back her hair and threw a skeptical glance at the man, but her gaze was also full of curiosity.

– I'll give you an example, said the man, sit in the chair next to mine, to study the clouds on the horizon before they vanish you need to sit and focus carefully.

He pointed toward the sea.

– Can you see that white little cloud, down there? Follow my finger, more to the right, near the promontory.

– I see it, said Isabella.

It was a little puff rolling in the air, very far away, in the lacquered sky.

– Watch carefully, said the man, and consider it, in *nefelomanzia* you need quick intuition but consideration is indispensable, don't lose sight of it.

Isabella shaded her eyes with her hand. The man lit a cigarette.

– Smoking isn't good for your health, said Isabella.

– Don't worry about what I'm doing, think about the cloud, in this world there are lots of things that aren't good for your health.

– It's opened at the sides, exclaimed Isabella, as if it's taken on wings.

– Butterfly, said the man confidently, and the butterfly has only one meaning, there's no doubt.

– Which is? asked Isabella.

– People with existential disagreements stop having them, people separated will be reunited and their life will be gracious like the flight of a butterfly, Strabo, page twenty-six of the main book.

– What book is that? asked Isabella.

– The main book of Strabo, said the man, that's the title, unfortunately it was never translated into modern languages, it's only studied in the last semester of college because you can only read it in ancient Greek.

– Why was it never translated?

– Because modern languages are too hurried, said the man, in the haste to communicate they become synthetic and grow less precise, for instance ancient Greek uses the dual in conjugating verbs, we only have the plural, and when we say *we*, in this case you and I, we can also mean many people, but for the ancient Greeks, who were quite exact, if only you and I are doing or saying that thing, only a pair of us, the dual was used. For instance, the *nefelomanzia* of that cloud is being done only by the two of us, only we know about it, and for this they had the dual.

– Really awesome, said Isabella, and let out a little shriek, putting a hand over her mouth, look at the other side, at the other side!

– It's a cirrus, the man said, a beautiful baby cirrus that in a moment will be swallowed by the sky, ordinary people would mistake it for a nimbus, though a cirrus is a cirrus, too bad for them, and the form of a cirrus can't have any other meaning but its own, which other clouds don't have.

– Which is? asked Isabella.

– Depends on the shape, said the man, you have to interpret it, and here's where I need you, otherwise what kind of *nefelomanti* are we?

– It seems to be splitting in two, said Isabella, look, it really is split in two, they seem like two little sheep trotting side by side.

– Two *cirrinus* lambs, without a doubt.

– I just don't get it.

– It's easy, said the man, the meek lamb by itself represents the evolutions of humankind, Strabo, page thirty-one of the main book, watch carefully, but when it splits, it becomes two parallel wars, one is just and the other unjust, they're impossible to distinguish, which ultimately isn't all that important to us, what matters is to understand how they'll both end up, what their future holds.

Isabella glanced at him like someone awaiting an urgent response.

– A miserable end, I can assure you, dear Isabèl.

– Are you really sure? she asked in an anxious voice.

– You tell me, whispered the man, I'm closing my eyes now, you have to interpret them, watch them, be patient, but try to catch just the right moment, because after that you'll be too late. The man closed his eyes, extended his legs, lowered a cap over his face, and remained still, as though falling asleep. Perhaps a minute passed, even more. Over the beach was a great silence, the bathers had gone to the restaurant.

– They're flaking in a kind of *stracciatella* soup, said Isabella in a low voice, like when the trail of a jet breaks up, now you can hardly see them, how weird, I can hardly see them, you look too.

The man didn't move.

– It's not necessary, he said, Strabo, page twenty-four of the main book, he wasn't ever wrong, two thousand years ago he prophesied the end of all war, but nobody up to now has fully grasped it, and today we've finally deciphered it on this beach, the two of us.

– You know you're an awesome man? said Isabella.

– I'm perfectly aware of that, answered the man.

– I think it's time to go to the restaurant, she went on, maybe my mom is already waiting at our table and she gets angry, can we keep talking this afternoon?

– I don't know, *nefelomanzia* is a very tiring art, maybe this afternoon I'll have to sleep, otherwise this evening I won't even make it to dinner.

– Is this why you take so many pills? asked Isabella, because of the *nefelomanzia*?

The man raised the cap from his face and looked at her.

– And what do you think? he asked.

Isabella had gotten up, she stepped out of the circle of shade, her body shone in the sunlight.

– I'll tell you tomorrow, she replied.

Translated by Martha Cooley and Antonio Romani

Letter From
Casablanca

Lina,

I don't know why I'm starting this letter off by discussing a palm tree when you haven't heard anything from me for eighteen years. Maybe because of all the palm trees here, I can see them from the hospital window, their long fronds waving in the scorching wind along blazing boulevards vanishing into white. Our house, when we were children, had a palm tree out front. Maybe you don't remember, because it was chopped down, if memory serves, the year it happened – so it had to be '53, that summer, I think – I was ten years old. We had a happy childhood, Lina, you can't remember, and no one could tell you about it, our aunt who raised you wouldn't know, oh, sure, she can tell you something about Papa and Mama, but not about your childhood that she couldn't have known and you don't remember. She lived too far away, up north, her husband worked at a bank, and they considered themselves superior to the family of a signalman, so they never came to our house. The palm tree was taken down by order of the Ministry of Transport claiming that it impeded the view of the trains and could cause an accident. God knows what sort of accident that palm tree could have caused, it was so tall, with a tuft of fronds brushing our second-floor window. The only thing that might have been slightly annoying: from the house, you saw the trunk, a trunk thinner than a light pole, that certainly didn't impede the view of the trains. Anyway, we had to take it down, there was nothing else to do, it's not like the land was ours. One night at dinner Mama, who from time to time had great ideas, proposed writing a letter directly to the Minister of Transport that the whole family would sign, a sort of petition. It went like this: "Dear Mr. Minister: In relation to the circular number such-and-such, protocol such-and-such, regarding the palm tree situated on the small piece of land in front of signal house number such-and-such for the Rome–Turin line, the signalman's family informs your Excellency that the abovementioned palm tree does not constitute any obstacle to the view of the passing trains. So we beg you to leave standing the abovementioned palm tree, being the only tree on the land (apart from a sparse vine on a pergola by the door) and being greatly loved by the signalman's children, and in particular keeping our little boy company, who's delicate by nature and often forced to stay in bed and can at least see a palm tree out the window and not just empty space, which would make him sad, and to testify to the love the signalman's children have for the abovementioned palm tree, suffice it to say that they have baptized it and do not call it palm tree but Josephine, this name owing to our once taking them to the city to see the movie *Quarantasette morto che parla* with Totò, and in the newsreel, they saw the famous French Negro singer with the abovementioned name who danced with a gorgeous headdress made out of palm leaves, and ever since, when the wind blows and the palm tree seems to dance our children call the tree their Josephine."

This letter's one of the few things I have left of Mama, a draft of the petition we sent, that Mama wrote out by hand in my composition notebook, and so, when I was sent to Argentina, I just happened to bring it along, never realizing, never imagining how precious that page would become for me. Something else I have left of Mama, a picture, but you can barely see her, a photo Mr. Quintilio took of us under our pergola, at the stone table, it must be summer, there's Papa, and Mr. Quintilio's daughter, a thin girl with long braids and a flowered dress, I'm playing with a wood rife, pretending to shoot into the camera lens, there are glasses on the table and a bottle of wine, Mama's just leaving the house with a soup tureen, she's just entered the photo that Mr. Quintilio's already snapped, she's entered by accident, in motion, and this is why she's a bit out of focus and in profile – she's hard to recognize – so much so, I prefer to think of her as I remember her. Because I remember her well, that year, the year we took down the palm tree, I was ten, it was definitely summer, and the event happened in October, a person remembers perfectly well at age ten, and I'll never forget what happened that October. But Mr. Quintilio, do you remember him? He was the overseer on the farm about two kilometers from the signal house, where we used to pick cherries in May, a small, nervous man who was always cracking jokes, Papa would tease him because under fascism he'd been deputy provincial party secretary, or something or other, and he was ashamed about it, would shake his head, say that was all water under the bridge, and Papa would laugh and slap him on the back. And his wife, do you remember her, that sad, heavy woman? She suffered terribly in the heat, and when they came for lunch, she brought a fan, and she'd sweat and pant, then go sit outside under the pergola and fall asleep on the stone bench, her head against the wall, not even waking to the passing freight trains. It was splendid when they came after dinner, and sometimes there was also Miss Palestro, an elderly spinster who lived alone in a large house affiliated with the farm, surrounded by a battalion of cats, and she was obsessed with teaching me French, because when she was young she'd been governess to the children of a count, she was always saying, *"pardon," "c'est dommage,"* and then her favorite, for all occasions, to emphasize something important or simply if she dropped her glasses: "*oh-là-là!*" Those evenings, Mama would sit down at the small piano – how she carried herself at that piano, it testified to her upbringing, to her comfortable childhood, her chancellor father, their vacations in the Tuscan Apennines – the stories she told of those vacations. And then she graduated in home economics.

If you only knew, my first years in Argentina, how I longed to have experienced those vacations! I longed for them so much, had imagined them so vividly, that sometimes I felt as though under a strange spell, and I'd recall vacations in Gavinana and San Marcello, the two of us there, Lina, when we were little, only you weren't you but Mama as a little girl and I was your brother who loved you very much, and I remembered when we went to a stream down from Gavinana to catch tadpoles, and you, meaning Mama, had a net and a huge goofy hat with flaps, like the wimple of the Vincenzine nuns, you were always running ahead, chattering, "We have to run, we have to run – the tadpoles are waiting!" and this sounded so funny to me, and I'd laugh like crazy, I couldn't keep up I was laughing so hard, and you disappeared into the chestnut trees by the stream and shouted, "Catch me, catch me!" and I did my best to catch up and took you by the shoulders, you cried out, and down we went, down the slope, rolling, and I hugged you and whispered, "Mama, Mama, hold me tight, Mama," and you held me tight, and as we rolled, you became the Mama I knew, I smelled your perfume, kissed your hair, everything merged, grass, hair, sky, and in that ecstatic moment came Uncle Alfredo's baritone voice: "*entonces niño, ¿los platinados están prontos?*" No, they weren't ready. And I found myself in the yawning maw of an old Mercedes, a box of spark-plug points in one hand and a screwdriver in the other, the ground dotted with watery blue oil, "now, what's this kid dreaming about," he said, giving me an affectionate slap. We were in Rosario, in 1958, and Uncle Alfredo, after all those years in Argentina, spoke a strange mix of Italian and Spanish. His garage was called The Motorized Italian, and he repaired everything, but mainly tractors, old Ford wrecks, as an emblem, next to Shell's shell, he had a leaning tower of neon, though only half-lit, as the gas in the tubes was used up and no one ever bothered to replace them. Uncle Alfredo was a corpulent man, ruddy, patient, a food connoisseur, and his nose was covered in blue spider veins and he was prone to hypertension – the exact opposite of Papa – you'd never have said that they were brothers.

Ah, but I was telling you about those evenings after dinner at our house, when we had visitors and Mama would sit down at the piano. Miss Palestro went into raptures over Strauss waltzes, I really preferred when Mama sang, it was so difficult to get her to sing, she was shy and would blush, "I don't have a voice anymore," she'd say, smiling, but then she'd give in at the insistence of Mrs. Elvira, who also preferred ballads and songs to waltzes, and finally Mama would give in, then there was a long silence. Mama would start with some amusing little ditties, to liven things up, "Rosamunda," say, or "Eulalia Torricelli," Mrs. Elvira would laugh with delight, breathlessly, clucking like a brood hen and puffing out her enormous chest as she fanned herself. Then Mama would play an interlude, not singing, Miss Palestro would ask for something more challenging, Mama would look up at the ceiling, as if for inspiration or trying to remember, her hands caressed the keys, there were no trains at that time, no disturbing sounds, the window thrown open to the marshland, the call of crickets, moths beating the screen with their wings, desperate to get in, Mama would sing "*Luna Rossa*," "*All'alba se ne parte il marinaro*," or a Beniamino Gigli ballad, "*Occhi di Fata*." How lovely it was to hear her sing! Miss Palestro's eyes would shine, Mrs. Elvira would even stop fanning herself, everyone was watching Mama in her filmy blue dress, you'd be asleep in your room, unaware, you didn't have these moments to remember. I was happy. Everyone applauded. Papa, brimming with pride, would go around with the bottle of vermouth and fill the guests' small glasses, saying, "please, please, this is no house of a Turk." Uncle Alfredo always used this strange expression, too, it was funny hearing him say this mixed in with Spanish, I remember we'd be at the table, he loved tripe *alla parmigiana* and thought Argentines were foolish for only liking cuts of steak from cattle, and he'd take a generous helping from the enormous steaming tureen, saying, "*Anda a comer*, niño, this is no house of a Turk." It was a phrase from their childhood, Uncle Alfredo and Papa's, who knows what it dated back to, I understood the concept, that this was a house of abundance, with a generous host, and who knows why the opposite was attributed to the Turks, maybe it dated back to the Saracen invasions. And Uncle Alfredo really was generous with me, he raised me like I was his own son, and actually, he had no children of his own: generous and patient, just like a real father, and probably with me plenty of patience was necessary. I was a sad, absentminded little boy, I got into a lot of trouble as a result, the only time I saw him lose his patience was awful, but it wasn't my fault, we were having our lunch, I'd crashed a tractor, I was doing a difficult maneuver, trying to get it into the shop, maybe I was distracted, and right then Modugno started singing "*Volare*" on the radio and Uncle Alfredo turned up the volume because he was crazy about that song, and I scraped the side of a Chrysler, doing quite a bit of damage. Aunt Olga wasn't mean, she was talker, a grumbling Venetian who clung to her dialect, you could barely understand her when she spoke, Venetian mixed with Spanish, a disaster. She and my uncle met in Argentina, and when they decided to marry, they were already getting on in years, so you couldn't really say it was a love match, let's just say it was convenient for them both, because she got to give up working in a meat-canning factory and Uncle Alfredo got a woman to keep his house tidy. But they did care for each other, or at least there was fondness, and Aunt Olga respected him, spoiled him. Who can say why she blurted that out that day, maybe she was tired, annoyed, had grown impatient, what

I do know is she shouldn't have, Uncle Alfredo had reprimanded me earlier, and I was already mortified, just staring down at my plate, and Aunt Olga, out of the blue, but not meaning to hurt my feelings, poor thing, almost like she was just making an observation, said, "he's the son of a madman – only a madman could do that to his wife." And then I watched as Uncle Alfredo stood up, calm, white in the face, and gave her a terrifying back-handed slap. The blow was so violent it knocked Aunt Olga off her chair, and falling, she grabbed onto the tablecloth, dragged down all the dishes behind her. Uncle Alfredo slowly walked out, returning to the garage. Aunt Olga got to her feet like nothing had happened, she gathered up the broken dishes, swept the floor, laid out a new tablecloth because the other was a mess, set the table, and went out to the stairwell. "Alfredo," she shouted, "lunch is on the table!"

When I left for Mar del Plata I was sixteen years old. Sewn into my undershirt I had a roll of pesos, and in my pocket, a business card from the Pensione Albano, "*agua corriente fria caliente*," and a letter for the owner, an Italian friend of Uncle Alfredo's, a friend from his youth, they'd come to Argentina on the same ship and always kept in touch. I was going to attend an Italian Salesian boarding school that had a conservatory of some sort. My aunt and uncle had pushed me to go, I'd finished my early schooling, I wasn't cut out to be a mechanic, that was clear, and Aunt Olga hoped the city would change me, I overheard her one night saying, "his eyes scare me sometimes, they're so frightened, who knows what the poor boy saw, who knows what he remembers." The way I behaved must have been somewhat troubling, I can see that. I never spoke, I'd turn red, grow flustered, cry a lot. Aunt Olga complained that popular songs and their foolish lyrics were ruining me, Uncle Alfredo tried to rouse me by explaining camshafts and clutches and at night, he'd try to get me to join him at the Florida café where a lot of Italians played *scopone*, but I preferred hanging out listening to music on the radio, I adored old Carlos Gardel tangos, Wilson Baptista's melancholy sambas, Doris Day songs, but, really, I loved all music. Maybe it was better for me to go study music, if that was my path: but far from the plains, somewhere civilized.

Mar del Plata was a fascinating, strange city, deserted when it was colder, crowded over the vacation months, with mammoth white hotels, twentieth-century style, that radiated sadness in the off-season, when it was a city of exotic seamen and old people who'd decided to spend their last years there and who tried to keep each other company by taking turns inviting each other for tea on hotel terraces or at café concerts, where shabby little orchestras caterwauled popular songs and tangos. I was at the Salesian conservatory for two years. I studied organ with Father Batteo, an old, half-blind man with deathly pale hands: Bach, Monteverdi, and Pierluigi da Palestrina. The classes on general culture were with Father Simone for science and Father

Anselmo for classics, which I had a real knack for. I didn't mind Latin but preferred History, the lives of saints and famous men, especially Leonardo da Vinci and Ludovico Antonio Muratori, who'd gotten his education by eavesdropping under a school window, until the teacher discovered him one day and said, "come into the classroom, dear boy!"

Evenings, I returned to Pensione Albano, where my job awaited, because the monthly allowance Uncle Alfredo sent wasn't enough. I'd slip on a jacket that Señora Pepa had washed twice a week and station myself in the *Comedor*, a room painted pale blue, with around thirty tables and views of Italy on the walls. Our clients were retirees, traveling salesmen, Italian emigrants living in Buenos Aires who could allow themselves the luxury of a couple of weeks in Mar del Plata. Mr. Albano ran the kitchen, he knew how to make *pansoti con salsa di noci* and *trenette al pesto*, he was Ligurian, from Comogli, a Perón supporter, said he'd freed a country from lice. Plus, Evita was a knockout.

When I found steady work at the Bichinho, I wrote Uncle Alfredo to stop sending my allowance. Not that I was earning a crazy amount of money, but it was enough anyway, and it didn't seem fair for Uncle Alfredo to fix tractors to send me a few pesos every month. O Bichinho was a supper club run by a plump, cheerful Brazilian, Senhor João Paiva, where you could have dinner at midnight and listen to music typical of Brazil. It was a place that claimed to be respectable, different from other clubs, though someone going there to find some company would find it easily enough, through the waiters' discrete complicity, because that business wasn't out in the open, everything looked respectable, forty candlelit tables; at the back, near the coatroom, two young women sat at tables, empty plates in front of them, sipping a cocktail, as if waiting for their order: and if a gentleman walked in, the waiter would guide him over and discretely ask: "Do you prefer dining alone or would you like a lady's company?" I understood these tricks, because I worked back there, while Ramón attended to the tables near the stage platform. These propositions had to be made with tact, with grace, you had to understand the customer so you didn't strike a nerve, and for some reason, I understood the customer straight off, I just had a flair for it, and by month's end, I made more tips than salary. Not to mention, Anita and Pilar were both generous girls. The highlight of the show was Carmen del Rio. Sure, her voice wasn't what it used to be, but she was still a draw. With the passing years, the huskiness to her voice, what made her anguished tangos so appealing, had faded, her voice had brightened, and she tried in vain to get that huskiness back by smoking two cigars before each performance. But it wasn't her voice that was so spectacular, that drove the audience wild, it was many things: her repertoire, the way she moved, her makeup, her outfits. Behind the stage curtain she had a little dressing room crammed with junk and a majestic wardrobe that held all the outfits she used in the Forties, when she was the great Carmen del Río: long chiffon gowns, wonderful white sandals with extremely high heels of cork, feather boas, tanghista shawls, a blond wig, a red wig, and two that were raven black and parted down the middle with a large chignon and a white comb, Andalusia-style. The secret to Carmen del Río was her makeup, and she knew it, spent hours on it, down to the smallest detail: her foundation, her long, false eyelashes, her glittering lipstick that she wore back in the day, her extremely long, bright-red, fatale nails. She often asked for my help, said I had a light touch and exquisite taste, I was the one person in the place she trusted, she'd open the doors to her wardrobe and want my advice. I'd go over the night's repertoire, she knew what to wear for the tangos, but I decided for her more sentimental set, I usually went pale: filmy, pastel dresses, oh, I don't know, apricot, which was lovely on her, or pale indigo, incomparable for "Ramona." Then I did her nails and lashes, she'd shut her eyes and settle into her makeup chair, lie back on the head rest and whisper, as if in dream, "I once had a gentle lover like you, he spoiled me like a child, Daniel, from Quebec, I wonder whatever became of him." Up close, without makeup, she showed her years, but under the spotlight, after I worked on her, Carmen was still a queen. I packed on the foundation and greasepaint, of course, and for powder, I insisted on a very pink Guerlain, not those overly white Argentine brands that brought out her wrinkles: the effect was stunning, and she was extremely grateful, told me I'd erased time. And for her perfume, I converted her to violet, a good amount, a very good amount of violet, and at first she protested, because violet's so ordinary, a perfume for schoolgirls, she didn't realize it was exactly this contrast that drew the audience: an old, worn-out beauty singing the tango, done-up like a pink doll. This is what created pathos, what brought on tears.

Then I'd return to my work at the back of the room, circulating among the tables, stepping lightly, "*más carabineros a la plancha, señor?*" "*le gusta el vino rosado, señorita?*" I knew that while she sang, Carmen was searching for me, and I'd hold out the boss's gold cigar lighter for customers as they brought their cigarette to their lips and let that lighter burn at heart level, our agreed-upon signal that her singing was divine, that she went right to the heart, and I'd hear her voice quiver even more, grow warmer. She needed encouragement, splendid old Carmen, "O Bichinho" would be nothing without her.

The night Carmen stopped singing was filled with panic. Of course it wasn't her choice to stop: we were in her dressing room, I was doing her makeup, she was lying back in her chair in front of the mirror, smoking a cigar, eyes closed, when the powder was suddenly sticky on her forehead, and I realized she was sweating and touched her: she was clammy, "I don't feel well," she whispered and said nothing else, raising her hand to her chest, I checked her pulse, couldn't find it anymore, and went for the manager,

Carmen was shaking like she had a fever, but she didn't have a fever, she was icy. We called a taxi to bring her to the hospital, I helped her to the back entrance, so the audience wouldn't see her, "Bye, Carmen," I said, "it's nothing, I'll come see you tomorrow," and she tried to smile. It was eleven o'clock, the customers were eating dinner, and onstage, the spotlight shone a circle of empty light, the pianist was playing softly to fill the void, and there came a scattered, impatient clapping, demanding Carmen. Behind the curtain, Mr. Paiva was extremely nervous, sucking on his cigarette, he called for the manager and told him to serve complimentary sparkling wine, to keep the audience quiet. But right then a low chant went up, "Car-men! Car-men!" and then I don't know what came over me, it wasn't thought out, some force seemed to drive me into the dressing room, I turned on the makeup lights around the mirror, chose a very tight, sequined dress with a slit up the side, campy, then white stilettos, black, elbow-length evening gloves, the red wig with flowing curls. I put on heavy eyeshadow, silver, but chose a light bâton for my lips, a muted apricot. When I stepped onstage, the spotlight hit me full-force, people stopped eating, eyes on me, forks raised, that audience I knew but had never faced, a half-circle, like I was under siege. I started with *Caminito verde*, the pianist was quick, knew my vocal timbre right away, quietly accompanied me, entirely in low notes, and then I nodded to the technician, who hit the blue spotlight, I gripped the microphone and whispered into it, I let the pianist play two interludes to prolong the song, because the audience couldn't take its eyes off me; and while he played, I moved slowly onstage and that blue cone of light followed, now and then I'd wave my arms like I was swimming in that light, and I'd stroke my shoulders, legs parted, head swaying so my curls caressed my shoulders, like Rita Hayworth in *Gilda*. And then people were wildly clapping, I knew it had gone well, that I'd caught them off guard: to keep up the energy, before the applause died down, I launched into another song, this time *"Lola Lolita la Piquetera,"* and then a Buenos Aires tango from the Thirties, *"Pregunto,"* that sent them into raptures. The kind of applause Carmen only got on her best nights. And then I had an inspiration, something crazy, I went over to the pianist, had him give me his jacket, I put it on over my dress, and as if joking, though very sorrowfully, I started singing Beniamino Gigli's ballad, *"Oh begli occhi di fata,"* as if to an imaginary woman I was pining over; and while I sang, that woman I was evoking slowly came forward, drawn by my song, and I peeled off the jacket, and I was whispering the last line into the microphone, *della mia gioventù cogliete il fiore*, my lover was abandoning me, but my lover was the audience, I stared at everyone, enthralled, I was me again, and I kicked the jacket away that I'd dropped onto the stage. But before the spell was broken, rubbing the microphone on my lips, I slipped into *"Acércate más."* And something indescribable happened, men jumped to their feet, clapping, an old gentleman in a white jacket threw me a carnation, an English officer sitting at a front table walked up and tried to kiss me. I escaped to the dressing room, I felt a mad excitement, joy, a jolt to my entire body, I locked myself in, panting, stared at myself in the mirror: I was beautiful, young, happy, and then, on impulse, I put on the blond wig, slipped the blue feather boa around my neck so it dragged along behind me, and I skipped off like an elf to the stage.

First I did *"Que será será"* Doris-Day style, then *"Volare"* to a chá-chá rhythm, wiggling, inviting the audience to clap along to the beat, and I sang "vo-la-re!," a chorus answered "oh-oh" and I "can-ta-re!," and they "oh-oh-oh-oh!" It felt like the end of the world. I left behind the excitement and noise, went back to the dressing room, and sat there, in Carmen's armchair, crying with happiness, listening to the audience chanting, *"nombre! nombre!"* Mr. Paiva entered, speechless, beaming, eyes shining, "You have to go out there and give them your name," he said, "we can't calm them down." And I exited once more, the technician put on a pink spotlight and I was awash in warm light, I took the microphone, two songs surged in my throat, and I sang *"Luna rossa"* and *"All'alba se ne parte il marinaro."* And when the long applause was finally dying down, I whispered into the microphone a name that just came to my lips. "Josephine," I said. "Josephine."

Lina, many years have passed since that night, and I've lived my life as I felt I had to. While I've traveled the world, I've always thought about writing you and never had the courage. I'm not sure if you ever found out what happened when we were kids, maybe our relatives weren't able to tell you, some things can't be said, whatever the case, that you already know or will come to know, remember that Papa wasn't a bad man, forgive him as I have. And I, from here, from this hospital in this distant city, let me ask you a favor. If what I'm about to face of my own volition should turn out badly, please claim my body. I've left precise instructions with a notary and the Italian Embassy so my body can be brought back home, if so, you'll receive sufficient funds to cover the funeral, and an extra sum as a reward, because in my life, I've earned plenty of money. Lina, the world is foolish, nature is foul, and I don't believe in the resurrection of the flesh. I do believe in memories, though, and I ask you to let me satisfy mine. Around two kilometers from the signal house where we spent our childhood, halfway between town and the farm where Mr. Quintilio used to work, there's a path by the fields that once had a sign, TURBINES, because it led to the pumping station for the reclaimed land, and after the locks, a few hundred meters from a group of red houses, you'll come to a small cemetery. That's where Mama lies. I want to be buried beside her and for you to have an enlarged photo put on my tombstone of me when I was six years old. It's a picture that's been with our aunt and uncle, you must've seen it a number of times, it's of the two of us, you're extremely small, a baby lying on a blanket, and I'm sitting beside you holding your hand, they dressed me in a pinafore and my curls are tied with

a bow. I don't want any dates. Please, nothing on the stone except a name –
but not Ettore – the name I sign below, with the affection of our common
blood that binds me to you, your

Josephine

Translated by Janice M. Thresher

The Cheshire Cat

In the first place, it wasn't true. Let's just say palpitations instead, even though palpitations are merely a symptom. But not fear, no, he told himself, how stupid, it's simply excitement, that's all. He opened the window and looked out. The train was slowing down. The overhanging roof of the station platform quivered in the torrid air. A scorching heat, but if it's not hot in July, when will it be? He read the sign for Civitavecchia, lowered the window shade, heard voices, then the stationmaster's whistle and doors slamming shut. He thought that if he pretended to be asleep, no one would enter the compartment. He closed his eyes and said: I don't want to think about it. And then: I have to think about it, this thing doesn't make sense. But why, do things ever make sense? Maybe they do, but an undisclosed sense, that you understand later on, much later, or that you don't understand, but things have to make sense: a sense of their own, of course, that at times has nothing to do with us, even if it seems to. For example, the phone call. "Hello Cat, it's Alice, I'm back, I can't explain now, I have only a couple of minutes to leave you a message." (A few seconds of silence.) ". . . I have to see you, I absolutely must see you, it's what I want most now, I've thought about it constantly these past years." (A few seconds of silence.) "How are you, Cat, do you still laugh that way? Sorry, that's a stupid question, but it's so hard to talk and know that your voice is being recorded, I must see you, it's very important, please." (A few seconds of silence.) "The day after tomorrow, July 15th, at 15:00, Grosseto station, I'll be waiting for you on the platform, there's a train that leaves Rome around 13:00." Click.

You come home and you find a message like that on the answering machine. After all that time. All swallowed up by the years: that period, that city, friends, everything. And the name "Cat" as well, that too swallowed up by the years, that floats up in your memory along with the smile that was worn by that cat, because it was the smile of the Cheshire cat. Alice in Wonderland. It was a wonderland time. But was it? She was Alice, and he was the Cheshire cat: all in jest, like an amusing story. But in the meantime the cat had disappeared, just like in the book. Who knows, maybe the smile has remained, but only the smile, without the face it belonged to. Because time passes and devours things; perhaps only the idea remains. He stood up and looked at himself in the small mirror hanging above the center seat. He smiled. The mirror reflected back the image of a forty-year-old man, with a thin face, blond mustache, and a strained, embarrassed smile, like all smiles in front of a mirror: no longer arch, no longer roguish, no longer the know-ing smile of one who ridicules life. Cheshire cat, my foot!

The woman entered the compartment with a timid air. Is that seat free? Of course it was, they were all vacant. She was an elderly lady with a hint of blue in her white hair. She pulled out her knitting and began clicking away. She wore a pair of crescent spectacles on a chain, and looked as if she'd stepped out of a TV commercial. Are you going to Turin too? she asked at once. Train questions. He said no, that he was getting off sooner, but he did not say which station. Grosseto. What sense did it make? And why Grosseto, what was Alice doing in Grosseto, why had she summoned him there? He felt his heart beating rapidly and thought again about fear. But fear of what? It's excitement, he told himself. Fear of what, go on, fear of what? Of time, Cheshire cat, time that has made everything evaporate, in-cluding your superb little smile like that of the Alice in Wonderland cat. And now here she was again, his Alice of wonders, July 15th, at 15:00 hours, the numbers typical of her, since she loved numerical games and mentally collected incongruous dates. Such as: *Forgive me, Cat, it's no longer possi-ble. I will write to you and explain everything. 10 of 10 of 10 (two days before the discovery of America). Alice.* It was her farewell message, she had left it tucked in the bathroom mirror. The letter had arrived almost a year later: it explained everything down to the last detail, but in reality it didn't explain a thing. It only described how things go, their superficial mechanisms. That was why he had thrown it away. The note, however, he still kept in his wallet. He took it out and looked at it. It had yellowed along the folds and had split open in the middle.

2

He would have liked to open the window, but maybe the woman would be bothered by it. Besides, a little metal sign requested it remain closed for the sake of the air conditioning. He got up and stepped into the corridor. He was just in time to see the sunlit cluster of Tarquinia's houses before the train slowly entered a curve. Whenever he passed Tarquinia, Cardarelli came to mind. And then the fact that Cardarelli was the son of a railwayman. And after that the poem "Liguria." Certain memories of school days die hard. He noticed that he was perspiring. He went back into the compartment and got his small travel bag. In the lavatory, he sprayed some deodorant under his arms and changed his shirt. Maybe he could even shave, for no reason, just to pass the time. There really wasn't much need to, but maybe it would freshen him up. He had brought his toiletry kit and electric razor; he hadn't dared admit it to himself, but it was in case he were to spend the night away. He shaved solely against the grain, taking great care, and patted his face with aftershave. Then he brushed his teeth and combed his hair. While he was combing his hair, he tried smiling, and it seemed to go a little better, it wasn't the slightly idiotic smile that he'd produced before. He said to himself: you have to come up with some hypotheses. But he didn't feel up to doing it in his mind, the theories crossed over one another, the words got tangled and confused; it was impossible.

He returned to the compartment where his traveling companion had fallen asleep with her knitting on her lap. He sat down and took out a notebook. If he wanted to, he could imitate Alice's handwriting with a certain approximation. He thought of writing a note as she might have written it, composed around his absurd hypotheses. He wrote: *Stephen and our child died in a car accident in Minnesota. I can't live in America anymore. Please, Cat, comfort me at this terrible moment of my life.* A tragic hypothesis, with a grief-stricken Alice who has understood the meaning of life, thanks to a terrible fate. Or a breezy, self-assured Alice, with a hint of cynicism: *That life had become hell, an unbearable prison, let that big baby Stephen take care of the kid, they're two of a kind, so long, America.* Or a note somewhere between maudlin and sentimental, in romance-novel style: *Despite all the time that has passed, you never left my heart. I can't live without you anymore. Believe me, your Alice, a slave to love.*

He tore the page out of the notebook, crumpled it into a ball and stuck it in the ashtray. He looked out the window and saw a flock of birds flying over a stretch of water. They had already passed Orbetello, so this was Alberese.

For Grosseto it would only be about ten minutes more. His heart raced again and he felt a kind of anxiety, like when you realize you're late. But the train was right on time, and he was on it, so he was on time too. Only he hadn't expected to be arriving so soon, his own self was running late. In his bag he had a linen jacket and a tie, but it seemed ridiculous to get off the train looking all spruced up, he was fine in shirtsleeves. With that heat besides. The train swerved brusquely at a switch point and the car swayed. The last car always sways more, it's always a little annoying, but at Termini station he hadn't felt like going all the way to the front of the platform and had slipped into the last car, partly hoping that there would be fewer people in it. His traveling companion's head bobbed affirmatively, as if nodding her approval, but it was only the rocking effect, because she went on sleeping peacefully.

He put the notebook away, straightened his slightly rumpled shirt, ran a comb through his hair again, and zippered up the bag. Through the window in the corridor he could see the first buildings of Grosseto and the train began to slow down. He tried to imagine how Alice would look, but by then there was no time left for such hypotheses; he should have considered them before, maybe it would have passed the time more enjoyably. Her hair, he thought, how will she be wearing her hair? She used to wear it long, but maybe she cut it, yes, she definitely must have cut it, long hair is no longer in style now. He imagined her dress would be white, for some reason.

3

The train entered the station and stopped. He stood up and lowered the window shade. He peeked out through the crack, but he was too far from the station building, he couldn't see anything. He got his tie and took his time knotting it, then put on his jacket. He looked at himself in the mirror and smiled slowly. It was better. He heard the stationmaster's whistle and the shutting of the doors. Then he raised the shade, lowered the window, and stood there. As the platform began to slide slowly alongside the moving train, he leaned out to see who was there. The passengers who had gotten off were filing into the underpass; under the projecting roof of the station platform were an old woman dressed in black, holding a child by the hand, a porter sitting on his baggage cart, and an ice-cream vendor in a white jacket, the ice-cream chest slung over his shoulder. He thought, it's not possible. It's not possible that she wouldn't be there, under the platform canopy, with short hair and a white dress. He rushed out into the corridor to lean out the other window, but by then the train had left the station behind and was on its way again; he only had time to glimpse the sign GROSSETO as it was moving away. It's not possible, he thought again, she must have been in the café-bar. She couldn't stand this heat and she went into the café-bar, so sure was she that I'd come. Or else she was in the underpass, propped against the wall, with her absent yet astonished gaze of an eternal Alice in Wonderland, her hair still long and slightly ruffled, wearing the same blue sandals that he had given her one time at the shore, and she would tell him: I dressed like this, like old times, just for you.

He walked down the corridor in search of the conductor. He found him in the first compartment, sorting some papers: evidently the man had come on board with the new shift and hadn't yet begun his round to check tickets. Looking in, he inquired when there would be a train going back. The conductor looked at him with a slightly puzzled expression and asked: back where? In the opposite direction, he said, back to Rome. The conductor began leafing through the timetables. There would be one in Campiglia, but I don't know if you'd make it in time to catch it, or . . . He studied the schedule more carefully and asked: do you want an express or would a local be all right? He thought about it and didn't answer immediately. It doesn't matter, he said then, you can tell me later, there's plenty of time.

Translated by Anne Milano Appel

Night, Sea, or Distance

There, from where things originate, they return, each paying the punishment of having come according to the unjust ordering of time.
— Anaximander

Every time he imagined how that night might have gone, he'd hear Tadeus's voice, nasal and ironic, making one of those comments of his that meant everything and nothing: because it's a good viaticum. And immediately everything would start to take shape, outlines would emerge: the Jardim do Príncipe Real, with its ancient tree and ring of yellow houses, the narrow street a tram rattled over, that cold evening of a far-off year, November, 1969, that third-floor room, tiny, crammed with books, and his friends in that room, the four of them, their faces back then, already grown men and women, sure, but they always looked younger in those days, who knows why, maybe it was how they dressed or wore their hair, anyway, they were kids, barely twenty, the four of them, full of hope and goodwill, there to speak with the famous poet, practically an old man now, who, in his youth was bellicose, ferocious, but then his will bent to events, to life, his ferocity turned to sarcasm and disappointment, and when it came to battles, he'd developed the skepticism of one who'd fought and lost and now believed the fight was in vain.

And at times, when he imagined that night, he even tried to avoid Tadeus's insidious comment; as if a strange reluctance, almost nausea, pushed him toward the final outcome, toward the breakdown and pain the victims would have to go through; and then he saw them already out on the street, that poor group of kids, saying goodnight to each other, then one of them telling a joke or saying one last thing, still three or four minutes like this, just by chance, no real reason for it that night, and just then the car would come, inescapable, for that rendezvous awaiting them, for that experience they truly had to go through, because they were the ones who'd gone through it. But also just then and just as inescapable, came Tadeus's comment, almost meaningless yet devious, if you really thought about it, and then his imagination, the imagination of the one who, after so much time, was imagining that night, would push the four friends backwards, like a film projected in reverse, and he saw them climb the stairs backwards, return to Tadeus's landing, reenter the apartment, that's it: they were in the doorway, ready to leave again, everything taking shape again, and they had to relive the preamble, the introit to what they went through that night, they were in the doorway saying goodnight to the old poet, after an evening spent talking about poetry.

Because it's a good viaticum, Tadeus would repeat, one of those comments of his that meant everything and nothing. Is it poetry that's a good viaticum? – but a viaticum for what – that would remain a mystery to them all: already in the doorway, coats on now, then goodnight, right, kids, bye, Luisa, Tiago, Tadeus, *au revoir* Michel, but then someone said: to night, sea, faraway. Maybe it really was Tiago, who was always returning to conversations that seemed finished, one of his traits, apparently referring to the viaticum, they all understood this, and it was also this, for some reason, that made one of them shut the door again. There's still another glass, what a pity not to finish Michel's bottle, you always arrive with a bottle, Michel, come help finish it off, but then, that isn't exactly the line, it would have to be: to night, sea, distance – not faraway – distance – there is a difference, said Tadeus. But that's not why they stayed, to go back to one of the books of poetry they'd read from that night, to check a line that was actually: if it's night, sea, or distance. No, they all knew they were staying for something else, because outside it really was night, sea, or distance, and Tiago's comment had revealed something they all felt but no one had the courage to express: a discomfort, like a slight illness; not fear; no, more a mix of insecurity and longing, like feeling exiled in their own city and feeling homesick for their real city, which was the same city, but at a different moment, not that hostile evening, not that night, with its dark, pulsing waves ready to break. This is what they'd felt in the doorway, while they were saying goodnight; and so they took off the coats they'd just put on and reentered that small room crammed with books. Tadeus didn't expect much more than their complicity in staying up to the early hours: when he read poetry, he'd lose all notion of time. He said: it's like when I write poetry, time goes fsssss, like a deflating balloon, I'm in a world with no atmosphere, a vacuum – when I read it, too – don't you find it has the same effect? He threw himself into an armchair, book in hand, and went: fsssss!, and they all laughed, because at that moment, Tadeus was acting like a kid, which he was good at. Not that he was old, but he definitely showed his fifty years, with the life he'd had. And now he was acting like a twenty-year-old, like the other twenty-year-olds. He went: fssssss, and said: that's my soul leaking everywhere, my soul wants out, it just needs a hole, or it'll suffocate. And the others laughed because they knew what he meant. And because laughter was called for that night. Now and then a car went by, the streetlights were off, a police ploy for keeping the subversives from gathering outside; the only light on the entire street came from the entranceway of the Adega Val do Rio and then further on, the Guitarra Dourada, with a neon guitar, one string burned out, and below, also in neon: CRUSTÁCEOS E MARISCOS. Tiago went to the window and said it felt like curfew, and then he placed his hand on his chest, like he was taking a strange oath or something was weighing on him, and he said: they won't get to win this time, they won't be able to rig these elections, too. But then he turned toward the glass and whispered: why would they let us win? – they've been in control for forty years. And then someone laughed, who can say, maybe no one, maybe just a sigh that sounded like nervous laughter, and at that moment there came a siren's distant wail, ambulance or police, and Joana, perhaps wanting to cover up that grim sound, said: maybe we could read some more, and she looked around, her eyes anxious, the eyes of a young woman who wanted to believe in life and poetry, and her hands nervous, perhaps because she sensed that the others understood her entreaty but just couldn't do it, couldn't find any hope or illusion in reading lines of poetry.

It had reached that point, the evening. Still early, though it felt more like the middle of the night; and the early evening was still present, still filled that space, and had formed a stagnant pool, a curse, like a spell to be broken, that made the people within those walls feel like captives. Who knows if one of them moved to break the spell, and if it was Tiago or Michel, who can say, and maybe, it was because he mysteriously sensed the spell holding them captive that he uttered those words as an incantation, raising his glass, with a voice that should have been full of good cheer but instead was grim: to November 1969, the month of the fall of Salazarism. Strange how November seemed present, conjured by those words. It had been a clear October day, and they spent it on the beach, with a picnic of fruit and sandwiches. Someone got up the nerve to dive into the ocean, the sun was hot and on the way home they felt their faces burning. And now, suddenly, you could feel November, could hear the trees rustling in the botanical garden, a nasty wind had risen, whistling in the cracks, and leaves flew past the windows.

They should toast again, they sensed it, to the newly printed book that lay on the table, a small book of poems that Tadeus had picked up that night from the printers so he could read to them before it was published; but he seemed to be avoiding that toast, as though he felt embarrassed or reluctant or slightly ashamed for writing those poems and getting them published that November full of others' illusions when he had no illusions left, a month already marked by defeat, which no one should pin their hopes on. Until someone, maybe Luisa or Joana, or maybe both, by strange coincidence, owing to a shyness that often results in trite phrases, raised their glasses and said in unison: to poetry. And Tadeus muttered, his voice nasal and ironic: because it's a good viaticum.

And just then, the one imagining how that night might have gone suddenly realized that Tadeus's words were creating a vicious cycle; because it was then that the friends, detecting a hint of goodbye in those words, slipped on their coats, went to the door, opened it, stood there a moment saying goodnight, and just then, as if it were a goodbye, an incantation, an ironic omen, Tadeus repeated: because it's a good viaticum. And then someone responded: to night, sea, or faraway; maybe Tiago, and it was also because of this, who knows why, but someone was shutting the door again and Tadeus was saying: there's still another glass, what a pity not to finish Michel's bottle.

And everything began again, in the imagination of the one imagining that night, like a pantomime or witch's spell: from the door to the armchairs, from the armchairs to the door, like poor creatures, bewitched and condemned to senseless repetition, forced to mime and run through yet again the prelude to the horrible experience awaiting them in the night, that an imagination didn't have the courage to make them endure the way they had to endure.

Until: enough. Now they've left, are finally headed down the stairs, the lightbulb on the second-floor landing is burned out, someone trips, someone laughs, Tiago, stop pushing (that's Luisa or Joana), oh, stop being such little old ladies (that's Tiago), and finally they're on the main floor, the button pushed that operates the lock, a click, and now they're outside, ah, finally free from the vicious circle of a comment holding them captive in the imagination of the one imagining how that night might have gone; finally outside, in the night, standing in front of the dimly lit Príncipe Real garden, almost no one passing, no, no one was out there, like a real curfew, a phantom city all around, barred windows, and them on the sidewalk, saying goodnight, a harmless joke or two, trying to rid themselves of the evening's gloom still clinging to them like a damp veil.

The car approached, headlights off, silently, and by the time they noticed, it had already pulled deftly to the curb, window partway down, dark inside, impossible to see the driver, just a gun barrel pointed in their direction, just barely shifting, in small ticks, taking aim at each of them in turn as if trying to decide which one to shoot. And then a very deep, calm voice: hold it right there, boys and girls, just stay where you are, but turn and face the wall, and raise your tiny hands. That's what the voice said exactly – your tiny hands – and there was a hard violence to that strange diminutive, they heard it, something horrific and evil that hit them in the back and made them tremble, like a blast of icy wind. They stayed like that for some time, staring at the wall, hard to say how long, but long, it felt endless, and absurd: a few minutes before, talking about poetry, and now an unfamiliar voice and a pistol pinning them to the wall. Now your jackets, the voice commanded, one at a time, and back up. Tiago was first, held his jacket out, arm extended, not turning around, as though trying to avoid any contact with that menacing figure. He heard the jacket being turned inside out, heard coins and keys falling, said: there's nothing in my jacket, if you want money, it's in my pants pocket. The laughter he heard was almost pleasant, and then the voice, cutting: you communist faggot – did you think I was a thief? And Tiago found the strength to ask: then who are you, and what do you want? And the voice: you'll find out later, little rat. The hand out the car window was rummaging through both boys' jackets, then afterwards, dropped each into the gutter between the sidewalk and the car. And now your purses, little ladies, said the voice. To Joana: you first, princess, I'm curious to dig through your little secrets, with that Virgin-Mary air of yours, I bet you've got plenty of little secrets in that purse, don't you? The hand thrust into the purse, a fat hand, the back slightly puffy, with short, strong fingers.

And at that moment, the seabass came. A fat, shiny, oily seabass writhing in the dark depths like the darkness of the car threatening the victims of the night: out the window, along with that swollen, stumpy-fingered hand, there was now a gasping seabass. So odd, a hand and a seabass out the window of a black car on Rua Dom Pedro Quinto on a November night in 1969.

But this came from the imagination of the one thinking about how that night might have gone. And so, just then, his imagination produced a seabass. And stranger still: this seemed fitting, in the middle of this dismal, quasi-curfewed night, with a drizzling rain starting and leaves blowing about, it only seemed fitting that out the window of that menacing car, there was now a seabass. Plop. Out slipped the fish, down into the gutter between the car and sidewalk, into the same spot where the hand pointing the pistol had dropped the boys' jackets and the girls' handbags. And there, in the filthy gutter, the seabass lay, almost still, just a weak twitch of the tail now, and a gasping mouth. It was dying. A fat, gasping, dying seabass. Don't touch it! Tiago shouted. He shouted at Joana, who'd knelt and taken the fish in her arms, foolishly, like she was cradling a baby. Don't touch it, Tiago repeated, it's filthy! But Joana didn't seem to hear his cry of disgust and alarm. We can't let this poor animal die, she said, bewildered; and Tiago continued: I'm not a communist, I'm a democrat, and I want to know who you are right now; and the voice in the car squealed, look who's talking, then screamed: you democrat faggot – did you think I was a thief?

Because of course that's what Tiago said: he was a democrat and he wanted to know who this man was. That's what he really must have said that night, of course he hadn't talked about any seabass, because there wasn't any seabass, right then, except in the mind of the one imagining how that night must have gone. That night, instead, there was only darkness by the Jardim do Príncipe Real, and the four of them, terrified, frozen, facing a pistol pointed at them out a car widow. Even the rest of the neon GUITARRA DOURADA sign was out now, the waiter in his white apron stood in the doorway, looked around, and of course, he saw a stopped car, headlights off, and four people with their hands up, so he quickly lowered the restaurant's rolling shutter, and stayed in there, lights out.

At this point, however, along with them, there's a fish. Even if that night there wasn't, now, in this conjured night, it's right there, and Joana takes it in her arms, seems to cradle it, and she looks around, bewildered, and Tiago is telling her: what are you doing? – put it down, leave it in the gutter, can't you see that fish is diseased?

Joana knelt by the gutter and picked up her purse that the hand had dropped out the window; a hand now gripping a letter: here's a little secret, right, princess? came the voice. Probably, Joana stifled a sob, or a moan, and tried to speak but couldn't, so Tiago spoke for her: that's a letter from her fiancé – you have no right to touch it. Ah, said the voice, now isn't that interesting. The hand tore open the envelope, took out the letter, and the voice, in that darkness, as if guided by the eyes of a cat, read: dearest Joana, the paperwork's almost all ready now, I think we can get married in a month, in December. The voice interrupted the letter, laughing: oh, isn't that romantic. You have no right to read that letter, Tiago said and walked up to the window. And then the fat hand holding the letter and gun sprang forward, incredibly agile, flying, and the gun barrel struck Tiago in the mouth, there was the sound of teeth breaking, Tiago buckled over, spitting teeth and blood, the car door opened and a man stepped out, a wide-brimmed hat covering his face, and he said: secret police – get your identity papers out. He turned to Tiago, his pistol put away now, his hands in his pockets and his face down, like he was studying his prisoners' shoes, but he turned to Tiago, because he repeated: your identity papers, you little faggoty democrat; and Tiago, his handkerchief in his mouth to staunch the blood, tried to mumble but it came out more of a wheeze, and then he shook his

head no, clutching his chin in both hands, for the pain of course, and perhaps, just then, Tadeus came down the stairs and stood in the entranceway
to the building.

So the one imagining what must have gone on that night saw Tadeus in
the entranceway, just then, while Tiago was spitting and wheezing into a
handkerchief, unable to talk, looking like he was done for. But how strange:
the one thinking all this couldn't help but imagine Tadeus behind the curtains, up there on the third floor, crouched in the darkness of his room. So
why didn't he come down sooner? he asked himself in his imagination; why
did he wait for things to come to this? But there was no point in dwelling on
such things: Tadeus was there now, that's what mattered, he'd come down,
he was there, he'd opened the door and said in a loud, clear voice: this gentleman is an acquaintance of mine – I can vouch for him.

What happened next? It was difficult to put into words, for the one who
was thinking that night. His imagination, at that point, was suffering from
something like paralysis or lack of sleep: the events were in suspension, im-
mobile, as were all the characters in that scene. And up to then he'd been
there, attentive, but now his eyes turned away, like something had dragged
his body away, a blast even stronger than that terrible icy wind, dropping
him onto a park bench in the Príncipe Real garden, beside tufts of papyrus
sprouting up along the pond: and at that distance, he couldn't figure out
who moved, who spoke, who decided, who wanted to go with Tiago, who

had to collect his documents left in his car, on Rua Sampaio Pina, right in front of Joana's building, maybe twenty blocks away, not even a kilometer as the crow flies, if you thought about it. Maybe Tadeus said he wanted to go with Tiago, and the others, too, all of them, sure, that must be how it went. But the man was shrewd and cruel and probably said: you, poet, just stay in your little apartment, with all your little books and poems. That must be what he said. And he probably told Luisa: make yourself scarce, little lady – get home. And why he only ordered Michel and Joana to get in with Tiago remains a mystery; he certainly wasn't concerned that Michel was a foreigner, because if he really thought this through, he'd have realized this wasn't an episode that should be known abroad, with the publicity the foreign press could give to the matter. Anyway, Tadeus went back inside and stood there, in the light, leaning on the doorjamb; Luisa stepped onto the street and hurried off toward the river, while Tiago, Michel, and Joana got into the car, and they all sped away; and the one imagining what happened that night kept imagining their departure from a park bench, and just then he noticed the car was a black Mercedes, an older model, decent but a bit out of style, the kind chauffeurs normally drive, with an old lady in the back.

But right after, he was with them. He was there now, too, between Joana and Michel, and Tiago sat up front, handkerchief pressed to his mouth, and the man was racing along, hugging the curves, or on the tight curves, jumping the sidewalk. Maybe he was drunk or on drugs, to tear along like that – but maybe not – maybe it was just another expression of his savagery, his disdain for life.

Here was the church of São Mamede, and the homes around Rato Square, where they drove down the wrong side of the street, and then the arches of Amoreiras Park, and further on the Ritz, with two doormen in green livery, ghostlike, and the Ritz seemed deserted too, the lights off in the grand salons. And finally, Rua Sampaio Pina. But then, almost like he knew his three prisoners were breathing a sigh of relief, the man braked sharply, veered to the sidewalk, and said: first political lesson – love your own country. He'd pulled his pistol out of his pocket now, and was rubbing it along his pants. You know what that means, boys and girls? he said, you don't know – you don't know anything. And Tadeus answered: I know as much as you, maybe more, I've known this country for fifty years, so spare me your lessons. His voice was low, restrained, and furious; he was the one who spoke, because he was in that car, too, how could he not have thought this, the one imagining what went on that night: would Tadeus ever let those three kids leave on their own with that loathsome fellow? No, of course Tadeus insisted on going too, maybe he'd stood in front of the car with his arms outstretched, a touch dramatic, absurd under these circumstances, and said firmly: I'm going with them.

And so the one imagining what happened that night had to imagine that scene again, and in the darkness of Rua Pedro Quinto, the last restaurant's lit signs going out, he saw Tadeus in front of that black Mercedes, blinded by the headlights, glowing, ghostly; and then he saw them silently climb into the car, all four of them, the three young people and Tadeus; but he, the one imagining watching, had now been carried off by a gust of wind, onto a park bench in Jardim do Príncipe Real, and at that distance, couldn't possibly tell where they were sitting in the car.

Don't play the hero now, the man said, my job is handing out life lessons, and if you've already memorized the lesson, then run through it again, it'll always do you some good. That's what he said, and he seemed calmer, less hysterical, and he'd spoken politely to Tadeus, and at that point the gun was in his pocket, and he told Tiago to go get his identity papers, because he clearly knew Tiago's car.

Tiago returned and said: here. The man studied the papers carefully, handed them back, and everything seemed to be over now. So, goodnight, kids, Tadeus said; he clearly couldn't bear anymore, he was exhausted, his presence was no longer needed: he walked off, hands in his pockets, almost cocky, at least in the view of the one imagining how that night must have gone. And when Tadeus was faraway, on the corner of Rodrigo da Fonseca, right in front of the kosher butcher's, the man pulled out his pistol again and said: all of you, back in the car. They got in, the three of them squeezed onto the backseat, and the man, standing outside, said: now, listen up, because the political lesson starts now: love your own country. And you know what it takes to love your own country? No, you don't, because you're three dirty communists, or democrats, whatever, same thing. All right, I'll tell you what it takes. It takes hatred. Hatred, to defend our civilization and our race. And you know how to tell a true civilization, a true race? When it dominates another race. And so forthwith, if you'll allow me such an old-fashioned word, forthwith: to dominate another race, first they have to be dominated sexually, yours truly, a full-blown Portuguese citizen in the service of Luanda and Lorenço Marques in the years of our Lord 1964–1968. Like so, my dear little fuckers, with this cock. And as he spoke, he undid his trousers, took out his organ, waved it around, and urinated into the night. Then he redid his trousers and said: I defended our race with this cock, raped the little daughters of those MPLA sonsofbitches waiting to ambush our heroic soldiers who'd left hearth and home to go out and defend those Zulu villages from communism. And I thoroughly raped them, as one must, and they were all of an uncertain age, but take my word for it, all less than thirteen, because by thirteen, Black girls are already grown women. And after I'd thoroughly enjoyed them, with this friend of mine, my pistol that I named Maria de Lourdes – because she's always protected me – with my pistol-friend, I finished the job, testing out the backsides of those little whores, meaning, I shoved my gun up each little ass, and how they squirmed, oh, you should've seen it, and me, bang bang, two shots, just two, just to puncture their intestines, and after this in-depth treatment, you should've seen how much their fathers talked, they even denounced their brothers, they spilled their guts after they got their little girls back with two bullets in their tummy, because those militants had plenty of daughters, that's right, plenty, Blacks have loads of kids, but lucky us, we also have loads of bullets.

That's when Joana got out of the car, staggered to a tree and bent over double, like she might vomit, and they heard her moan, then laugh, almost hysterical or having some kind of fit, and then the other two ran out to help her, and the Mercedes was already faraway, silent, they saw its brake lights at the Parque Eduardo VII intersection, and Michel and Tiago said: Joanna, let's get you home. But she said no, she wanted to collect herself, take in the cool night air, she didn't want to go home and see her family right now, no thanks, she didn't want them to walk her home and leave her at her door, she just felt like being alone. So the other two left, together, heads down, like they were guilty, but guilty of what, then, and as they turned to wave goodbye, they saw that on her face, she wore a strange, disturbing smile.

This story should end right here, when everyone walked off, going their separate ways, into the night: gone, the people that grim night had drawn together into a singular fate; gone, that car and its obscene occupant; and gone, even the night, once at its peak, now yielding to the break of day. But right then, the one imagining how that night must have gone felt an undefinable yearning, a sense of torment, as if that cycle had to end, break apart, or find a crease where it might hide, and hide as well what it had triggered in someone else's soul. And then, out of temptation, out of pure temptation, the one imagining that night let his imagination follow Joana as she walked down the street, because Joana didn't go home, she started down toward Braancamp, and he followed her as she crossed Alexandre Herculano, Joana walking slowly, unhurried, as if there were no escape; he watched her walk along that last stretch of Rodrigo da Fonseca with its jacaranda trees, turn onto Rua de São Mamede, take Rua da Escola Politécnica, and then Rua Dom Pedro Quinto, click click, her heels on the pavement, there was absolutely no one out that cold night in 1969, Joana arrived at Tadeus's building and there in the entranceway, leaning against the doorjamb, was Tadeus, who didn't speak, just smiled as if to say: I've been expecting you, I knew you'd come, that you wouldn't be able to resist. And then she nodded, as though admitting she'd come because she had to, because you can't resist the things you have to do; she stooped in the gutter by the sidewalk and took the gasping seabass in her arms and told Tadeus: we can't let this poor animal die, we have to bring it inside, get it some water, and he silently stepped aside for her. And while Tadeus was shutting the door, the one imagining that night imagined, oddly, that they went up the stairs astride that dying fish: and, funny, that seabass, with exhausted flicks of its tail, climbed the spiral stairs, once, twice, three times, until it entered a vortex that was escaping the building, passing through walls and time; willful, oily, dying, but untiring: forward, seabass, year after year, life passing, years and years, leading finally, one day, up to him; the one who was now imagining that night from so many years before. Up to him, and where?

Translated by Elizabeth Harris

Message from
the Shadows

In these latitudes night falls suddenly, hard upon a fleeting dusk that lasts but an instant, then the dark. I must live only in that brief space of time, the rest of the day I don't exist. Or rather, I am here, but it's as if I weren't, because I'm elsewhere, in every place on earth, on the waters, in the wind that swells the sails of ships, in the travelers who cross the plain, in the city squares with their merchants and their voices and the anonymous flow of the crowd. It's difficult to say what my shadow world is made of and what it means. It's like a dream you know you are dreaming, that's where its truth lies: in its being real beyond the real. Its structure is that of the iris, or rather of fleeting gradations, already gone while still there, like time in our lives. I have been granted the chance to go back over it, that time no longer mine, which once was ours; it runs swiftly inside my eyes; so fast that I make out places and landscapes where we lived together, moments we shared, even our conversations of long ago, do you remember? We would talk about parks in Madrid, about a fisherman's house where we would have liked to live, about windmills and the rocky cliffs falling sheer into the sea one winter night when we ate bread soup, and of the chapel with the fishermen's votive offerings: madonnas with the faces of local women and castaways like puppets who save themselves from the waves by holding on to a beam of sunlight pouring down from the heavens. But all this flickers by inside my eyes and although I can decipher it and do so with minute exactness, it's so fast in its inexorable passage that it becomes just a color: the mauve of morning in the highlands, the saffron of the fields, the indigo of a September night with the moon hung on the tree in the clearing outside the old house, the strong smell of the earth and your left breast that I loved more than the right, and life was there, calmed and measured out by the cricket who lived nearby, and that was the best night of all nights, liquid as the pulp of an apricot.

In the time of this infinitesimal infinite, which is the space between my now and our then, I wave you goodbye and I whistle "Yesterday" and "*Guaglione.*" I've laid my pullover on the seat next to mine, the way I used to when we went to the cinema and I waited for you to come back with the peanuts.

Translated by Tim Parks

The Woman of Porto Pim

A Story

I sing every evening, because that's what I'm paid to do, but the songs you heard were *pesinhos* and *sapateiras* for the tourists and for those Americans over there laughing at the back. They'll get up and stagger off soon. My real songs are *chamaritas*, just four of them, because I don't have a big repertoire and then I'm getting on, and I smoke a lot, my voice is hoarse. I have to wear this *balandrau*, the traditional old Azores costume, because Americans like things to be picturesque, then they go back to Texas and say how they went to a tavern on a godforsaken island where there was an old man dressed in an ancient cloak singing his people's folksongs. They want the *viola de arame*, which has this proud, melancholy sound, and I sing them sugary *modinhas*, with the same rhyme all the time, but it doesn't matter because they don't understand, and then as you can see, they're drinking gin and tonics. But what about you, though, what are you after, coming here every evening? You're curious and you're looking for something different, because this is the second time you've offered me a drink, you order *cheiro* wine as if you were one of us, you're a foreigner and you pretend to speak like us, but you don't drink much and then you don't say anything either, you wait for me to speak. You said you were a writer, and that maybe your job was something like mine. All books are stupid, there's never much truth in them, still I've read a lot over the last thirty years, I haven't had much else to do, Italian books too, all in translation of course. The one I liked most was called *Canaviais no vento*, by someone called Deledda, do you know it? And then you're young and you have an eye for the women, I saw the way you were looking at that beautiful woman with the long neck, you've been watching her all evening, I don't know if she's your girlfriend, she was looking at you too, and maybe you'll find it strange but all this has reawakened something in me, it must be because I've had too much to drink. I've always done things to excess in life, a road that leads to perdition, but if you're born like that you can't do anything about it.

In front of our house there was an *atafona*, that's what they're called on this island, a sort of wheel for drawing up water that turned round and round, they don't exist anymore, I'm talking about years and years ago, before you were even born. If I think of it now, I can still hear it creaking, it's one of the childhood sounds that have stuck in my memory, my mother would send me with a pitcher to get some water and to make it less tiring I used to sing a lullaby as I pushed and sometimes I really would fall asleep. Beyond the water wheel there was a low whitewashed wall and then a sheer drop down to the sea. There were three of us children and I was the youngest. My father was a slow man, he used to weigh his words and gestures and his eyes were so clear they looked like water. His boat was called *Madrugada*, which was also my mother's maiden name. My father was a whaleman, like his father before him, but in the seasons when there were no whales, he used to fish for moray eels, and we went with him, and our mother too. People don't do it now, but when I was a child there was a ritual that was part of going fishing. You catch morays in the evening, with a waxing moon, and to call them there was a song that had no words: it was a song, a tune, that started low and languid, then turned shrill. I never heard a song so sorrowful, it sounded like it was coming from the bottom of the sea, or from lost souls in the night, a song as old as our islands. Nobody knows it anymore, it's been lost, and maybe it's better that way, since there was a curse in it, or a destiny, like a spell. My father went out with the boat, it was dark, he moved the oars softly, dipping them in vertically so as not to make any noise, and the rest of us, my brothers and my mother, would sit on the rocks and start to sing. Sometimes the others would keep quiet, they wanted me to call the eels, because they said my voice was more melodious than anybody else's and the morays couldn't resist it. I don't believe my voice was any better than theirs: they wanted me to sing on my own because I was the youngest and people used to say that the eels liked clear voices. Perhaps it was just superstition and there was nothing in it, but that hardly matters.

Then we grew up and my mother died. My father became more taciturn and sometimes, at night, he would sit on the wall by the cliffs and look at the sea. By now we only went out after whales; we three boys were big and strong and Father gave us the harpoons and the lances, since he was getting too old. Then one day my brothers left. The second oldest went to America, he only told us the day he left, I went to the harbor to see him off, my father didn't come. The other went to be a truck driver on the mainland, he was always laughing and he'd always loved the sound of engines; when the army man came to tell us about the accident I was at home alone and I told my father over supper.

We two still went out whaling. It was more difficult now, we had to take on casual labor for the day, because you can't go out with less than five, then my father would have liked me to get married, because a home without a woman isn't a real home. But I was twenty-five and I liked playing at love; every Sunday I'd go down to the harbor and get a new girlfriend. It was wartime in Europe and there were lots of people passing through the Azores. Every day a ship would moor here or on another island, and in Porto Pim you could hear all kinds of languages.

I met her one Sunday in the harbor. She was wearing white, her shoulders were bare and she had a lace cap. She looked as though she'd climbed out of a painting, not from one of those ships full of people fleeing to the Americas. I looked at her a long time and she looked at me too. It's strange how love can find a way through to you. It got to me when I noticed two small wrinkles just forming round her eyes and I thought: she isn't that young. Maybe I thought like that because, being the boy I still was then, a mature woman seemed older to me than her real age. I only found out she wasn't much over thirty a lot later, when knowing her age would be of no use at all. I said good morning to her and asked if I could help her in any way. She pointed to the suitcase at her feet. Take it to the *Bote*, she said in my own language. The *Bote* is no place for a lady, I said. I'm not a lady, she answered, I'm the new owner.

Next Sunday I went down to town again. In those days the *Bote* was a strange kind of bar, not exactly a place for fishermen, and I'd only been there once before. I knew there were two private rooms at the back where rumor had it people gambled, and that the bar itself had a low ceiling, a large ornate mirror, and tables made out of fig wood. The customers were all foreigners, they looked as though they were on holiday, while the truth was they spent all day spying on each other and pretending to come from countries they didn't really come from, and when they weren't spying they played cards. Faial was an incredible place in those days. Behind the bar was a Canadian called Denis, a short man with pointed sideburns who spoke Portuguese like someone from Cape Verde. I knew him because he came to the harbor on Saturdays to buy fish; you could eat at the *Bote* on Sunday evening. It was Denis who later taught me English.

I want to speak to the owner, I said. The owner doesn't come until after eight, he answered haughtily. I sat down at a table and ordered supper. She came in toward nine, there were other regulars around, she saw me and nodded vaguely, then sat in a corner with an old man with a white mustache. It was only then that I realized how beautiful she was, a beauty that made my temples burn. This was what had brought me there, but until then I hadn't really understood. And now, in the space of a moment, it all fell into place inside me so clearly it almost made me dizzy. I spent the evening staring at her, my temples resting on my fists, and when she went out I followed her at a distance. She walked with a light step, without turning; she didn't seem to be worried about being followed. She went under the gate in the big wall of Porto Pim and began to go down to the bay. On the other side of the bay, where the promontory ends, isolated among the rocks, between a cane thicket and a palm tree, there's a stone house. Maybe you've already noticed it. It's abandoned now and the windows are in poor shape, there's something sinister about it; some day the roof will fall in, if it hasn't already. She lived there, but in those days it was a white house with blue panels over the doors and windows. She went in and closed the door and the light went out. I sat on a rock and waited; halfway through the night a window lit up, she looked out and I looked at her. The nights are quiet in Porto Pim, you only need to whisper in the dark to be heard far away. Let me in, I begged her. She closed the shutter and turned off the light. The moon was coming up in a veil of red, a summer moon. I felt a great longing, the water lapped around me, everything was so intense and so unattainable, and I remembered when I was a child, how at night I used to call the eels from the rocks: then an idea came to me, I couldn't resist, and I began to sing that song. I sang it very softly, like a lament, or a supplication, with a hand held to my ear to guide my voice. A few moments later the door opened and I went into the dark of the house and found myself in her arms. I'm called Yeborath, was all she said.

Do you know what betrayal is? Betrayal, real betrayal, is when you feel so ashamed you wish you were somebody else. I wished I'd been somebody else when I went to say goodbye to my father and his eyes followed me about as I wrapped my harpoon in oilskin and hung it on a nail in the kitchen, then slung the viola he'd given me for my twentieth birthday over my shoulder. I've decided to change jobs, I told him quickly, I'm going to sing in a bar in Porto Pim, I'll come and see you Saturdays. But I didn't go that Saturday, nor the Saturday after, and lying to myself I'd say I'd go and see him the next Saturday. So autumn came and the winter went, and I sang. I did other little jobs too, because sometimes customers would drink too much and to keep them on their feet or chase them off you needed a strong arm, which Denis didn't have. And then I listened to what the customers said while they pretended to be on holiday; it's easy to pick up people's secrets when you sing in a bar, and, as you see, it's easy to tell them too. She would wait for me in her house in Porto Pim and I didn't have to knock anymore now. I asked her: who are you? Where are you from? Why don't we leave these absurd people pretending to play cards? I want to be with you forever. She laughed and left me to guess the reasons she was living the way she was, and she said: wait just a little longer and we'll leave together, you have to trust me, I can't tell you any more. Then she'd stand naked at the window, looking at the moon, and say: sing me your eel song, but softly. And while I sang she'd ask me to make love to her, and I'd take her standing up, leaning against the window-sill, while she looked out into the night, as though waiting for something.

It happened on August 10. It was São Lourenço and the sky was full of shooting stars, I counted thirteen of them walking home. I found the door locked and I knocked. Then I knocked again louder, because there was a light on. She opened and stood in the doorway, but I pushed her aside. I'm going tomorrow, she said, the person I was waiting for has come back. She smiled, as if to thank me, and I don't know why but I thought she was thinking of my song. At the back of the room a figure moved. It was an old man and he was getting dressed. What's he want? he asked her in the language I now understood. He's drunk, she said; he was a whaler once but he gave up his harpoon for the viola, while you were away he worked as my servant. Send him away, said the man, without looking at me.

There was a pale light over Porto Pim. I went around the bay as if in one of those dreams where you suddenly find yourself at the other end of the landscape. I didn't think of anything, because I didn't want to think. My father's house was dark, since he went to bed early. But he wouldn't sleep, he'd lie still in the dark the way old people often do, as if that were a kind of sleep. I went in without lighting the lamp, but he heard me. You're back, he murmured. I went to the far wall and took my harpoon off the hook. I found my way in the moonlight. You can't go after whales at this time of night, he said from his bunk. It's an eel, I said. I don't know if he understood what I meant, but he didn't object, or get up. I think he lifted a hand to wave me goodbye, but maybe it was my imagination or the play of shadows in the half dark. I never saw him again. He died long before I'd done my time. I've never seen my brother again either. Last year I got a photo of him, a fat man with white hair surrounded by a group of strangers who must be his sons and daughters-in-law, sitting on the veranda of a wooden house, and the colors are too bright, like in a postcard. He said if I wanted to go and live with him, there was work there for everybody and life was easy. That almost made me laugh. What could it mean, an easy life, when your life is already over?

And if you stay a bit longer and my voice doesn't give out, I'll sing you the song that decided the destiny of this life of mine. I haven't sung it for thirty years and maybe my voice isn't up to it. I don't know why I'm offering, I'll dedicate it to that woman with the long neck, and to the power a face has to surface again in another's, maybe that's what's touched a chord. And to you, young Italian, coming here every evening, I can see you're hungry for true stories to turn them into paper, so I'll make you a present of this story you've heard. You can even write down the name of the man who told it to you, but not the name they know me by in this bar, which is a name for tourists passing through. Write that this is the true story of Lucas Eduino who killed the woman he'd thought was his, with a harpoon, in Porto Pim.

Oh, there was just one thing she hadn't lied to me about; I found out at the trial. She really was called Yeborath. If that's important at all.

Translated by Tim Parks

Islands

He thought he might put it this way: Dear Maria Issunta, I am well and hope the same is true of you. Here it's already hot, it's nearly summer, but with you, on the other hand, good weather perhaps hasn't yet come; we're always hearing about fog, and then there's all that big-city and industrial waste. Anyhow I'm expecting you if you want to come for a holiday, with Giannandrea, too, of course, and God bless you. I want to thank you for his and your invitation, but I've decided not to come, because, you know, your mother and I lived here together for thirty-five years. When we first came we felt as if we were in a different world, as if in the North, and in fact it was, but now I've grown fond of the place and it's filled with memories. Then, since your mother's death I've grown accustomed to living alone and even if I miss my work I can find a lot of distractions, like looking after the garden, something I've always enjoyed doing, and also after the two blackbirds, which keep me company, too, and what would I do in a big city, and so I've decided to stay in these four rooms, where I can see the harbor and if I feel like it I can take the ferry to go and visit my old friends and have a game of briscola. It's only a few hours by ferry, and I feel at home on board, because a man misses the place where he spent his whole life, every week for a lifetime.

He peeled the orange, dropped the peel into the water, watched it float in the boat's foaming wake parting the blue and imagined that he had finished one page and was starting another, because he simply had to say that he was missing his work already; it was his last day of service and already he missed it. Missed what? A lifetime aboard the boat, the trip out and the trip in, I don't know whether you remember, Maria Assunta, you were very little and your mother used to say: how is this little one ever going to become a big girl? I got up early; in winter it was still dark and I gave you a kiss before going out; it was bitterly cold and they never gave us decent coats, only old horse blankets dyed blue, those were our uniforms. All those years made for a habit, and I ask you again what would I do in a big city, what would I do in your house at five o'clock in the morning? I can't stay in bed any later; I get up at five, as I did for forty years, it's as if an alarm clock rings inside me. And then you've had schooling and school changes people even if they're from the same family; and your husband, too – what would we have to talk about? He has ideas, which can't be mine, from this point of view we don't exactly get along. You're educated, both of you; that time when I came with your mother and after dinner some friends of yours arrived, I didn't say a word the whole evening. All I could talk about were things I know, that I learned in the course of my life, and you'd asked me not to mention my job. Then there's something else, which may seem silly to you, I'm sure Giannandrea would laugh, but I couldn't live with the furniture in your house. It's all glass, and I bump into it because I don't see it. So many years, you understand, with my own furniture and getting up at five o'clock.

But, mentally, he crumpled up this last page, just as he had written it and threw it into the sea where he imagined he could see it floating, together with the orange peel.

2

I sent for you so that you'd take off the handcuffs, the man said in a low voice.

His shirt was unbuttoned and his eyes were closed as if he were sleeping. He seemed to have a yellow complexion, but perhaps it was the curtain strung across the porthole that gave the whole cabin this color. How old was he; thirty, thirty-five? Perhaps no older than Maria Assunta; prison ages a man quickly. And then that emaciated look. He felt a sudden curiosity and thought to ask the fellow his age. He took off his hat and sat down on the opposite bunk. The man had opened his eyes and was looking at him. The eyes were blue and, who knows why, this touched him. How old are you? he asked in a formal manner. Formal, perhaps because this was the end of his service. And the man was a political prisoner, which was something special. Now the man sat up and looked at him hard out of his big blue eyes. He had a blond mustache and ruffled hair. He was young, yes, younger than he seemed. I told you to take off my handcuffs, he said, in a weary voice. I want to write a letter, and my arms hurt. The accent was from the North, but he didn't know one northern accent from another. Piedmontese, perhaps. Are you afraid I'll escape? he asked ironically. Look here, I won't run away, I won't attack you, I won't do anything. I wouldn't have the strength. He pressed one hand against his stomach, with a quick smile that traced two deep furrows in his cheeks. And then it's my last trip, he added.

When the handcuffs were off he poked about in a small canvas bag, taking out a comb, a pen and a yellow notebook. If you don't mind I'd rather be alone to write, he said; your presence bothers me. I'd appreciate it if you'd wait outside the cabin. If you're afraid I may do something you can stay by the door. I promise not to make trouble.

3

And then he'd surely find something to do. When you have work you're not so alone. But real work, which would yield not only satisfaction but also money. Chinchillas, for instance. In theory he already knew all about them. A prisoner who had raised them before his arrest had told him. They're charming little creatures; just don't get too close. Chinchillas are tough and adaptable, they reproduce even in places where there isn't much light. Perhaps the closet in the cellar would do, if the landlord would allow it. Or you could hide what you're doing. The man on the second floor kept hamsters.

He leaned against the rail and loosened his shirt collar. Hardly nine o'clock and it was already hot. It was the first day of real summer heat. He fancied he smelled scorched earth and with the smell came the picture of a country road running among prickly pears, a yellow landscape under the sun, a barefoot boy walking toward a house with a lemon tree: his childhood. He took another orange from the bag he had bought the evening before and began to peel it. The price was impossibly high at this season, but he had allowed himself a treat. He threw the peel into the sea and caught a glimpse of the shining coast. Currents outlined bright strips in the water, like the wake of other ships. Quickly he calculated the time. The prison guard would be waiting at the pier and the formality of turning the prisoner over to him would take a quarter of an hour. He could reach the barracks toward noon; it wasn't far. He fingered the inside pocket of his jacket to check that his discharge papers were there. If he were lucky enough to find the sergeant in the barracks he'd finish by one o'clock. And by half-past one he'd be sitting under the pergola of the restaurant at the far end of the harbor. He knew the place well but had never eaten there. Whenever he'd gone by, he paused to look at the menu displayed on a sign surmounted by a swordfish painted in metallic blue. He had an empty feeling in his stomach, but it couldn't be hunger. At any rate he let his imagination play over the dishes listed on the sign. Today it will be fish soup and red mullet, he said to himself, and fried zucchini, if he chose. To top it off, a fruit cup or, better still, cherries. And coffee. Then he'd ask for a sheet of paper and an envelope and spend the afternoon writing the letter. Because you see, Maria Assunta, when a man works he is not so alone, but it must be real work, which yields not only satisfaction but also a bit of money. And so I've decided to raise chinchillas, they're charming creatures as long as you don't get too close. They're tough and adaptable and they reproduce even in places where there isn't much light. But in your house it would be impossible, you can see that, Maria Assunta, not because of Giannandrea, whom I respect even if we don't have the same ideas; it's a question of space and here I have the cellar closet. It may not be ideal, but if the man on the floor above me raises hamsters in a closet I don't see why I can't do the same thing.

A voice from behind caused him to start. Officer, the prisoner wants to see you.

4

The guard was a lanky fellow with a pimpled face and long arms sticking out below sleeves that were too short. He wore his uniform awkwardly and spoke the way he had been trained to. He didn't say why, he added.

He told the guard to take his place on deck and went down the stairs leading to the cabins. As he crossed the saloon he saw the captain chatting with a passenger at the bar. For years he'd seen him there and now he waved his hand in a gesture that was less a greeting than a sign of agreement, that they'd see each other that night, on the return trip. He slowed his pace wanting to tell the captain that he wouldn't see him that evening: it's my last day of service and tonight I'll stay on the mainland, where I have some things to attend to. Then it suddenly seemed ridiculous. He went down the next flight of stairs to the cabin deck, then along the bare, clean passageway, taking the master-key off his chain. The prisoner was standing near the porthole, staring out to sea. He wheeled around and looked at him out of those childlike blue eyes. I want to give you this letter, he said. He had an envelope in his hand and held it out with a timid but peremptory gesture.

Take it, he said; I want you to mail it for me. He had buttoned up his shirt and combed his hair and his face was not as haggard as before. Do you realize what you're asking? he answered. You know quite well I can't do it.

The prisoner sat down on the bed and looked at him in a manner that seemed ironical, or perhaps it was just his childlike eyes. Of course you can do it, he said, if you want to. He had unpacked his canvas bag and lined up the contents on his bunk as if he were making an inventory. I know what's wrong with me, he said. Look at my hospital admission card, have a look. Do you know what it means? It means I'll never get out of that hospital. This is a last trip, do you follow me? He emphasized the word "last" with an odd intonation, as if it were a joke. He paused as if to catch his breath and once more pressed his hand against his stomach, nervously or as if in pain. This letter is for someone very dear to me and, for reasons I'm not going to bother explaining, I don't want it to be censored. Just try to understand, I know you do. The ship's siren sounded as it always did when the harbor was in sight. It was a happy sound, almost a snort.

He answered angrily, in a hard, perhaps too hard voice, but there was no other way to end the conversation. Repack your bag, he said hurriedly, trying not to look him in the eyes. In half an hour we'll be there. I'll come back when we land to put your handcuffs in place. That was the expression he used: put them in place.

5

In a matter of seconds the few passengers dispersed and the pier was empty. An enormous yellow crane moved across the sky toward buildings under construction, with blind windows. The construction yard siren whistled, signaling that work should stop, and a church bell in the town made a reply. It was noon. Who knows why the mooring operation had taken so long. The houses on the waterfront were red and yellow; he reflected that he'd never really noticed them and looked more closely. He sat down on an iron stanchion with a rope from a boat wound around it. It was hot, and he took off his cap. Then he started to walk along the pier in the direction of the crane. The usual old dog, with his head between his paws, lay in front of the combined bar and tobacco shop and wagged his tail feebly as he went by. Four boys in T-shirts, near the jukebox, were joking loudly. A hoarse, slightly masculine woman's voice carried him back across the years. She was singing *Ramona* and he thought it was strange that this song should have come back into fashion. Summer was really here.

The restaurant at the far end of the harbor was not yet open. The owner, wearing a white apron, with a sponge in hand, was wiping the winter's salt and sand from the shutters. The fellow looked at him and smiled in recognition, the way we smile at people we've known for most of our life but for whom we have no feelings. He smiled back and walked on, turning into a street with abandoned railway tracks, which he followed to the freight yard. At the end of one of the platforms there was a mailbox, red paint eaten away by rust. He read the hour of the next collection: five o'clock. He didn't want to know where the letter was going but he was curious about the name of the person who would receive it, only the Christian name. He carefully covered the address with his hand and looked only at the name: Lisa. She was called Lisa. Strange, it occurred to him: he knew the name of the recipient without knowing her, and he knew the sender without knowing his name. He didn't remember it because there's no reason to remember the name of a prisoner. He slipped the letter into the box and turned around to look back at the sea. The sunlight was strong and the gleam on the horizon hid the points of the islands. He felt perspiration on his face and took off his cap in order to wipe his forehead. My name's Nicola, he said aloud. There was no one anywhere near.

Translated by Frances Frenaye

The Translation

It's a splendid day, you can be sure of that, indeed I'd say it was a summer's day, you can't mistake summer, I'm telling you, and I'm an expert. You want to know how I knew? Oh, well, it's easy, really, how can I put it? All you have to do is look at that yellow. What do I mean by that? Okay, now listen carefully, you know what yellow is? Yes, yellow, and when I say yellow I really do mean yellow, not red or white, but real yellow, precisely, yellow. That yellow over there on the right, that star-shaped patch of yellow opening across the countryside as if it were a leaf, a glow, something like that, of grass dried out by the heat, am I making myself clear?

That house looks as if it's right on top of the yellow, as if it were held up by yellow. It's strange one can see only a bit of it, just a part, I'd like to know more, I wonder who lives there, maybe that woman crossing the little bridge. It would be interesting to know where she's going, maybe she's following the gig, or perhaps it's a barouche, you can see it there near the two poplars in the background, on the left-hand side. She could be a widow, she's wearing black. And then she has a black umbrella too. Though she's using that to keep off the sun, because as I said, it's summer, no doubt about it. But now

I'd like to talk about that bridge – that delicate little bridge – it's so graceful, all made of bricks, the supports go as far as the middle of the canal. You know what I think? Its grace has to do with that clever contrivance of wood and ropes that covers it, like the scaffolding of a cantilever. It looks like a toy for an intelligent child, you know those children who look like little grown-ups and are always playing with Meccano and things like that, you used to see them in respectable families, maybe not so much now, but you've got the idea. But it's all an illusion, because the way I see it that graceful little bridge, apparently meant to open considerably to let the boats on the canal go through, is really a very nasty trap. The old woman doesn't know, poor thing, she's got no idea at all, but now she's going to take another step and it'll be a fatal one, believe me, she's sure to put her foot on the treacherous mechanism, there'll be a soundless click, the ropes will tighten, the beams suspended cantilever fashion will close like jaws and she'll be caught inside like a mouse – if things go well, that is, because in a worst-case scenario all the bars that connect the beams, those poles there, rather sinister if you think about it, will snap together, one right against the other with not a millimeter between and, wham, she'll be crushed flat as a pancake. The man driving the gig doesn't even realize, maybe he's deaf into the bargain, and then the woman's nothing to him, believe me, he's got other things to think about, if he's a farmer he'll be thinking of his vineyards, farmers never think about anything but the soil, they're pretty self-centered, for them the world ends along with their patch of ground; or if he's a vet, because he could be a vet too, he'll be thinking about some sick cow on the farm, that must be back there somewhere, even if you can't see it, cows are more important than people for vets, everybody has his work in this world, what do you expect, and the others had better look out for themselves.

I'm sorry you still haven't understood, but if you make an effort I'm sure you'll get there, you're a smart person and it doesn't take much to work it out, or rather, maybe it does take a bit, but I think I've given you details enough; I'll repeat, probably all you have to do is connect together the pieces I've given you, in any event, look, the museum is about to close, see the custodian making signs to us, I can't bear these custodians, they give themselves such airs, really, but if you want let's come back tomorrow, in the end you don't have that much to do either, do you? and then Impressionism is charming, ah these Impressionists, so full of light, of color, you almost get a smell of lavender from their paintings, oh yes, Provence . . . I've always had a soft spot for these landscapes, don't forget your stick, otherwise you'll get run over by some car or other, you put it down there, to the right, a bit farther, to the right, you're nearly there, remember, three paces to our left there's a step.

Translated by Tim Parks

Wanderlust

for Sergio Vecchio, vecchio amico

It sometimes began like that, with an imperceptible sound, like a faint music; and with a color as well, a fleck that started in the eyes and swept over the landscape, then flooded the eyes again and from there went on to the soul: indigo, for example. Indigo conveyed the sound of an oboe, sometimes of a clarinet, on better days. Yellow instead summoned the sound of an organ.

He watched the rows of poplars emerge from the blanket of fog like pipes of an organ, and on them he saw the yellow music of sunset, with a few golden notes. The train streaked through the countryside, the horizon an uncertain filament that appeared and disappeared among the waves of mist. He pressed his nose against the window, then with his finger wrote on the vapor condensed on the glass: *indigo, in the violet of the night.* Someone tapped him on the shoulder and he started.

"Did I scare you?" a man asked. He was an elderly, corpulent gentleman, with a gold chain on his vest. He looked surprised and annoyed at the same time. "Sorry, I didn't think. . ." "Oh, not at all," he said, hurriedly erasing the words on the pane with his hand.

The man introduced himself, stating his last name first. He was a livestock broker from Borgo Panigale. "I'm on my way to the cattle fair in Modena," he said. "And you, are you traveling far?"

"I don't know," he replied, "I have no idea where this train is going."

"Then why did you take it," the man asked logically, "if you don't even know where it's going?"

"To travel," he said, "because trains travel."

The broker laughed and pulled out a cigar. He lit it and puffed out the smoke. "Of course trains travel, and we travel in them. What's your name?"

"Dino."

"A fine name. And?"

"And what?"

"And what's your last name?"

"Artista."

"That's your last name?"

"Yes, it's Artista. Mr. Dino Artista."

"It's a curious name. I'd never heard of it before."

"I made it up, it's a nom de plume."

"What do you mean?"

"I mean it's a pen name. And since it's a pen name, I chose Artista."

"So you're an artist?"

"That's exactly right," he said. And he wrote on the steamed up window glass: Dino Artista.

"And what type of artist, a variety artist?"

"Anything and everything. A juggler, mainly, and also an acrobat. Just now I've thought of an acrobatic feat that someday I'll perform. Sooner or later, I'll go to America."

"To perform as an acrobat?"

"No, I'll go there by tram, and that's the acrobatic feat."

"By tram?! You can't go to America by tram, there's an ocean."

"You can, you can," he said, "it's tricky but it's possible."

"Oh, really," the cattle broker said, "and how is it done?"

"Magic," he said, "the magic of art." Then he abruptly changed the subject and looked around warily. "The conductor hasn't come by yet, has he?"

The broker shook his head no and immediately understood. "You don't have a ticket, young man, do you?"

He nodded in admission, and lowered his eyes as if he were ashamed. "I'll have to lock myself in the lavatory, at least until he's passed by."

The broker laughed. "We're approaching Modena," he said, "if you want to get off with me I'll treat you to lunch at Molinari Brothers."

2

The cattleman did not stop talking. He was a jovial man, and he liked sitting in the carriage, giving orders to the driver, assuming the hospitable tone of a generous person. You could see it gave him satisfaction. He told the coachman to go through the old center, because he wanted to show his guest the Ghirlandina: you can't come to Modena without seeing the cathedral and the bell tower. And with a gloved hand he pointed out the city's splendors through the window, illustrating them with the plain words of a man who is not very cultured but whose warmth displays a love for people and things to see.

"This is Piazza Reale," he said, "and now we're going around Piazza Grande. Look up, lean out the window."

Then the carriage turned onto a very long street flanked by buildings. "This is the Corso of the Via Emilia," the broker said. "It's called that because it follows the route outside the walls, on one side toward Bologna and on the other toward Reggio. Our restaurant is over there, on the corner of Strada San Carlo."

Molinari Brothers was a big, crowded brasserie, with marble tables and large coat stands on which the diners' cloaks were hung. The cattle broker was well-known, and many people greeted him. There was a flurry of commotion, because of the following day's fair. They chose a corner table, and the host arrived with a carafe of wine on the house. It was customary in that establishment. The young man looked around wide-eyed. All that bustle cheered him. The place was warm and smoke-filled, and through the windows you could see a wall with sprigs of capers in the cracks between the stones. The fog had lowered even further, making outlines seem unreal.

With the food and wine, the broker's cheeks had turned red and his eyes shone. "My son was a young man like you, his name was Pietro," he said, clearly moved. "He died of a fever in 1902, it's been four years now." Then he blew his nose with his napkin and said, "He too had a mustache."

By the time they left, evening was falling and the lamp-lighters were lighting the first street lamps. Some shops had lit torches near their signs and there were laurel branches on the doorposts of some of the taverns. A little boy with a cardboard mask passed under the arcades holding a woman's hand. It was February.

"It's the last day of Mardi Gras," the broker said, "stay and keep me company. I have a room at the Hotel Italy and you can be my guest. Let's go have some fun together."

The young man followed him silently through the already deserted streets. Their steps resounded on the pavement and neither one spoke. They walked through some porticos and came to a gray stone building with an imposing entrance. The broker pulled a bell handle and a smaller door opened within the bigger one. They went up a long flight of stairs and entered a vestibule with a colorful stained glass window. An improbably blond lady wearing a flowered dress received them, and led them to a seat in a small parlor. There were pictures of beautiful girls on the walls and the young man began studying them with interest.

"Now it's not like it used to be," the broker whispered, "when Anna Ferrarina was the madam. She was a true connoisseur, she always had top-quality girls. But she married an old fool from Rome, a professor, and she's become a respectable lady. Now we have to settle for whatever is available." He laughed briefly and began looking at the picture of a brunette photographed with her hands over her heart. "I choose this one," he said, "I like her eyes. Which one do you choose?"

The young man looked at him goggle-eyed. "Why do I have to choose?" he stammered.

"What do you mean, why?"

"I mean why, what for?"

"What for?! What do you mean, what for?"

"To do what?"

The broker slapped a hand to his forehead and said, "Oh dear God!" Then he asked, "Is this the first time?"

"Yes," the young man murmured.

"But how old are you, my boy?"

"Twenty-one."

"And you've never done it?"

"No."

"Well, look, it doesn't matter, they'll teach you themselves, you'll see, it's the easiest thing in the world."

He shook the little bell that was on the table and sounds and giggles could be heard in the corridor. "We're coming, we're coming, have a little patience," a woman's voice called out.

3

The fair was closing down. The ground was littered with trash and the stands were clearing out. A child passed by with a paper trumpet that unrolled as he blew it. Waiting near the post house were carriages and carts full of wares ready to leave for Bologna or Reggio. A peddler stood at the door of the post house. He was a skinny drifter, with a small concertina and a parrot in a little cage. He wore a cheap wool jacket and carried a case slung over his shoulder.

"This is Regolo," the broker said, introducing him to the young man. "He's going to Reggio and even farther. He makes the rounds of all the fairs. He'll keep you company."

The young man and the peddler shook hands.

"I leave him in your hands," the broker whispered to the peddler, "look after him for a while. He reminds me of my son. He's an artist, his name is Dino."

The wagon driver cracked the whip and the draft horse slowly started shuffling forward. The two men sat on the cart, with their backs to the driver and their legs dangling.

"Bye-bye," the cattleman called, "have a good trip."

Just then the young man leaped down and ran toward him. "I forgot to give you this," he said hurriedly, "it's a sketch of the woman I met last night. I'm giving it to you as a souvenir." And he went chasing after the cart that was already turning onto Via Emilia.

The broker unfolded the sheet of paper. It was a crumpled scrap of wrapping paper. On it was written: *Prostitute. . . Who beckoned you to life? Where do you come from? From the rank Tyrrhenian ports, from the singing fairs of Tuscany or was your mother rolled over in burning sands under siroccos? Immensity impressed stupor on your feral Sphynx-like face. The teeming breath of life tragically shakes your black mane as if you were a lioness. And you watch the sacrilegious blond angel who does not love you and you do not love and who suffers for you and wearily kisses you.*

4

Regolo sold *arruffi* of all colors, which were skeins of thread for mending; along with serialized novels in monthly installments and "fortune planets." The "planets" were yellow, pink, and green slips of paper that bore the lunar phases and the fortune, which the parrot Anacletus, the fisherman of Destiny, chose at random and handed to the buyer with his beak. Anacletus was very old and had a bad leg. Regolo treated him with a Chinese ointment bought at the Sottoripa arcade, in Genoa, where the Chinese sometimes set up a market to sell odds and ends as well as remedies for arthritis, aging virility, and sores. But Anacletus was willful and protested the medications, squawking furiously. Then he fell asleep on his perch, with his head tucked under his wing, and every now and then he shuddered in his sleep and puffed up his feathers, as if he were dreaming.

Maybe even parrots dream of indigo, Dino thought. The wagon moved along slowly, jolting and swaying, the sound of its rimmed wheels monotonous. The countryside was beguiling and boundless, always the same, with rows of fruit trees and cultivated fields. Dino thought of indigo, and the music of indigo replaced the rhythmic creaking of the wheels. And when he woke up, Regolo was shaking him by the shoulder, because they had arrived in Reggio Emilia.

They continued down to Porta Santa Croce. It was a clear afternoon. The wagon driver barked "giddy-up!" and cracked the whip, and the horse plodded on slowly. Regolo had to pick up some items from a dealer behind the public baths; so they agreed to meet at Caffè Vittorio in Piazza Cavour, and Dino roamed around the city by himself, because he wanted to see the house where Ariosto was born. He brought along Anacletus, sitting on his perch – the bird was a hindrance to Regolo, whereas he kept Dino company. He felt happy to be walking through the streets of that unfamiliar city accompanied by a parrot. And so, as he strolled along, he began to match his steps in time to a little tune he made up on the spot, which went: "I go walking through the streets mysterious dark and narrow: behind the windowpanes I see Gemmas and Rosas looking out. . ."

5

When Regolo arrived at Caffè Vittorio, Dino had just completed what he was working on. Arranged on the table were three stacks of fortune planets, sorted by color.

"I want to tell you something," Dino said. "If I stay with you a few days, I want to make my contribution to the business. So I've put the finishing touches on the planets: for each planet I have created a verse."

Regolo sat down and Dino explained to him that his contribution consisted of embellishing each sheet with an artistic phrase, because that's how art should come to people, carried in the beak of a parrot who randomly selects among destiny's slips of paper. And that was the strange function of art: to touch people by chance, because everything is random in the world, and art reminds us of that. And for that reason it both saddens and comforts us. It doesn't explain anything, just as the wind does not explain: it blows in and stirs the leaves, then it sweeps through the trees and sails away.

"Read me a few verses," Regolo asked.

Dino chose a pink planet and read: "And I kept on wandering without love, leaving my heart from door to door." Then he picked up a yellow planet and read: "Gold, golden dusty butterfly, why have the flowers of the thistle bloomed?" Finally he selected a green planet and read: "You brought me a little bit of seaweed in your hair, and a smell of wind." And he explained: "These words are dedicated to a woman whom I will someday find in a port, but she doesn't yet know that we will meet."

"And how do you know that you will meet?" Regolo asked.

"Because I'm sometimes a little clairvoyant. Well, that's not really how it is."

"So how then?"

"I imagine something so vividly that afterwards it actually happens."

"So then, read another verse," Regolo said.

"What color do you want?"

"Yellow."

"It's the color of organ music. Violet, on the other hand, evokes the music of an oboe, sometimes of a clarinet."

"I'd like to hear a yellow one."

Dino picked a yellow planet and read: "Because a face appears, there is like an unknown weight on the flowing water, the chirring cicada."

6

They went from house to house, selling skeins and handing out planets. They crossed the Crostolo valley and took the road to Mucciatella and Pecorile.

At night they slept in farmers' barns and talked about many things, especially the celestial vault, because Regolo could identify all the stars and knew their names.

Regolo had a sweetheart in Casola who put them up for five days. Her name was Alba. She was an unmarried woman with an ailing, elderly father, and Regolo was a husband to her once a year.

During those days, Dino worked in the stable to repay Alba's hospitality. It was a paltry stable with a pig and two goats.

On the sixth day they left and followed the bed of the Campola River to reach Canossa.

There were scattered farmhouses around, but they skipped them to go see the ruins of the castle. From that elevation the view was magnificent, with the broad Po Valley spread out below them.

Down there, on that plain, ran Via Emilia, stretched out like a ribbon of promises, headed north toward Milan; after that came Europe, modern metropolises alive with electricity and factories where life throbbed like a fever. Dino, too, had a fever; it was once again pounding in his temples, as it had the day he'd boarded the train at the station in Bologna, driven by a restlessness to travel. The sky was yellow, with violet smudges. Dino heard the music of an oboe and told that to Regolo. The music was that distant road calling to him from afar. He set Anacletus' perch down on the ground and gripped Regolo in a hearty embrace. He left him sitting on a castle stone and ran hurriedly toward the plain, toward the road.

The road, and its alluring siren's call. He thought: "Harsh prelude of a muted symphony, quivering violin with electrified strings, trolley running in a line across an iron sky of curved wires. . ." And he said to himself, "Go Dino, walk faster, run far, life is restricted and too boundless is the soul."

Translated by Anne Milano Appel

The Trains That Go
to Madras

The trains from Bombay to Madras leave from Victoria Station. My guide assured me that a departure from Victoria Station was, of itself, as good as a trip through India, and this was my first reason for taking the train rather than flying. My guide was an eccentric little book, which gave utterly incongruous advice, and I followed it to the letter. My whole trip was incongruous and so this guidebook suited me to perfection. It treated the traveler not like an avid collector of stereotype images to be visited, as in a museum, by three or four set itineraries, but like a footloose and illogical individual, disposed to taking it easy and making mistakes. By plane, it said, you'll have a fast, comfortable trip but you'll miss out on the India of unforgettable villages and landscapes. With long-distance trains you risk unscheduled stops and may arrive as much as a whole day late, but you'll see the *true* India. If you have the luck to hit the right train it will be not only comfortable but on time as well; you'll enjoy first-rate food and service and spend only half as much for a first-class ticket as you would on a plane. And don't forget that on Indian trains you may make the most unexpected acquaintances.

These last points had definitely convinced me, and perhaps I'd been lucky to have hit the right train. We had crossed strikingly beautiful country, unforgettable, also, for the humanity I saw, the air-conditioning worked perfectly and the service was faultless. Dusk was falling as the train crossed an area of bare red mountains. The steward came in with tea on a lacquered tray, gave me a dampened towel, poured the tea and informed me, discreetly, that we were in the middle of India. While I was eating he made up my berth and told me that the dining car would be open until midnight and that, if I wanted to dine in my own compartment, I had only to ring the bell. I thanked him with a small tip and gave him back the tray. Then I smoked a cigarette, looking out of the window at the unfamiliar landscape and wondering about my strange itinerary. For an agnostic to go to Madras to visit the Theosophical Society, and to spend the better part of two days on the train to get there was an undertaking that would probably have pleased the odd authors of my odd guidebook. The fact was that a member of the Theosophical Society might be able to tell me something I very much wanted to know. It was a slender hope, perhaps an illusion, and I didn't want to consume it in the short space of a plane flight; I preferred to cradle and savor it in a leisurely fashion, as we like to do with hopes that we cherish while knowing that there is little chance of their realization.

An abrupt braking of the train intruded on my thoughts and probably my torpor. I must have dozed off for a few minutes while the train was entering a station and I had no time to read the sign displaying the name of the place. I had read in the guidebook that one of the stops was at Mangalore, or perhaps Bangalore, I couldn't remember which, but now I didn't want to bother leafing through the book to trace the railway line. Waiting on the platform there were some apparently prosperous Indian travelers in western dress, a group of women and a flurry of porters. It must have been an important industrial city; in the distance, beyond the rail lines, there were factory smokestacks, tall buildings and broad, tree-lined avenues.

The man came in while the train was just starting to move again. He greeted me hastily, matched the number on his ticket with that of the berth and, after he had found that they tallied, apologized for his intrusion. He was a portly, bulging European, wearing a dark-blue suit, quite inappropriate to the climate, and a fine hat. His luggage consisted only of a black leather overnight bag. He sat down, pulled a white handkerchief out of his pocket and, with a smile on his face, proceeded to clean his glasses. He had an affable, but reserved air, seemed almost apologetic. "Are you going to Madras too?" he asked, and added, without waiting for an answer, "This train is highly reliable. We'll be there at seven o'clock in the morning."

He spoke good English, with a German accent, but he didn't look German. Dutch, I thought to myself, for no particular reason, or Swiss. He looked like a businessman, around sixty years of age, perhaps a bit older. "Madras is the capital of Dravidian India," he went on. "If you've never been there you'll see extraordinary things." He spoke in the detached, casual manner of someone well-acquainted with the country, and I prepared myself for a string of platitudes. I thought it a good idea to tell him that we could still go to the dining car, where the probable banality of his conversation would be interrupted by the silent manipulations of knife and fork demanded by good table manners.

As we walked through the corridor I introduced myself, apologizing for not having done so before. "Oh, introductions have become useless formalities," he said with his affable air. And, slightly inclining his head, he added: "My name's Peter."

On the subject of dinner he revealed himself to be an expert. He advised me against the vegetable cutlets which, out of sheer curiosity, I was considering, "because the vegetables have to be very varied and carefully worked over," he said, "and that's not likely to be the case aboard a train." Timidly I proposed some other dishes, purely random selections, all of which he disapproved. Finally I agreed to take the lamb tandoori, which he had chosen for himself, "because the lamb is a noble, sacrificial animal, and Indians have a feeling for the ritual quality of food."

We talked at length about Dravidian civilization, that is, he talked, and I confined myself to a few typically ignorant questions and an occasional feeble objection. He described, with a wealth of details, the cliff reliefs of Kancheepuram, and the architecture of the Shore Temple; he spoke of unknown, archaic cults extraneous to Hindu pantheism, of the significance of colors and castes and funeral rites. Hesitantly I brought up my own lore: the legend of the martyrdom of Saint Thomas at Madras, the French presence at Pondicherry, the European penetration of the coasts of Tamil, the unsuccessful attempt of the Portuguese to found another Goa in the same area and their wars with the local potentates. He rounded out my notions and corrected my inexactness in regard to indigenous dynasties, spelling out names, places, dates, and events. He spoke with competence and assurance; his vast erudition seemed to mark him as an expert, perhaps a university professor or, in any case, a serious scholar. I put the question to him, frankly and with a certain ingenuousness, sure that he would answer in the affirmative. He smiled, with a certain false modesty, and shook his head. "I'm only an amateur," he said. "I have a passion that fate has spurred me to cultivate."

There was a note of distress in his voice, I thought, expressive of regret or sorrow. His eyes glistened, and his smooth face seemed paler under the lights of the dining car. His hands were delicate and his gestures weary. His whole bearing had something incomplete and indefinable about it, a sort of hidden sickliness or shame.

We returned to our compartment and went on talking, but now he was more subdued, and our conversation was punctuated by long silences. While we were getting ready for bed I asked him, for no specific reason, why he was traveling by train and not flying. I thought that, at his age, it would have been easier and more comfortable to take a plane rather than undergo so long a journey. I expected that his answer would be a confession of fear of air travel, shared by people who have not been accustomed to it from an early age.

He looked at me with perplexity, as if such a thing had never occurred to him. Then, suddenly, his face lit up and he said: "By plane you have a fast and comfortable trip, but you miss out on the real India. With long-distance trains you risk arriving as much as a day late, but if you hit the right one you'll be just as comfortable and arrive on time. And on a train there's always the pleasure of a conversation that you'd never have in the air."

Unable to hold myself back, I murmured, "India, A Travel Survival Kit."

"What's that?"

"Nothing," I said. "I was thinking of a book." And I added, boldly, "You've never been to Madras."

He looked at me ingenuously. "You can know a place without ever having been there." He took off his jacket and shoes, put his overnight bag under the pillow, pulled the curtain of his berth, and said goodnight.

I would have liked to tell him that he, too, had taken the train because he cherished a slender hope and preferred to cradle and savor it rather than consume it in the short space of a plane flight. I was sure of it. But, of course, I said nothing. I turned off the overhead light, leaving the blue night-lamp lit, pulled my curtain and said only goodnight.

◆ ◆ ◆

We were awakened by someone's turning on the ceiling light and speaking in a loud voice. Just outside our window there was a wooden structure, lit by a dim lamp and bearing an incomprehensible sign. The train conductor was accompanied by a dark-skinned policeman with a suspicious air. "We're in Tamil Nadu," said the conductor, smiling, "this is a mere formality." The policeman held out his hand: "Your papers, please."

He looked distractedly at my passport and quickly shut it, but lingered longer over my companion's. While he was examining it I noticed that it came from Israel. "Mr. . . . Shi. . . mail?" he asked, pronouncing the name with difficulty.

"Schlemihl," the Israeli corrected him. "Peter Schlemihl."

The policeman gave us back our passports, nodded coolly and put out the light. The train was running again through the Indian night and the blue night-lamp created a dreamlike atmosphere. For a long time we were silent, then I said: "You can't have a name like that. There's only one Peter Schlemihl, the shadowless man, he's a creation of Chamisso, as you know very well. You could pass it off on an Indian policeman, of course . . ."

My travel companion did not reply for a minute. Then he asked, "Do you like Thomas Mann?"

"Not everything," I answered.

"What, then?"

"The stories. Some of the short novels. *Tonio Kroger, Death in Venice.*"

"I wonder if you know the preface to Chamisso's *Peter Schlemihl*," he said. "An admirable piece of writing." Again there was silence between us. I thought he might have fallen asleep. But no, he couldn't have. He was waiting for me to speak, and I did.

"What are you doing in Madras?"

My travel companion did not answer at once. He coughed slightly. "I'm going to see a statue," he murmured.

"A long trip just to see a statue."

My companion did not reply. He blew his nose several times in succession. "I want to tell you a little story," he said at last. "I want to tell you a little story." He was speaking softly, and his voice was dulled by the curtain. Many years ago, in Germany, I ran across a man, a doctor, whose job it was to give me a physical examination. He sat behind a desk and I stood, naked, before him. Behind me there was a line of other naked men waiting to be examined. When we were taken to that place we were told that we were useful to the cause of German science. Beside the doctor there were two armed guards, and a nurse who was filling out cards. The doctor asked us very precise questions about the functioning of our male organs; the nurse made some measurements which she then wrote down. The line was moving fast because the doctor was in a hurry. When my turn was over, instead of moving on to the next room where we were to go, I lingered for a few seconds to look at a statuette on the doctor's desk which had caught my attention. It represented an oriental deity, one I had never seen, a dancing figure with the arms and legs harmoniously diverging within a circle. In the circle there wasn't much empty space, only a few openings waiting to be closed by the imagination of the viewer. The doctor became aware of my fascination and smiled, a tight-lipped, mocking smile. 'This statue,' he said, 'represents the circle of life into which all dross must enter in order to attain that superior form of life which is beauty. I hope that in the biological cycle envisaged by the philosophy which conceived of this statue you may attain, in another life, a place higher than the one you occupy in this one.'"

At this point my companion halted. In spite of the noise of the train I could hear his deep, regular breathing.

"Please go on," I said.

"There's not much more to say. The statuette was a dancing Shiva, but that I didn't know. As you see, I haven't yet entered the recircling circle of life, and my own interpretation of the figure is a different one. I've thought of it every day since; indeed, it's the only thing I've thought of in all these years."

"How many years has it been?"

"Forty."

"Is it possible to think of only one thing for forty years?"

"Yes, I think so, if you've been subjected to indignity." "And what is your interpretation of the figure?"

"I don't think it represents the circle of life. It's simply the dance of life."

"And how is that different?"

"Oh, it's very different," he murmured. "Life is a circle. One day the circle must close, and we don't know what day that will be." He blew his nose again and said, "Now, please excuse me. I'm tired, and if you wouldn't mind, I'd like to sleep."

◆　◆　◆

When I woke up we were drawing near to Madras. My travel companion was already shaved and fully dressed in his impeccable dark-blue suit. He had pushed up his berth and now, looking thoroughly rested and with a smile on his face, he pointed to the breakfast tray on the table next to the window.

"I waited for you to wake up so that we could drink our tea together," he said. "You were so fast asleep that I didn't want to disturb you."

I went into the washroom and made my morning toilet, gathered my belongings together and closed my suitcase, then sat down to breakfast. We were running through an area of clustered villages, with the first signs of the approaching city.

"As you see, we're right on time," said my companion. "It's exactly a quarter to seven." Then, carefully folding his napkin, he added: "I wish you'd go to see that statue. It's in the Madras museum. And I'd like to hear what you think of it." He got up, reached for his bag, held out his other hand and pleasantly said goodbye. "I'm grateful to my guidebook for the choice of the best means of transportation," he said. "It's true that on Indian trains you may make the most unexpected acquaintances. Your company has given me pleasure and solace."

"The feeling is mutual," I answered. "I'm the one who's grateful to the guidebook."

We were entering the station, alongside a crowded platform. The train's brakes went on and we glided to a stop. I stepped aside and he got off first, waving his hand. As he started to walk away I called out to him, and he turned.

"I don't know where to send my reaction to the statue," I stated. "I don't have your address."

He had the same perplexed expression I had seen on his face before. After a moment's reflection, he said: "Leave me a message at the American Express. I'll pick it up."

Then we went our separate ways, into the crowd.

◆　◆　◆

I stayed only three days in Madras. Intense, almost feverish days. Madras is an enormous agglomeration of low buildings and immense uncultivated spaces, jammed with bicycles, animals, and random buses; getting from one end of the city to another took a very long time. After I had fulfilled my obligations I had only one free day and I chose to go, not to the museum but to the cliff reliefs of Kancheepuram, some kilometers from the city. Here, too, my guidebook was a precious companion.

On the morning of the fourth day I was at the depot for buses to Kerala and Goa. There was an hour before departure time, it was scorchingly hot and the shade of the roofed platforms afforded the only relief from the heat, off the streets. In order to while away the time I bought the English-language newspaper, a four-page sheet that looked like a parish bulletin, containing local news, summaries of popular films, notices, and advertisements of every kind. Prominently displayed on the front page there was the story of a murder committed the day before. The victim was an Argentine citizen who had been living in Madras since 1958. He was described as a discreet, retiring gentleman in his seventies, without close friends, who had a house in the residential section of Adyar. His wife had died three years before, from natural causes. They had no children.

He had been killed with a pistol shot to the heart. The murder defied explanation, since no theft was involved: everything in the house was in order and there was no sign that anything had been broken into. The article described the house as simple and plain, possessing a few well-chosen art objects and with a small garden. It seemed that the victim was a connoisseur of Dravidian art; he had taken part in the cataloguing of the Dravidian section of the local museum. His photograph showed a bald old man with blue eyes and thin lips. The report of the episode was bland and factual. The only interesting detail was the photograph of a statuette, alongside that of the victim. A logical juxtaposition, since he was an expert on Dravidian art, and the Dance of Shiva is the best-known work in the Madras museum, and a sort of symbol as well. But this logical juxtaposition caused me to connect one thing with another. There were twenty minutes left before the departure of my bus; I looked for a telephone and dialed the number of the American Express, where a young woman answered politely. "I'd like to leave a message for Mr. Schlemihl," I told her. The girl asked me to wait a minute and then said, "At the moment we have no such name on record, but you can leave your message all the same, if you like, and it will be delivered to him when he comes by."

"Hello, hello!" the operator repeated when she did not hear any reply.

"Just a minute, operator," I said. "Let me think."

What could I say. My message had a ridiculous side. Perhaps I had understood something. But exactly what? That, for someone, the circle had closed?

"It doesn't matter," I said. "I've changed my mind." And I hung up.

I don't deny that my imagination may have been working overtime. But if I guessed correctly what shadow Peter Schlemihl had lost, and if he ever happens, by the same strange chance that brought about our meeting on the train, to read this story, I'd like to convey my greetings. And my sorrow.

Translated by Frances Frenaye

The phrase that follows this is false:
the phrase that precedes this is true

Madras, 12 January 1985

Dear Mr. Tabucchi,

Three years have gone by since we met at the Theosophical Society in
Madras. I will admit that the place was hardly the most propitious in which
to strike up an acquaintance. We barely had time for a brief conversation,
you told me you were looking for someone and writing a little diary about
India. You seemed to be very curious about onomastics; I remember you
liking my name and asking my permission to use it, albeit disguised, in the
book you were writing. I suspect that what interested you was not so much
myself as two other things: my distant Portuguese origins and the fact that
I knew the works of Fernando Pessoa. Perhaps our conversation was somewhat eccentric: in fact its departure point was two adverbs used frequently

in the West (*practically* and *actually*), from which we attempted to arrive at the mental states which preside over such adverbs. All of which led us, with a certain logic, to talk about pragmatism and transcendence, shifting the conversation, perhaps inevitably, to the plane of our respective religious beliefs. I remember your professing yourself to be, it seemed to me with a little embarrassment, an agnostic, and when I asked you to imagine how you might one day be reincarnated, you answered that if ever this were to happen you would doubtless return as a lame chicken. At first I thought you were Irish, perhaps because the Irish, more than the English, have their own special way of approaching the question of religion. I must say in all honesty that you made me suspicious. Usually Europeans who come to India can be divided into two groups: those who believe they have discovered transcendence and those who profess the most radical secularism. My impression was that you were mocking both attitudes, and in the end I didn't like that. We parted with a certain coldness. When you left I was sure your book, if you ever wrote it, would be one of those intolerable Western accounts which mix up folklore and misery in an incomprehensible India.

I admit I was wrong. Reading your *Indian Nocturne* prompted a number of considerations which led me to write you this letter. First of all I would like to say that if the theosopher in Chapter Six is in part a portrayal of myself, then it is a clever and even amusing portrait, albeit characterized by a severity I don't believe I deserve, but which I find plausible in the way you see me. But these are not, of course, the considerations that prompted me to write to you. Instead I would like to begin with a Hindu phrase which translated into your language goes more or less like this: the man who thinks he knows his (or his own?) life, in fact knows his (or his own?) death.

I have no doubt that *Indian Nocturne* is about appearances, and hence about death. The whole book is about death, especially the parts where it talks about photography, about the image, about the impossibility of finding what has been lost: time, people, one's own image, history (as understood by Western culture at least since Hegel, one of the most doltish philosophers, I think, that your culture has produced). But these parts of the book are also an initiation, of which some chapters form secret and mysterious steps. Every initiation is mysterious, there's no need to invoke Hindu philosophy here because Western religions believe in this mystery too (the Gospel). Faith is mysterious and in its own way a form of initiation. But I'm sure the most aware of Western artists do sense this mystery as we do. And in this regard, permit me to quote a statement by the composer Emmanuel Nunes, whom I had occasion to hear recently in Europe: "*Sur cette route infinie, qui les unit, furent bâties deux cités: la Musique et la Poésie. La première est née, en partie, de cet élan voyageur qui attire le Son vers le Verbe, de ce désir vital de sortir de soi-même, de la fascination de l'Autre, de l'aventure qui consiste à*

vouloir prendre possession d'un sens qui n'est pas le sien. La seconde jaillit de
cette montée ou descente du Verbe vers sa propre origine, de ce besoin non moins
vital de revisiter le lieu d'effroi où l'on passe du non-être à l'être."

But I would like to turn to the end of your book, the last chapter. During my most recent trip to Europe, after buying your book, I looked up a few newspapers for the simple curiosity of seeing what the literary critics thought about the end. I could not, of course, be exhaustive, but the few reviews I was able to read confirmed what I thought. It was evident that Western criticism could not interpret your book in anything but a Western manner. And that means through the tradition of the 'double,' Otto Rank, Conrad's *The Secret Sharer*, psychoanalysis, the literary 'game' and other such cultural categories characteristic of the West. It could hardly be otherwise. But I suspect that you wanted to say something different; and I also suspect that that evening in Madras when you confessed to knowing nothing about Hindu philosophy, you were – why, I don't know – lying (telling lies). As it is, I think you are familiar with Oriental gnosticism and with those Western thinkers who have followed the path of gnosticism. You are familiar with the Mandala, I'm sure, and have simply transferred it into your culture. In India the preferred symbol of wholeness is usually the Mandala (from the Latin *mundus*, in Sanskrit 'globe,' or 'ring'), and then the zero sign, and the mirror. The zero, which the West discovered in the fourth century after Christ, served in India as a symbol of Brahma and of Nirvana, matrix of everything and of nothing, light and dark; it was also an equivalent of the 'as if' of duality as described in the Upanishads. But let us take what for Westerners is a more comprehensible symbol: the mirror. Let us pick up a mirror and look at it. It gives us an identical reflection of ourselves, but inverting left and right. What is on the right is transposed to the left and vice versa with the result that the person looking at us is ourselves, but not the same self that another sees. In giving us our image inverted on the back-front axis, the mirror produces an effect that may even conceal a sort of sorcery: it looks at us from outside, but it is as if it were prying inside us; the sight of ourselves does not leave us indifferent, it intrigues and disturbs us as that of no other: the Taoist philosophers call it *the gaze returned*.

Allow me a logical leap which you perhaps will understand. We are looking at the gnosis of the Upanishads and the dialogues between Misargatta Maharaj and his disciples. Knowing the Self means discovering in ourselves that which is already ours, and discovering furthermore that there is no real difference between being in me and the universal wholeness. Buddhist gnosis goes a step further, beyond return: it nullifies the Self as well. Behind the last mask, the Self turns out to be absent.

I am reaching the conclusion of what, I appreciate, is an overly long letter, and probably an impertinence that our relationship hardly justifies. You will forgive me a last intrusion into your privacy, justified in part by the confession you made me that evening in Madras vis-à-vis your likely reincarnation, a confession I haven't the audacity to consider a mere whim. Even Hindu thinking, despite believing that the way of Karma is already written, maintains the secret hope that harmony of thought and mind may open paths different from those already assigned. I sincerely wish you a different incarnation from the one you foresaw. At least I hope it may be so.

I am, believe me, your

Xavier Janata Monroy

Vecchiano, 18 April 1985

Dear Mr. Janata Monroy,

Your letter touched me deeply. It demands a reply, a reply I fear will be considerably inferior to the one your letter postulates. First of all, may I thank you for allowing me to use part of your name for a character in my book; and furthermore for not taking offense at the novelistic portrayal of the theosopher of Madras for which you provided the inspiration. Writers are not to be trusted even when claiming to practice the most rigorous realism: as far as I am concerned, therefore, you should treat me with the maximum distrust.

You confer on my little book, and hence on the vision of the world which emerges from it, a religious profundity and a philosophical complexity which unfortunately I do not believe I possess. But, as the poet we both know says, "Everything is worth the trouble if the spirit be not mean." So that even my little book is worth the trouble, not so much for itself, but for what a broad spirit may read into it.

Still, books, as you know, are almost always bigger than ourselves. To speak of the person who wrote that book, I am obliged, in spite of myself, to descend to the anecdotal (I wouldn't dare to say biographical), which in my case is banal and low caste. The evening we made each other's acquaintance in the Theosophical Society, I had just survived a curious adventure. Many things had happened to me in Madras: I had had the good fortune to meet a number of people and to meditate on various strange stories. But what happened to me had to do with me alone. Thanks to the complicity of a temple guard, I had managed to get inside the compound of the temple of Shiva the Destroyer, which, as you know, is strictly forbidden to non-Hindus, my precise intention being to photograph the altars. Since you appreciate the meaning I attribute to photography, you will realize that this amounted to a double sacrilege, perhaps even a challenge, since Shiva the Destroyer is identified with Death and with Time, is the *Bhoirava*, the Terror, and manifests himself in sixty-four forms, which the temple of Madras illustrates and which I wanted to photograph for myself. It was two in the afternoon, when the temple shuts its gates for siesta, so that the place was entirely deserted with the exception of a few lepers who sleep there and who paid not the slightest attention. I know this will arouse a profound sense of disapproval on your part, but I do not want to lie. The heat was oppressive, the big monsoon had only just finished and the compound was full of stagnant puddles. Swarms of flies and insects wandered about in the air, and the stench of excrement from the cows was unbearable. Opposite the altars to Shiva the traitor, beyond the troughs for the ablutions, is a small wall for votive offerings. I climbed upon it and began to take my photos. At that moment a piece of the wall I was standing on, being old and sodden with rain, collapsed. Of course I am giving you a 'pragmatic' explanation of what happened, since considered from another point of view the affair could have another explanation. In any event, when the wall crumbled I fell, skinning my right leg. A few hours later, when I'd got back to my hotel, the scratches had developed into an incredible swelling. It was only the following morning, though, that I decided to go to the doctor, partly because I hadn't had myself vaccinated at all before coming to India and I was afraid I might have got infected by tetanus – certainly my leg showed every sign that that was what it was. To my considerable amazement, the doctor refused to give me an anti-tetanus shot. He said it was superfluous since, as he said, tetanus runs its course much faster in India than in Europe, and 'if it were tetanus you would already be dead.' It was just 'a simple infection,' he said, and all I needed was some streptomycin. He seemed quite surprised that I hadn't been infected by tetanus, but evidently, he concluded, one occasionally came across Europeans who had a natural resistance.

I'm sure you will find my story ridiculous, but it's the story I have to tell. As far as your gnostic interpretation of my *Nocturne,* or rather of its conclusion, is concerned, allow me to insist in all sincerity that I am not familiar with the Mandala and that my knowledge of Hindu philosophy is vague and very approximate, consisting as it does in the summary found in a tourist guide and in a pocket paperback I picked up at the airport called *L'Induisme* (part of the 'Que sais-je?' series). As regards the question of the mirror, I started doing some hurried research only after getting your letter. For help I went to the books of a serious scholar, Professor Grazia Machianò, and am finding it hard work to grasp the basics of a philosophy of which I am woefully ignorant.

Finally I must say my own feeling is that on the most immediate level my *Nocturne* reflects a spiritual state which is far less profound than you so generously suppose. Private problems, of which I will spare you the tedious details, and then of course the business of finding myself in a continent so remote from my own world, had provoked an extremely strong sense of alienation toward everything: so much so that I no longer knew why I was there, what the point of my journey was, what sense there was in what I was doing or in what I myself might be. It was out of this alienation, perhaps, that my book sprang. In short, a misunderstanding. Evidently misunderstandings suit me. In confirmation of which allow me to send you this most recent book of mine, published a few days ago. You know Italian very well and may wish to take a look at it.

I am, believe me, your

Antonio Tabucchi

Dear Mr. Tabucchi,

My thanks for your letter and gift. I have just finished *Little Misunderstandings of No Importance* and your other book of short stories, *Reverse Side*, which you were generous enough to enclose. You did well, since the two complement each other and this made reading them more pleasant.

I am perfectly well aware that my letter caused you some embarrassment, just as I am also aware that you, for reasons of your own, wish to elude the gnostic interpretations that I have of your books and which you, as I said, deny. As I mentioned in my first letter, Europeans visiting India can usually be divided into two categories: those who believe they have discovered transcendence and those who profess the most radical secularism. I fear that despite your search for a third way, you do fall into these categories.

Forgive me my insistence. Even the philosophical position (may I so define it?) which you call 'Misunderstanding' corresponds, albeit dressed up in Western culture (the Baroque), to the ancient Hindu precept that the misunderstanding (the error of life) is equivalent to an initiatory journey around the illusion of the real, that is, around human life on earth. Everything is identical, as we say; and it seems to me that you affirm the same thing, even if you do so from a position of skepticism (are you by any chance considered a pessimist?). But I would like to abandon my culture for a moment and draw on yours instead. Perhaps you will remember Epimenides' paradox which goes more or less like this: 'The phrase that follows this is false: the phrase that precedes this is true.' As you will have noticed, the two halves of the saying are mirrors of each other. Dusting off this paradox, an American mathematician, Richard Hoffstadter, author of a paper on Gödel's theorem, has recently called into question the whole Aristotelian-Cartesian logical dichotomy on which your culture is based and according to which every statement must be either true or false. This statement in fact can be simultaneously both true and false; and this because it refers to itself in the negative: it is a snake biting its own tail, or, to quote Hoffstadter's definition, 'a strange loop.'

Life too is a strange loop. We are back to Hinduism again. Do you at least agree on this much, Mr. Tabucchi?

I am, believe me, your

Xavier Janata Monroy

Dear Mr. Janata Monroy,

As usual your letter has obliged me to make a rapid and I fear super-ficial attempt to assimilate some culture. I only managed to track down something about the American mathematician you mention in one Italian periodical, a column written from the USA by journalist Sandro Stille. The article was very interesting and I have promised myself to look into the mat-ter more deeply. I do not, however, know much about mathematical logic, nor perhaps about any kind of logic; indeed I believe I am the most illogical person I know, and hence I don't imagine I will make much progress in studies of this variety. Perhaps, as you say, life really is 'a strange loop.' It seems fair that each of us should understand this expression in the cultural context that best suits him.

But allow me to give you a piece of advice. Don't believe too readily in what writers say: they lie (tell lies) almost all the time. A novelist who writes in Spanish and who perhaps you are familiar with, Mario Vargas Llosa, has said that writing a story is a performance not unlike a strip-tease. Just as the girl undresses under an immodest spotlight revealing her secret charms, so the writer lays bare his intimate life to the public through his stories. Of course there are differences. What the writer reveals are not, like the unin-hibited girl, his secret charms, but rather the specters that haunt him, the ugliest parts of himself: his regrets, his guilt and his resentments. Another difference is that while in her performance the girl starts off dressed and ends up naked, in the case of the story the trajectory is inverted: the writer starts off naked and ends up dressed. Perhaps we writers are simply *afraid*. By all means consider us cowards and leave us to our private guilt, our private ghosts. The rest is clouds.

Yours
    Antonio Tabucchi

Translated by Tim Parks

Bucharest Hasn't Changed a Bit

Not to mention, he was doing well there – too well. Was he exaggerating? No, he wasn't exaggerating in the least. I feel better here than at home, he said, my meals served, the bed made, sheets changed once a week, and a room all to myself, there's even a small balcony, true the view isn't much, a stretch of cement buildings, but from the common terrace with its little tables and wicker chairs you can enjoy a splendid panorama, the whole city, and to the right, the sea, it's not a nursing home, he said, it's a hotel. He almost sounded irritated, the way old people sometimes do, and his son didn't dare contradict him. Dad, he murmured, don't get worked up, I know you're doing well here, I realize that. You don't know anything, mumbled the old man, what do you know, you're just saying that to make me happy, you had the good luck to be born in this country, when your mother and I were finally able to leave she had a belly out to here, did you ever think that if we hadn't made it out, you might've become some fervent kid with a red neckerchief, one of those boy scouts lining the street when the presidential car would go by, the magnificent couple inside, blessing the crowd? Do you know what you would've yelled, waving your little flag? Long live the conducător who leads our people toward a radiant future. And you'd have grown up like that, forget all the languages you've learned here and all your culture and linguistics, forget linguistics, they'd have sewn up your *lingua* if you weren't obedient to the ideals of the magnificent *conducatrix* couple who were conducting the people toward a radiant future.

Perhaps he's finished, thought the son, now he's done venting, he's tired, the son would've liked to say something rather than just repeating the obvious stuff he'd said last time, fine, Dad, don't get worked up, you just said you're doing well here, better than at home, I think so too, leave the past alone, don't think about it, it happened so long ago, please, Dad. But he couldn't find any other words: fine, Dad, don't get worked up, you just said you're doing well here, better than at home, I think so too, leave the past alone, don't think about it. The old man didn't let him finish, he was entitled to speak, that's how it should be, now he was staring blankly, he caressed his knees as though wanting to press the creases of his pants, he was sitting on that little padded chair with a white pillow behind his neck, gazing at a photograph in a silver frame that he kept on the side table. It was an image of a young man and woman hugging each other, he had his right arm around her waist, she had a hand on his shoulder almost without touching it, as if she were embarrassed by having her picture taken, she had a ribbon in her fluffy hair, wore a modest dress in a style that made him think of certain movies from before the war, how strange, he'd always seen that picture on the big bureau in his parents' bedroom, once when he was young he'd asked his mom who they were and she'd answered: no one you knew.

You know that atrocious couple was received everywhere with every honor right up till yesterday? The old man went on with his thoughts, did you know that? He didn't answer, just nodded slightly, it wasn't yesterday, Dad, he dared to mumble, they killed them more than fifteen years ago, Dad. The old man didn't hear. They kept giving her honorary degrees, the great scientist, he continued, she'd invented a magic potion, a rejuvenating gelatin that stopped time much better than the monkey's glands of that other charlatan, the Russian, a semolina flatbread, royal jelly, and sludge from the Black Sea, and for this wonderful discovery of hers, the heads of state in the countries where you now spend your time welcomed her like a benefactress to mankind, tons of honorary degrees, in France in Italy in Germany, I can't remember, in your Europe, anyhow, you, where are you teaching now, Rome? Don't forget that racial laws were invented right there, in this beautiful country where we made sure you were born, some sinister types, real fascists, are making official appearances, are being received with every honor, everything upside down, and meanwhile, in the country where your mother and I were born, the fervent believers in the radiant future showed up instead, the fake scientist's eternal-youth gelatin is what attracted them, these old people like me who resisted aging, who planted themselves in a nice hotel on the Black Sea, feasted on lavish meals but every day, first thing, took two spoonfuls of the magic royal jelly, then shamelessly went down to the private beach, progressives and nudists, to check beneath their bellies to see if the treatment was having any effect. She was a nurse, she began her scientific career by sticking bedpans under old people's asses in places like this one, then she married the *conducător* of the people and became a scientist, did you tell me you're going back to Rome tomorrow? If you get a chance, wave at that guy for me when he leans out the window, the television showed him when he traveled to the same place where they used to take me on vacation as a boy, he wore lovely loafers and a white outfit, just the right color for that place, innocence, if only he'd worn a monk's habit, which is serious clothing in certain circumstances, and as if that weren't enough, guess what he suddenly thought to utter in his castrato voice? To ask the Lord, his Lord of course, why He was absent, why He wasn't there, and where He was. What on earth kind of questions were those? *Gott mit uns*, my son, that's where He was, He was with them, He was there, next to the sentries guarding the barbed wire, in case any of us got the idea to escape, even if we could barely stand.

He lit a cigarette he'd hidden under a napkin in the drawer where he kept his medicines. When you leave, open the window, he said, if the nurse realizes, she'll make a fuss about it, she's a softie but she sticks to the rules, here everyone's obsessed with rules, in any case I do feel much better here than at home, besides, it wasn't a palace, and of course you remember the social worker assigned to me by the municipality to look after me four hours a week, can you imagine, that pigheaded Ukrainian used to look at me as though I were an official document, and not a word of Romanian, and then giving people like us – I'm thinking of your mother's family now, after all they had to go through in Ukraine – giving people like that a Ukrainian as a social worker, a pigheaded person who pretends not to understand if you talk to her in Romanian and answers in her own language. He wanted to tell him: Dad, please, don't say absurd things, she didn't talk to you in her language, she was talking to you in Hebrew, and she didn't pretend not to understand Romanian, she really didn't understand it, it's you who never wanted to learn how to speak Hebrew correctly, you always insisted on speaking Romanian, even with me, I'm grateful for that because you gave me your language, though you can't make a chauvinistic matter out of it, I understand your problem, when you and Mom arrived here you were more than forty years old, it wasn't easy, but you can't blame the social work-er if she doesn't talk to you in Romanian. Instead he preferred not to say anything since the old man had launched into his soliloquy again, going back to a seemingly finished subject, as he tended to do now. Please don't make me repeat myself, he said, I feel like I'm in a hotel here, and if you want to remain in Rome to teach, don't let your conscience disturb you, see this nice room? I've never in my life been in a hotel as nice as this, you can't even imagine when your mother and I were able to crawl out of that sewer, you can't imagine the place where I left my brother, after his illness, that was no nursing home, it was a *lager*, the *lager* of the great *conducător* of the Romanian people, I left him in a wheelchair in the hall, he tried to follow us to the exit but he didn't move a millimeter, the wheelchairs of the *conducător*'s nursing homes were nailed down, and then he began praying out loud, he called after me, reciting the Talmud to make us stop, you understand? If your mother and I left, nobody else would go see him, take care of him, but in that moment, as I was crying and trying to hide my tears, with all those witches in white uniforms staring at me, all of them spies dressed up like nurses, I mean, in that moment, hey, a brother can't be treated like that, you, would you do that to a brother even if you don't have one? And then I turned and said clearly, so the spies in white uniforms could hear: we both managed to avoid the Codreanu camps, but this one, the great *conducător r*'s, I did all by myself, for five years, my dear brother, and since I've been reeducated, now I can leave, because sometimes they allow visas for reeducated people, and I'll preserve an entirely personal memory of my reeducation.

He grew quiet, as if he'd finished, but he hadn't, it was only a pause, he only needed to get his wind back. You know, my son, he went on, you can go ahead and tell your memories to others, they're eager to listen to your account and perhaps they get everything, even the smallest nuances, but that memory will still be yours and yours alone, it doesn't become someone else's memory just because you've told it to others, memories are told but not transmitted. And then, since it seemed like the right moment, he said: speaking of memory, Dad, the doctor told me you refuse to take your medicine, the nurse realized that you pretend to swallow the pills and then spit them out in the sink, why do you do that? These doctors I don't like, murmured the old man, they don't understand a thing, believe me, they are ignorant know-it-alls. I don't think there's much to understand, Dad, he replied, they're only trying to help a person of your age, that's all, besides, the diagnosis is encouraging, there is no serious pathology as we feared, if there were, your attitude would be understandable since it wouldn't be an attitude but the indicator of a progressive pathology, in your case it's an attitude, or rather a purely psychological fact, so the doctors say, that's the reason they prescribed these pills for you, it's a very light psychoactive drug, nothing much, just a little help. The old man looked at him with an expression that struck him as indulgent, perhaps his voice had an ironic tone. A helping hand, sure, a helping hand, those people think they can polish your memory like a mirror, this is the point, to make it function not the way it wants but the way they want, so it doesn't obey itself anymore, its own nature, which has no geometric shape, you can't represent memory with a nice geometric drawing, it takes the shape it wants according to the moment, to the time, to who knows what, and they, the big doctors, they want to make it trigonometrical, that's the right word, so it's easily measured, like dice, this is reassuring for them, a die has six sides, you turn it over and can see them all, does memory seem like a die to you? He waved as though whisking away a fly. He grew quiet. He'd stopped smoothing the creases of his pants. His eyes closed, his head on the pillow of the armchair, he seemed to have fallen asleep. Many years ago, he whispered, I had a recurring dream, I started having it when I was fifteen, in the *lager*, and I carried it with me for half my life. A night rarely passed without that dream, to tell the truth it wasn't even a dream, because dreams, even the most disjointed dreams, have a story, and mine was only an image, like a photo, actually, my head was snapping that photo, if I can put it that way, because I was standing there looking at the fog and at a certain point, click, my brain snapped a photo, and in front of me a landscape would be displayed, or rather, there was no landscape at all, it was a landscape made of nothing, mainly there was a gate, a beautiful white gate, thrown open onto a landscape that wasn't there, nothing other than that image, the dream was mostly what I felt while looking at that image my brain had photographed, because dreams aren't so much what happens as the emotion one feels while living what happens, and I wouldn't know how to tell you about the emotion I was feeling, because emotions aren't explainable, to be explained they have to transform into feelings, as Baruch knew, but a dream isn't the right place for transforming emotions into feelings, I can tell you this was real torment for me, because while I longed to take off running, go through that wide-open gate, and dive into the unknown beyond, fleeing toward I don't know where, at the same time I also felt a sense of shame, like guilt for something I didn't do, the fear of hearing my father's voice scolding me, but there was no voice in that dream, it was a silent dream, with the fear of hearing a voice. That dream vanished the first night we got to this country. We slept in Jaffa at the house of some friends you never met, they died soon after, your mother couldn't fit into her clothes anymore, we had only two suitcases and there was a feeling of war in the air, for that matter it's always felt like war in this country, we slept on the terrace, on two makeshift beds, it was hot, you could hear sirens in the distance and noise coming from the streets, which wasn't reassuring for people used to the silence of Bucharest nights, but even so, I slept like a child that night and never had that sort of dream again.

He broke off. Opened his eyes for a moment and then shut them again. Began talking in a voice so low that the son leaned forward to hear him. Last week the dream came back, he whispered, exactly the same, the same iron gate, really white, apparently dreams don't rust, and neither do the emotions that go with them, exactly like what I used to feel, the same torment, the desire to take off running and cross over, to run in order to see what lies hidden beyond, but something holds me back, and it's not my father's voice, my film is silent like photos are silent, it's not the voice of my father, if only I could hear his voice, it's the fear of hearing it, but enough now.

He opened his eyes and in a firm voice asked: when are you leaving? On Wednesday, Dad, he answered, but I'll come back to see you in a month. Don't throw your money away, said the old man, I bet the airfare from Rome is really pricey. Dad, he said, getting ready to go, don't be the cheap old Jewish man, please. I am a cheap old Jewish man, said the old man, what else could I be if not a cheap old Jewish man? Before you go, open the window, please, if the nurse smells the stink of smoke, she gets angry.

◆　◆　◆

Fortunately he had only a carry-on bag, enough for a weekend, otherwise he'd have lost who knows how much time waiting at the luggage carousel, he knew that. When he emerged from the arrivals lounge into the main airport hall, he was hit by a glaring light much fiercer than the one in Rome, and above all he felt the heat, which was almost shocking to him, as though he'd forgotten that the end of April in Tel Aviv is practically summertime, and he sniffed some familiar scents that piqued his appetite. There must have been a cart nearby of some street vendor frying falafel, he looked around because he had the idea of buying a bagful to bring to his father, he knew well that he'd be told the falafel didn't stand comparison with the Romanian *covrigi* his mother had cooked all her life, but at the Ben Gurion Airport one couldn't expect to find *covrigi*, he could find them at a Romanian bistro near the Carmel Market, but who knows how much time he'd lose because of the traffic. He spotted the falafel vendor, bought a small bagful, and got in line for the taxi. A cab turned up, driven by a young Palestinian, a beardless guy with a tentative mustache on his upper lip, who at first sight didn't even seem to be of age. He spoke to him in Arabic, so as not to force him to speak Hebrew. A driver's license, d'you have one? he asked. The young guy looked at him, wide-eyed. Do you think I'd like to get myself arrested, sir? he answered, these people arrest everybody, you go to jail for even less. The answer disturbed him: these people arrest everybody, these people who? His country, he thought, "these people" were his country. He gave his destination imprecisely. Around Ben Yehuda, he said, then I'll tell you exactly where. An elegant place, observed the young guy with a shrewd smile. Very elegant, he answered, it's a home for old people. The car had just slipped into the traffic when he had an idea. Do you know a good Palestinian bakery? The falafel he had, the *covrigi* he didn't feel like looking for, why not bring his father a Palestinian specialty? All during his childhood he'd heard his father say that Romanian Jews were the other Palestinians of Israel. I know a great one, the young man answered enthusiastically, my brother works there, they even make a baklava like you can't find anywhere these days. Baklava isn't Palestinian, it's Iraqi, he replied, sorry, it's Iraqi, no offense intended. No way it's Iraqi, said the young guy, that's a good one.

The nurse at the lodge told him his father was probably on the common terrace, at that hour tea was served to the guests. He found him sitting at a small table with three friends. Next to the cup there was a pack of cards, perhaps they'd played a game. He was almost surprised to see the old man get up and head toward him, arms spread wide, cheerful.

They sat at a small table to the side, he put the two little bags on the table, had no time to say a word since his father was already asking if he wanted tea or coffee, he'd never seen his father so courteous. How are you feeling? he asked. Very well, answered the old man, I've never felt so good. He had a shrewd look in his eyes, he was practically winking, almost seeking complicity in something. Are you sleeping well? he asked, and the old man answered, better than a child. The terrace extended around the building on the top floor, but from the table where they were seated the sea wasn't visible, the city was resplendent under the afternoon sun. They were silent. His father asked him for a cigarette. He himself didn't smoke, but he'd bought a pack at the airport, like he always did when he came to visit. The old man leaned back in his chair, inhaled a mouthful of smoke with pleasure, and then made a sweeping gesture with his arm, like someone showing a visitor something he owns, pointing to the city spread out at their feet. I'm glad you came back to my country, he said, it was time you did. He made the same sweeping gesture. In all these years Bucharest hasn't changed a bit, he said smiling, don't you agree?

Translated by Martha Cooley and Antonio Romani

Little Misunderstandings
of No Importance

The clerk called the court to order and there was a brief silence as the nearly white-haired Federico, in his judge's robe, led the little procession through the side door into the courtroom. At that very moment the tune of *Dusty Road* surged up in my mind. I watched them take their seats as if I were witnessing a ritual, remote and incomprehensible, but projected into the future. The image of those solemn men, sitting on a bench with a crucifix hanging over it, faded into the image of a past that, like an old film, was my present. Almost mechanically my hand scribbled *Dusty Road*, while my thoughts traveled backwards. Leo, confined like a dangerous animal in the prisoner's cage, lost his sickly, unhappy look. I saw him leaning on his grandmother's Empire-style console with that old bored and knowing expression which made for his special charm. Tonino, he was saying, put *Dusty Road* on again, will you? And I put the record back on. Yes, Leo deserved to dance with Maddalena, known as the Tragic Muse because as Antigone in the school play she had broken into uncontrollable sobs. This was the appropriate record, yes it was, for dancing so passionately in the drawing room of Leo's grandmother. And so the trial began, that evening when Leo and Federico had taken turns dancing with the auburn-haired Tragic Muse, gazing into her eyes and swearing that they weren't rivals, that they didn't give a damn for her. They were dancing for the sake of dancing, that was all. But they were mad about her, of course, and so was I as I changed the records, looking as if I didn't care.

From one dance to another a year went by, a year marked by a certain phrase, one that we ran into the ground because it fit any and every occasion. Missing an appointment, spending money you didn't have in the bank, forgetting a solemn promise, finding a highly recommended book a total bore, all these mistakes and ambiguities were described as "little misunderstandings of no importance." The original example was something that happened to Federico and roused us to memorable gales of laughter. Federico, like the rest of us, had planned his future and signed up for Classics; he was already a whiz at Greek and had played the part of Creon in *Antigone*. We, instead, had opted for Modern Literature. It's closer to us, said Leo, and you can't compare James Joyce with those boring ancients, can you? We were at the Caffè Goliardico, the students' meeting place, each of us with our registration book, looking over the schedule of courses, stretched out on the billiard table. Memo had joined us; he was a fellow from Lecce with political commitments and anxious that politics be handled *the way it should be*, so we called him Little Pol and the nickname stuck throughout the year. At a certain point Federico appeared on the scene, looking very upset and waving his registration book in the air. He was so breathless and beside himself that he was barely able to explain. They had signed him up, by mistake, for Law and he simply couldn't get over it. To give him moral support we went with him to the administrative office, where we tangled with an amiable but indifferent old codger who had dealt with thousands of students over the years. He looked carefully at Federico's book and then at his worried face. Just a little misunderstanding that can't be corrected, he said. No use worrying about it. Federico stared at him in dismay, his cheeks reddening. A little misunderstanding that can't be corrected? he stammered. The old man did not lose his composure. Sorry, he said, that's not what I meant. I meant a little misunderstanding of no importance. I'll get it fixed for you before Christmas. Meanwhile, if you like, you can take the Law courses. That way you won't be wasting your time. We went away choking with laughter: a little misunderstanding of no importance! And Federico's angry look made us laugh all the more.

Strange, the way things happen. One morning a few weeks later, Federico turned up at the café looking quite pleased with himself. He had just come out of a class on the philosophy of law, where he had gone merely to pass the time, and well, boys, believe it or not, he'd grasped certain problems he'd never grasped before. The Greek tragedians, by comparison, had nothing to say. He already knew the classics, anyhow, so he'd decided to stay with Law.

Federico the judge said something in a questioning tone, his voice sounded faraway and metallic as if it were coming through a telephone. Time staggered and took a vertical fall, and the face of Maddalena, ringed by tiny bubbles, floated in a puddle of years. Perhaps it's not such a good idea to go and see a girl you've been in love with on the day they're amputating her breasts. If only in self-defense. But I had no desire to defend myself, I'd long since surrendered. And so I hung about in the hall outside the operating room, where patients are made to wait their turn. She was wheeled in, wearing on her face the innocently happy look of pre-anesthesia, which I've heard stirs up a sort of unconscious excitement. Her eyes were glazed and I squeezed her hand. There was an element of fear, I could see, but dulled by drugs. Should I say something? What I wanted to say was: Maddalena, I was always in love with you, I don't know why I've never managed to tell you before. But you can't say such a thing to a girl entering the operating room for an operation like that. Instead I broke out at full speed with some lines from *Antigone*, which I'd spoken in the performance years before:

Many wonders there be, but naught more wondrous than man. Over the surging sea, with a whitening south wind wan, through the foam of the firth man makes his perilous way.

God knows how they came to mind so exactly, and whether she remembered them, whether she was in a condition to understand, but she squeezed my hand before they wheeled her away. I went down to the hospital coffee shop, where the only alcohol was Ramazzotti bitters and it took a dozen glasses to get me drunk. When I began to feel a bit queasy I went and sat on a bench in front of the hospital, telling myself that it would be quite mad to seek out the surgeon, a madness born of drink. Because I wanted to find the surgeon and ask him not to throw those breasts into the incinerator but to give them to me. I wanted to keep them, and even if they were rotten inside I didn't care; there's something rotten in all of us and I cared for those breasts – how could I put it? – they had a special meaning for me; I hoped he understood. But a flicker of reason stopped me; I managed to get a taxi and go home, where I slept through the afternoon. It was dark when the telephone woke me – I didn't notice the time. Federico was on the line saying: Tonino, it's me. Can you hear, Tonino? It's me. Where are you? I asked in a gummy voice. I'm down south, in Catanzaro. Catanzaro? What are you doing there? I'm trying for the post of prosecutor. I've heard that Maddalena's ill, in the hospital. Exactly. Do you remember those breasts of hers? Well, snip, snip, they're gone. He said: what are you telling me, Tonino. Are you drunk? Of course I'm drunk, drunk as a drunk, and life makes me sick, and you make me sick, too, taking your exams there in Catanzaro. Why didn't you marry her, tell me that. She was in love with you, not with Leo, and you knew it; you didn't marry her because you were afraid. And why the devil did you marry that know-it-all wife of yours, tell me that! You're a bastard, Federico! There was a click as he hung up. I muttered a few more expletives into the telephone, then went back to bed and dreamed of a field of poppies.

And so the years continued to flutter back and forth, as they passed, while Leo and Federico continued to dance with Maddalena in the Empire-style drawing room. In the space of a second, just as in an old film, while they sat in the courtroom, the one wearing his judge's robe, the other in the prisoner's cage, the merry-go-round turned, leaves flew off the calendar and stuck to one another, and they danced with Maddalena, gazing into her eyes, while I changed the records. Up came a summer we all spent together in the mountain camp of the National Olympics Committee, the walks in the woods and the contagious passion for tennis. The only serious player was Leo, with his unbeatable backhand, his good looks, tight T-shirt, glossy hair, and the towel wound casually around his neck when the game was over. In the evening we stretched out on the grass and talked of one thing and another, wondering on whose chest Maddalena would lay her head. And then a winter that took us all by surprise. First of all on account of Leo.

Who could have imagined him, so well turned out and so ostentatiously futile, with an arm around the statue in the hallway leading to the university president's office, haranguing the students. He wore a very becoming olive-green parka, military style. I'd bought a blue one, which I thought went better with my eyes, but Maddalena didn't notice, or at least didn't say so. She was intent on Federico's parka, which was too big, with dangling sleeves and was bunched up round his ramrod body in a ridiculous fashion which, for some reason, women found endearing.

Now Leo started to talk in his low-pitched, monotonous voice, as if he were telling a story, in the ironical manner that I knew so well. In the courtroom you could have heard a pin drop; the newspaper reporters hunched over their notes as if he were telling the Great Secret, and Federico, too, followed him intently. Good God, I thought, why must you pretend to follow so closely? What he's saying isn't so strange; you were there that winter, too. I almost imagined Federico standing up and saying: Gentlemen of the jury, with your permission, I'd like to tell this part myself, because I knew it at first hand. The bookshop was called Nuovo Mondo; it was on the Piazza Dante where now, if I'm not mistaken, there's an elegant shop that sells perfumes and Gucci bags. It had a large room, with a closet, a smaller room and a toilet on the right side. We never kept explosives in the small room, only the strawberries Memo brought up from Apulia after he had been there on vacation. Every evening, in season, we got together to eat strawberries and olives. The chief topic of conversation was the Cuban Revolution – there was a poster of Che Guevara over the cash register – but we talked about revolutions of the past as well. As a matter of fact, I was the one to talk about them. My friends had no historical or philosophical background, whereas I was studying for an exam on political ideas (which I passed with top marks). And so I gave them lessons – seminars, we called them – on Babeuf, Bakunin, and Carlo Cattaneo. Actually revolutions didn't really interest me. I did it because I was in love with a red-haired girl called Maddalena. I was sure she was in love with Leo, or, rather, I knew she was in love with me but I was afraid she was in love with Leo. In short, it was a little misunderstanding of no importance, a phrase popular with us at the time. And Leo was always making fun of me; he had a gift for that. He was witty and ironical and plied me with tricky catch questions which conveyed the idea that I was a reformist but he was a true radical, a revolutionary. He wasn't all that radical, really; he put it on in order to impress Maddalena, but whether it was by chance or from conviction, he took on a prominent role and became the most important member of our group. Yet, for him, too, this was a little misunderstanding which he considered of no importance. And then you know how it is, the roles that we assume become real. In life things easily get locked in, and attitude freezes into choice.

But Federico said none of these things. He was listening attentively to the prosecutor's questions and Leo's answers. It's not possible, I thought to myself; it's all a play. But it wasn't a play, it was real. Leo was on trial; the things he had done were real and he was admitting to them, impassively, while Federico impassively listened. He couldn't do otherwise, I realized, because that was his role in the comedy that they were playing. At this point I was moved by an impulse to rebel, to interfere, to erase the prepared script and rewrite it. What could I do? I wondered, and the only recourse, it occurred to me, was Memo; yes, that was the only thing to do. I went out of the courtroom, showing my press card to the *carabinieri*. In the hallway, while I was dialing the number, I racked my brain for what I was going to say. They're going to sentence Leo, I'd tell him; come quickly, because you've got to do something. He's digging his own grave; it's totally absurd. Yes, he's guilty, I know, but not to that extent; he's just a cog in a machine that's crushed him. He's pretending he was at the controls, but that's just in order to live up to his reputation. He's never manipulated any machine and perhaps there's no proof of what he's saying. He's just Leo, the Leo that used to play tennis, with a towel wound around his neck. Only he's bright, I mean bright in a stupid way, and the whole thing's absurd.

The telephone rang and rang until a cold, refined woman's voice, with a marked Romanesco accent, answered. No, His Honor isn't home, he's at Strasbourg. What do you want? I'm a friend, I said, an old friend. Can you tell me how to reach him? It's something very important. I'm sorry, said the cold, refined voice, His Honor is at a meeting. If you like you can leave a message and I'll get it to him as soon as possible. I hung up and went back to the courtroom, but not to the place where I'd been sitting. I stayed at the upper edge of the semi-circular room, behind the *carabinieri*. At this particular moment there was widespread murmuring. Leo must have come out with one of his usual witticisms. His face wore the malicious expression of someone who has pulled a fast one. At the same time I detected a great sadness. Federico, too, as he shuffled the papers in front of him, seemed oppressed by sadness, like a weight on his shoulders. I had an urge to cross the courtroom, to stand in front of the judge's bench, amid camera flashes, to say something to the two of them and grasp their hands or something of the sort. But what could I say? That it was a little misunderstanding that couldn't be corrected? Because just as I thought of this I realized that everything was, indeed, an enormous little misunderstanding that couldn't be corrected and that life was taking away, that the roles had been allotted. It was impossible not to play them. I had come with my notebook and pen, hadn't I? Just looking at them play their parts I was playing one of my own. I was to blame for falling in with the game, because there's no escape and everyone of us is to blame in his own way. All of a sudden I was overcome by weariness and shame and, at the same time, I was struck by an idea I couldn't decipher, a desire for Simplification. In a split second, in pursuit of a dizzily unwinding skein, I realized that we were there because of something called Complication, which for hundreds and thousands and millions of years has piled up, layer upon layer, increasingly complex circuits and systems, forming us as we are and all that we live through. I longed for Simplification, as if the millions of years that had produced the beings named Federico, Leo, Maddalena, Little Pol, and myself had magically faded out into a split second of vacant time and I could imagine us, all of us, sitting on a leaf. Well, not exactly sitting, because we had become microscopic in size, and mononuclear, without sex, or history or reason, but with a flicker of awareness which allowed us to recognize one another, to know that we, we five, were there on a leaf, sucking up dewdrops as if we were sipping drinks at a table of the Caffè Goliardico, having no other function than to sit there while another kind of record player played another kind of *Dusty Road*, in a different form but with the same substance.

While I lingered, absorbed in my thoughts, on the leaf, the court rose, and so did the onlookers; only Leo remained seated in his cage and lit a cigarette. Perhaps it was a scheduled recess, I don't know, but I tiptoed outside. The air was clear and the sky blue; in front of the courthouse an ice-cream cart seemed to be abandoned, and few cars passed by. I started to walk toward the docks. On the canal a rusty barge, apparently without an engine, was gliding silently by. I passed near it, and aboard there were Leo and Federico, the one with his devil-may-care expression, the other grave and thoughtful. They were looking at me questioningly, obviously expecting an answer. And at the stern, as if she were holding the tiller, sat Maddalena, radiant with youth and smiling, like a girl who knows she's radiant with youth. Do you remember *Dusty Road?* I wanted to ask them. But all three were static and motionless, and I realized that they were overly colored, lifelike plaster figures, in the caricature poses of mannequins in a shop window. And so, of course, I said nothing but merely waved as the barge carried them away. Then I walked on, toward the docks, with slow, cadenced steps, trying not to tread on the cracks in the pavement, the way, as a child, I tried in a naive ritual to regulate by the symmetry of stones my childish interpretation of a world as yet without scansion or meter.

Translated by Frances Frenaye

Drip, Drop, Drippity-Drop

The pain that woke him ran down his left leg, from the groin to the knee, but its provenance was elsewhere, by then he knew this all too well. With his thumb he began to press from his tailbone upward, when he arrived between the third and fourth lumbar vertebrae, he felt a sort of electric current running through his body, as if right from that spot a radio station was broadcasting out from the neck to the toes. He tried rolling over in bed. At the first attempt the pain paralyzed him. He stayed on his side, actually not even on his side, on half his side, which isn't a precise position, it's a would-be position, a passage. He stayed suspended in this movement, if one can put it that way, as in certain Italian Baroque paintings where the saint, male or female, gracefully overexcited from fasting or from Christ, remains forever suspended within the painter's brushstrokes, because the craziest of painters, who are also the ones of genius, are marvelous at catching the unfinished movement of their depicted character, usually crazy himself, and the pictorial miracle happens as a kind of bizarre levitation that seems to dispense with the force of gravity.

He tried to wiggle his toes. With a little pain they moved, the big toe included, the one most at risk. He stayed like this, not daring to shift a millimeter, looking at his toes, and thought of that poor guy from Prague who one day awoke out of context, meaning that instead of lying on his back he was lying on his armor-plated shell, and watching the ceiling of his little room, which he imagined to be pale blue, who knows why, he helplessly waved his hairy little paws and wondered what to do. The thought irritated him, not so much because of the comparison but because of the reference to genre: literature, literature again. He tried out an experimental phenomenology of the situation. He got up his courage and shifted his side a centimeter. From the fourth vertebra a dart of pain shot to the base of the neck – he could almost hear the whistle – then it spun around, reached the groin, and spread along the entire leg. *How to Speak with Your Own Body* was a book he'd read with skepticism yet with a certain curiosity, he couldn't deny that, a popular book though probably not very reliable in scientific terms, but why shouldn't one talk to one's own body? There are people who talk to walls. As a young man he'd read a novel by a writer quite popular at the time, then unjustly neglected, quite a guy, who really got down to the nitty-gritty at times and who in that book spoke to his own body, indeed a specific part of his body, which he called his "him," and from there arose a dialogue that was anything but banal. Here though it wasn't the same, since his "him" wasn't involved, and so he simply said: leg, oh leg! He moved it and it responded with a lacerating pain. Dialogue was impossible. He stretched it very carefully and the pain concentrated in his spinal column. The column of infamy. He grew irritated again. He thought that if he called the doctor, who at this point he was all too familiar with, he'd tell him he was suffering from literature, an observation already made in the past. He pictured the doctor saying: my dear fellow, the problem is mainly due to the fact that you assume the wrong positions, actually you've assumed the wrong positions all your life, to write, because the problem unfortunately is that you write, don't be offended, instead of leading a life more consonant with hygiene and well-being, that is, going to a pool or jogging around in shorts like other men your age, you stay all bent over writing your books for whole days at a time, and not only bent over – I've seen you – you're all crooked too, like a misshapen biscuit, your spine looks like the sea when a southwest wind blows, all crooked, but it's too late to reform it now, you could try torturing it a bit less, you don't seem capable of reading the x-rays I brought you, so to make you really understand, tomorrow I'll bring you the plastic articulated spine I used to study with at college, and I'll shape it like yours, so you'll finally see what you've reduced it to.

◆ ◆ ◆

We gave her oxygen because she was having difficulty breathing, said the doctor, but her condition is stable, don't worry. Which meant: stay calm tonight, she'll get through it. He entered on tiptoe. The room was dim. The patient in the next bed was asleep. She was a chubby blond woman who yesterday had spent all afternoon on her cell phone while lying in bed in her robe, waiting for the operation she needed to have as soon as possible, she said. And added: I don't know why I decided to check myself into the hospital, today of all days, with the Easter holidays and our restaurant in Porto Venere packed, you know, dear sir (she said it like that, dear sir), ours is one of the very few Ligurian restaurants that appear in the Michelin Guide, and imagine that, I came here to have this little operation on this of all days, when diners are waiting in line to get in, could I be any stupider, just for a few gallstones, Armando, Armando (meanwhile Armando, who must have been her husband, was on the phone), please don't make Leopoldina set the tables, she does her best but she always mixes up the glasses, puts the wine glasses in the wrong spot, I spent the whole winter teaching her but she doesn't get it, she's a girl from the country, bye, Armando, *mi raccomando*. And having gotten rid of Armando with a rhyme, she went on: you'll understand, dear sir, demanding clients, they're almost always from Milan, or they're Lombards, anyway, and as you know better than I, it's Lombardy that pulls the cart in our country, they're rich because they work, and it's understandable that they're demanding, and if a Milanese says I'm paying and I demand, you can't object, because if someone's paying then he demands, dear sir, it stands to reason. And then she began describing in detail the specialty of the house, tagliatelle with lobster, but fortunately she was cut off by another call from Armando.

◆　◆　◆

He avoided passing too close, circled around her bed, and sat at the foot of the other one. His aunt wasn't sleeping, she always seemed to be sleeping yet as soon as she heard a rustle she'd open her eyes. When she saw him she removed her oxygen tube. She didn't want her body to look ravaged by illness, even flat on her back she was able to eye him up and down, she noticed the cane right away, perhaps she read the suffering on his face, even though the worst of it had passed with the painkillers. What happened to you? she asked. Yesterday you were fine. It's been since this morning, he said, I don't know, I talked with the doctor, it seems my spine has had another crash like last year in May, I need another x-ray, I'll do it when I can. She wagged her finger, a warning sign: in Italy the only good kind of crash is a financial one, she murmured, today the woman in the other bed spent the afternoon watching TV, she wanted a TV, she says it's her right since she's paying for the room, they gave her headphones so I wouldn't be disturbed, at a certain point they interviewed that show-off from Telecom who caused a shortfall of I don't know how many millions, he fixed himself right up with that crash. Unfortunately mine is only vertebral, he replied. The conversation was mouth to ear, so the restaurateur wouldn't wake up and start reciting the second part of the recipe for tagliatelle with lobster. Don't come anymore, she said, sitting in that chair day and night is destroying you, with that spine of yours, stay at home a few days. What are you saying? he said, excuse me, I stay home lazing away like the doctor would want while you're here in this bed, at home I get depressed, at least here we chat. Don't be silly, she said, what chatting, in a whole day I get out three words, I don't have the breath anymore. And she smiled. It was strange, the smile on her face; on the suffering mask drawn by illness the smile restored that beautiful woman with prominent cheekbones and enormous eyes whom the disease had buried in extensive swelling, as if she'd reemerge stubbornly, that young woman who had acted as a mother to him when he was a kid and his own wasn't able to. And an image returned that his memory had erased, a precise scene, the same expression on the aunt's face now, and her voice saying to the sister: don't worry, just go to the hospital, I'll take care of the boy like he's my own, I'll think only of him. And right after came the image of Enzo, surfacing from an eternity of time came Enzo, the judicious student of jurisprudence, Enzo, so proper and so polite, who after graduating was supposed to join the firm of his grandfather as an intern because he'd be marrying this aunt, and he was so earnest, Enzo, everybody used to say, and still surfacing from the well of memory here was Enzo now, waving his arms and shouting, he, who was so proper and polite, was yelling at the aunt, telling her that she was crazy: but you're crazy – I'm taking the bar exam and you're heading to the mountains for three months with the kid, and what about us, when are we supposed to get married! And he saw again his self from back then, a scrawny little kid, wearing glasses because he was nearsighted, he didn't understand, and then why was his left knee always hurting, he didn't want to go to the Dolomites, they were far away, and up in the mountains he couldn't play bandits with his friend Franco, his aunt whirled around, her voice was icy and low, he'd never heard her use that tone before, Enzo, you don't understand anything, you're broke, and you're also a bit of a fascist, I've heard that you and your friends criticize my father for his ideas, this kid has tuberculosis of the knee, he needs to be in the mountains, and I'm taking him to the mountains with my own money, not yours, which you don't have, except for what my father is kind enough to give you every month, and if you ever feel like taking a real curve, now's the moment. Go ahead and take the curve: was it possible his aunt had used this expression? And yet the words resounded in his ears: go ahead and take the curve.

For the rest of the afternoon the woman talked about her gallstones, his aunt murmured in his ear, it's not possible they'd put her in a ward like this for gallstones, it has to be more than gallstones, poor woman, and then she watched *Big Brother*, her favorite show, I pretended to sleep, so she took off her headphones and lowered the volume but I could hear too, I didn't want to call the nurses, what do you expect, educating people is a waste of time, besides, by now these people have made their money and *Big Brother* has educated them, that's why they vote for him, it's a vicious circle, they vote for those who educated them, you've lost the tail end of the tagliatelle with lobster, but I wanted to humor myself, you know how much she charges her demanding diners for a lobster tagliatelle? Fifty euros, and it's frozen lobster, I made her confess. She seemed to want to stop talking, turning her head on the pillow. But then she murmured: Ferruccio, I want to say several words I've never said in my life, or I haven't said them often, only when nobody could hear me, but now I'd really like to say them out loud, and if I wake that one up over there, too bad. He nodded and winked at her. What a fool, poor woman, she said. And then added: they're all a bunch of assholes. She closed her eyes. Perhaps she'd really fallen asleep.

◆　◆　◆

Ferruccio. He remembered that name, Ferruccio. She'd called him Ferruccio only a few rare times, when he was a child, though, then she stopped. His uncle's name was Ferruccio, but no one called him Ferruccio, it was his given name, the kind people are given but never use, that used to happen where they lived, the newborn would be given the name of some ancestor, to honor his memory, and then they'd call the baby something else. He'd always heard his aunt's brother called Cesare, sometimes Cesarino, maybe that was his middle name, Ferruccio Cesare, who knows, but on his gravestone there was no Cesare, just Ferruccio. His aunt was the only person who'd always called her brother by the name Ferruccio, he died in Mussolini's war, in the pictures sent from that Greek island where he'd refused to surrender to the Germans, he was a scrawny little lieutenant with an honest face and curly hair, he was studying engineering, when his draft card arrived in '39 the aunt had a terrible fight with him, she'd told him about it once, she didn't want her brother to leave, but where do you want me to go, he objected, are you crazy? Go into the mountains here behind us, she said, hide in the caves, don't go to war for these cockroaches. But in '39 nobody was in the mountains yet, there were only wild rabbits and foxes, the aunt was always ahead of her time, and so Ferruccio left for Il Duce and for the King.

He moved close enough to brush against her face. She wasn't sleeping: she suddenly opened her eyes and put a finger to his lips. The aunt's voice was a whisper, so feeble it seemed like the rustling wind. Pull up your chair and move closer to my mouth, she said, but don't think I'm dying, I'm talking like this so the restaurateur won't wake up, if we interrupt her dream she'll get upset, she's dreaming of lobster. He laughed softly. Don't laugh, she said,

I need to talk, I'd like to talk to you, and I don't know if there'll be another occasion. He nodded and whispered in her ear: what would you like to tell me? About your childhood, she said, when you were so small you can't remember. It was the last thing he expected. And she sensed it, his aunt didn't miss a thing. Don't be surprised, she said, it's not all that strange, you think you're so smart but it probably never occurred to you that memories of the time when someone is very young are kept by the grown-ups near him, you can't recall such far-off memories, you need the grown-ups from back then, if I don't tell you about it myself maybe something of it will remain but only in a confusing, thick fog, like when you've dreamed something but can't really remember what, so you don't even try to remember since it doesn't make sense to try remembering a dream you don't remember, this is how the past is made, especially if it's really past, I couldn't possibly remember when your uncle Ferruccio and I were children, yet I remember it like it was yesterday though more than eighty years have passed, because in her last days my grandmother thought to tell me what I was like before I knew who I was, when I wasn't aware yet of being myself, have you ever thought about this? He shook his head no, he never had, and said: so what years do you want to tell me about? When you were five and everyone at home had come to believe you were a bit retarded, as the kindergarten teacher said, but that just didn't make sense to me, how could you be retarded if you already knew how to write your name? I'd already taught you the alphabet and you'd learned it in the blink of an eye. I write the letters on the blackboard, the teacher said, I ask him to repeat them, like everybody else, and he stays silent, there are two possibilities, either he's a difficult boy and is refusing, or he just doesn't understand. I suddenly grasped the problem one July day, we were at Forte, a woman with a white apron and a basket on her arm was walking along the beach, yelling: doughnuts! We were under the beach umbrella, you wanted a doughnut, and your father was about to call her over, but I said to you: Ferruccio, go and get one by yourself, then I'll give you the money, do you remember? He said nothing, drifting back. Go on and try, she said, see if you can catch hold of the memory, you were sitting on a black-and-white rubber ring your father had made for you from the inner tube of a moped to which he'd stuck a waterproof, papier-mâché duck head he'd found in a warehouse for carnival floats, it must have been one of the first Viareggio carnivals after the disaster, you were hugging it all morning long but didn't have the courage to take it into the water, now can you see yourself? He could see himself. Or it seemed like he did, he saw a skinny little boy hugging an inner tube with a duck head attached to it and the little boy saying to his dad: I want a doughnut. I see him, Aunt, he confirmed, I think I'm back there. And then I told you to go and get the doughnut, she murmured, you left the duck and ran toward that white apron on the beach, hurrying hurrying, afraid that apron would go by, an imposing man was standing at the water's edge showing off how elegant he was in his white robe and he took you by the hand, not understanding, and called to us in a haughty voice, and I said to your father: the kid can't see distances, he mistook that man for the doughnut woman, he is really nearsighted, no way he's retarded, take him to an eye doctor.

The aunt's phrasing came back to him. She'd never say a game was nice, it was really nice, and she hadn't bought him a colorful book but a really colorful one, and we had to go for a walk because that day the sky was really blue. Meanwhile she'd moved on to another memory, murmuring in that silent room, all those devices over the bed: the tanks, the plastic tubes, and the needles inserted in her arms, then she went quiet and suddenly the silence grew heavy, the sounds of the city seemed almost from another planet, the vast grounds surrounding the hospital isolated it from everything. And in that silence he listened to her murmuring in his ear, leaning forward, curiously his back pain had ceased, and behind that feeble voice he found he was navigating in a self he'd lost, back and forth like a kite twisting on a string, and from up there, from that kite upon which he was seated, he began to discern: a tricycle, the voice of an evening radio broadcast, a Madonna everybody claimed was crying, a little girl from a "displaced" family, with bows in her braids, who as she hopped on a chalk pattern on the ground exclaimed: square one, bread and salami! and other things like that, the aunt by then was talking in the dark since even the dim overhead light had been shut off, only the pale blue lamp over the bed remained and a glowing slice of neon coming from under the door. She closed her eyes and fell silent, she seemed exhausted. He straightened up in the chair and felt a sharp pinprick of pain between his vertebrae. She's fallen asleep, he thought, now she's really fallen asleep. Instead she brushed his hand and beckoned for him to come closer again. Ferruccio, he heard her breath saying, do you remember how beautiful Italy used to be?

✦ ✦ ✦

How can the night be present? Composed only of itself, it's absolute, every space belongs to it, its mere presence is imposing, the same presence a ghost might have that you know is there in front of you but is everywhere, even behind you, and if you seek refuge in a patch of light you become its prisoner because all around you, like the sea surrounding your little lighthouse, is the impenetrable presence of the night.

Instinctively he dug in his pocket for his car keys. They were attached to a small black device as big as a matchbox with two buttons: one set off a dot of red light that opened and closed the car, from the other, a mini-eye with a convex lens, emerged a bright fluorescent beam. He pointed the white beam at the floor. It cut through the dark like a laser. He scribbled with the light until he found his shoes, how strange, he'd never realized that they were still *those* shoes. Italian shoes? the woman at the next table had asked, studying them with interest. It'd started like that, with the shoes. But of course they're Italian shoes, madame, he mumbled to himself, handmade, finest leather, just look at the uppers, shoes are judged mainly by their uppers, here, madame, put your finger inside, don't worry, no, it doesn't tickle, *do you like?* But why do people hold on to a pair of shoes for twenty years, even Italian shoes, they wind up ruined, old shoes must be thrown out. The fact is they're comfortable, madame, he continued mumbling, I wear them because they're comfortable, don't kid yourself that these worn-out shoes are the madeleine of your lovely lashes, the point is lately my feet get a bit swollen, particularly at night, bad circulation, this damn discopathy has brought on arterial stenosis in my leg, the capillaries have been affected and so, madame, my feet swell.

Cautiously he pointed the beam of light toward the wall, like a detective searching for clues in the dark, he avoided the patient, especially her body, slowly scrolling down over the bed. He began to catalog. One: the plastic bag full of that milky stuff, with a narrow tube leading to the stomach: food. Two: next to it some sort of intravenous drip that disappeared under the sheets. Three: the oxygen boiling soundlessly in the water, now emerging from the inhaler she'd removed. Four: a little white bottle hanging upside down from a rack, with a thin tube that made a U-turn, the drops falling one after another before descending in a fixed rhythm down to the arm: morphine. With that same rhythm, all day and all night, doctors administered an artificial peace to a body that otherwise would shake from a storm of pain. He would've liked to avert his gaze but couldn't, as if he were being drawn in, hypnotized by that monotonous rhythm of drops. He pushed the little button and turned off the light. And then he heard them, the drops. At first they were muffled sound, a subterranean thrum, as though coming from the floor or walls: drip, drop, drippity, drippity, drip, drop, drippity-drop. They reached into his skull, tapped against his brain, but with no echo, a snap that pops and disappears to make way at once for the next snap, seemingly similar to the previous snap, but actually with a different tone, the same way rain begins falling on a lakeshore but if you really listen you can hear there's a variation of sound from drop to drop, because the cloud doesn't make the drops identical, some are bigger, some smaller, you just have to listen: drip, drop, drippity-drop, according to their own musical scale, they sounded like that, and after arriving and getting muffled inside his head, began growing in intensity to the point where he heard them burst in his head as though his skull couldn't contain them anymore, and they burst from his ears into the surrounding space, like bells gone crazy whose sonic waves grew to a spasm. And then, by sorcery, as though his body were a magnet able to attract sonic waves, he felt they were swarming toward him, but no longer in the brain, in the vertebrae, at a precise point, as though his vertebrae were the well of water where the rod discharges the lightning bolt. And it was also right at that point, he felt, that they extinguished themselves, tearing through the pall that the night imposed on the earth, lacerating its presence. The chinks in the shutters began going pale. It was dawn.

◆ ◆ ◆

And if we were to play the *if* game? The memory came with a voice at the little table next to his, as though his uncle were there, hidden behind the hedge bordering the terrace of the coffee bar. It was his uncle's voice this time, actually his uncle was the one who'd invented that game. Why? Because the *if* game is good for the imagination, especially on certain rainy days. For instance we are at the beach, or in the mountains, it doesn't matter, since the kid is sick and the sea and the mountains are both good for him, it all depends, otherwise a bad worm will gnaw at his knee, and for instance it's September, and in September sometimes it rains, never mind, if it's raining and he's at home, a kid can find a lot to do, but during this forced vacation, especially in a poorly furnished rental cottage or even worse in a pensione, if it rains, boredom sets in, and with it melancholy. But fortunately there's the *if* game, and so the imagination gets to work, and the best player is the one who throws out the craziest ideas, totally crazy, mamma mia that laughter, listen to this: and what if the pope were to have landed in Pisa?

He asked for a double espresso in a large cup. The hospital grounds were coming to life: two young doctors in white uniforms were chatting, a little truck marked HOSPITAL SUPPLIES set off, a man in light-blue coveralls came down a side street carrying a whisk and a plastic bag, now and then he'd stop and sweep up some leaves, some butts. On his little table he spread out the paper napkin folded next to his cup and smoothed it carefully so he could write on it. On a corner of the napkin, a brand: Caffè Honduras. He circled it with his fountain pen. The paper, porous, absorbed a little ink but held up: he could try. The first sentence was obligatory: what if I were to go to Honduras? He continued numbering the sentences. Two: and what if I were to dance the Viennese waltz? Three: and what if I were to go to the moon and eat Cain's fritters? Four: and what if Cain hadn't made any fritters? Five: and what if I had left on the ship? Six: and what if the ship had already left? Seven: and what if at a whistle it would turn back? Eight: and what if Betta were to get married? Nine: and what if the Maltese cat were to play the piano and sing in French?

Read as a poem it had its own personality, maybe that woman who'd asked him to write something for a poetry anthology for children would like it, but that wouldn't be honest, it wasn't for children, it was a *poème zutique*. But children like *zutiques*, what matters is saying silly things, so even if it's done out of melancholy, children won't realize. I'll phone him, he said to himself. There was no need for a cell phone, besides, he'd never had one: right by the coffee bar was a phone booth, and some change left on the table, tempting him. Sure, it wouldn't be easy to explain himself, the conversation had to be set up right, like a teacher wants with an essay, because if you set up the theme correctly, you're safe, even if you express yourself poorly. Perhaps before approaching the topic you'd need a code, something that once suggested complicity, a sort of watchword, like sentinels in the trenches would use when they changed guard. He thought: hand hand square and there passed a crazy hare. Sure that he'd get it. And then he'd say: I know very well you can't wake up someone at this hour after not calling him for three years, but the fact is I went into hiding for a bit. Hand hand square and there passed a crazy hare. He went on: I set my mind on writing a big novel, let's put it that way, that novel everyone's waiting for, sooner or later, the publisher, the critics, because sure, they say, the short stories are splendid, and also those two books of meanderings, even that fake diary is a text of the first order, no doubt, but a novel, when are you going to write us a real novel? Everyone's fixed on the novel, so I was fixed on it too, and if you're going to write the novel everyone wants from you, which will be your masterpiece, you realize you need the right atmosphere, and the right place, and you need to search for the right place God knows where, because where you are is never the right place, and so I went into hiding to look for the right place to write my masterpiece, am I making myself clear? Hand hand square and there passed a crazy hare. Ingrid is in Göteborg, she went to see our daughter, I don't know if you know but she got married in Göteborg, she went back to her maternal roots, besides, she's better off there than here around someone dying, but I'll explain that later, no, I'll explain right now, I'm in my usual haunts, at the city hospital, no, no, I'm really fine, sure I'd like to see you, I'm coming to the point, because my call is nothing but an sos from a radio operator who turned off his radio, but it's not that there was a storm around me, if anything a dead calm, without even any shadow lines to cross, they had been crossed a long time ago, there was a sandbar instead on which the boat ran aground. Hand hand square and there passed a crazy hare. My aunt is dying, said en passant. Mine, not yours, we each have a mother, and our father didn't have sisters, so it's my aunt, though that's not really why I'm calling, it's that actually I wanted to read you a passage from the novel I've been working on these past three years of silence so you'll have some idea of the effort I've put into it, I'm sure you'll understand why I didn't show up earlier, you ready? It goes like this: and what if I went to Honduras? And what if I danced the Viennese waltz? And what if I went to the moon and ate Cain's fritters? And what if Cain hadn't made his fritters? And what if I left with the ship? And what if the ship had already left? And what if at a whistle it would turn back? And what if Betta got married? And what if the Maltese cat played the piano while singing in French? It cost me more than the Serchio River cost the people of Lucca, you like it?

✦   ✦   ✦

He sat there, with the coins in hand, staring at the phone booth, there's a world of difference between saying and doing, and doing was saying: listen, I'm back, I'm here at the hospital, no, I'm totally fine, well, not totally, the fact is these three years have heaped up one on top of the other as though they were all just one day, actually just one night, I know I'm not making myself clear, I'll try to be clearer, think of plastic bottles, the ones for mineral water, the bottle makes sense as long as it's full of water, but when you've drunk it you can scrunch it up and throw it out, that's what happened to me, my time has scrunched up, and my vertebrae too, if I can put it that way, I know I'm jumping around but I can't express myself any better, be patient. And while he was thinking of what he'd come up with, he noticed a nurse in white pushing a wheelchair coming out of the low pavilion not far from the coffee bar, its glass door opened from the inside. And on the door closing behind them was a yellow sign with three blades, like a fan. The nurse was moving forward slowly because the path from the pavilion to the coffee shop rose slightly, and in the wheelchair was a boy, or at least from a distance it seemed a boy because he had no hair, but gradually as they approached he realized it was a girl. The features of the face, even though it was a childish face, weren't male, because the difference is already clear at ten or twelve, which seemed roughly the age of that boy, which is to say, that girl, and also the voice was already female, since at that age the vocal cords are well differentiated, and she talked with the old nurse pushing the wheelchair, although from there he couldn't make out what they were saying, he caught only the sound of the voices. He'd stood up with the coins in his hand aimed at the phone, rather he'd almost stood, he half stood, just like the day before getting out of bed, when the same razor blade cut into his back again, slicing all the way down to below his navel. He stood very still, like that figure of Pontormo he liked so much, whose face is a landscape of pain almost as though he were bearing the cross instead of the one destined for such a task. The two female voices were still too feeble to be deciphered, but they were cheerful, this he got from the tone, they seemed to be twittering back and forth, like two little sparrows telling each other something, he shut his eyes and the twittering became a squeak and he thought instead of mice chattering together in their cage, those white mice that scientists experiment on, they were two guinea pigs for the science of so-called life, the most agonizing science of all, one of them was being subjected to it prematurely, the other, the old one, had endured the experiments and gone on. They fell silent, perhaps because the woman pushing the wheelchair was getting tired and the girl didn't want to wear her out, but as soon as they reached the top of the path the girl began talking again, and must have been responding to something the nurse had said, from her tone of voice it was clear she was affirming something, a solemn affirmation that nobody could prove wrong. Her voice was joyful, full of life, as when life, through the voice, is willful and affirms itself. The girl repeated what she'd said just as they were passing him, and while she spoke a broad smile lit up her face: but this is the most beautiful thing in the world! But this is the most beautiful thing in the world!

The path continued down toward a clinic in the middle of the grounds. They'd stopped talking, but he could hear the noise of the wheelchair rolling over the gravel. He wanted to turn around but was unable to. The most beautiful thing in the world. That's what the girl had said, this bald girl, being hauled in a wheelchair by a nurse. She knew what the most beautiful thing in the world was. He, however, did not. How was it possible at his age, with all he'd seen and experienced, that he still didn't know what the most beautiful thing in the world was?

Translated by Martha Cooley and Antonio Romani

The Flying Creatures
of Fra Angelico

The first creature arrived on a Thursday toward the end of June, at vespers, when all the monks were in the chapel for service. Privately, Fra Giovanni of Fiesole still thought of himself as Guidolino, the name he had left behind in the world when he came to the cloister. He was in the vegetable garden gathering onions, which was his job, since in abandoning the world he hadn't wanted to abandon the vocation of his father, Pietro, who was a vegetable gardener, and in the garden at San Marco he grew tomatoes, courgettes and onions. The onions were the red kind, with big heads, very sweet after you'd soaked them for an hour, though they made you cry a fair bit when you handled them. He was putting them in his frock gathered to form an apron, when he heard a voice calling: Guidolino. He raised his eyes and saw the bird. He saw it through onion tears filling his eyes and so stood gazing at it for a few moments, for the shape was magnified and distorted by his tears as though through a bizarre lens; he blinked his eyes to dry the lashes, then looked again.

It was a pinkish creature, soft looking, with small yellowish arms like a plucked chicken's, bony, and two feet that again were very lean with bulbous joints and calloused toes, like a turkey's. The face was that of an aged baby, but smooth, with two big black eyes and a hoary down instead of hair; and he watched as its arms floundered wearily, as if unable to stop itself making this repetitive movement, miming a flight that was no longer possible. It had got caught up in the branches of the pear tree, which were spiky and warty and at this time of year laden with pears, so that at every one of the creature's movements, a few ripe pears would fall and land splat on the clods beneath. There it hung, in a very uncomfortable position, feet straddled over two branches which must be hurting its groin, torso sideways and neck twisted, since otherwise it would have been forced to look up in the air. From the creature's shoulder blades, like incredible triangular sails, rose two enormous wings which covered the entire foliage of the tree and which moved in the breeze together with the leaves. They were made of different colored feathers, ochre, yellow, deep blue, and an emerald green the color of a kingfisher, and every now and then they opened like a fan, almost touching the ground, then closed again, in a flash, disappearing behind each other.

Fra Giovanni dried his eyes with the back of his hand and said: "Was it you called me?"

The bird shook his head and, pointing a claw like an index finger toward him, wagged it.

"Me?" asked Fra Giovanni, amazed.

The bird nodded.

"It was me calling me?" repeated Fra Giovanni.

This time the creature closed his eyes and then opened them again, to indicate yes once again; or perhaps out of tiredness, it was hard to say: because he was tired, you could see it in his face, in the heavy dark hollows around his eyes, and Fra Giovanni noticed that his forehead was beaded with sweat, a lattice of droplets, though they weren't dripping down; they evaporated in the evening breeze and then formed again.

Fra Giovanni looked at him and felt sorry for him and muttered: "You're overtired." The creature looked back with his big moist eyes, then closed his eyelids and wriggled a few feathers in his wings: a yellow feather, a green one and two blue ones, the latter three times in rapid succession. Fra Giovanni understood and said, spelling it out as one learning a code: "You've made a trip, it was too long." And then he asked: "Why do I understand what you say?" The creature opened his arms as far as his position allowed, as if to say, I haven't the faintest idea. So that Fra Giovanni concluded: "Obviously

I understand you because I understand you." Then he said: "Now I'll help you get down."

Standing against a cherry tree at the bottom of the garden was a ladder. Fra Giovanni went and picked it up, and, holding it horizontally on his shoulders with his head between two rungs, carried it over to the pear tree, where he leaned it in such a way that the top of the ladder was near the creature's feet. Before climbing up, he slipped off his frock because the skirts cramped his movements, and draped it over a sage bush near the well. As he climbed up the rungs he looked down at his legs, which were lean and white with hardly any hairs, and it occurred to him they looked like the bird creature's. And he smiled, since likenesses do make one smile. Then, as he climbed, he realized his private part had slipped out of the slit in his drawers and that the creature was staring at it with astonished eyes, shocked and frightened. Fra Giovanni did himself up, straightened his drawers and said: "I'm sorry, it's something we humans have"; and for a moment he thought of Nerina, of a farmhouse near Siena many years before, a blond girl and a straw rick. Then he said: "Sometimes we manage to forget it, but it takes a lot of effort and a sense of the clouds above, because the flesh is heavy and forever pulling us earthward."

He grabbed the bird creature by the feet, freed him from the spikes of the pear tree, made sure that the down on his head didn't catch on the twigs, closed his wings, and then with the creature holding on to his back, brought him down to the ground.

The creature was droll: he couldn't walk. When he touched the ground he tottered, then fell on one side, and there he stayed, flailing about with his feet in the air like a sick chicken. Then he leaned on one arm and straightened his wings, rustling and whirling them like windmill sails, probably in an attempt to get up again. He didn't succeed, so Fra Giovanni gripped him under the armpits and pulled him up, and while he was holding the creature those frenetic feathers brushed back and forth across his face tickling him. Holding him almost suspended under these things that weren't quite armpits, he got him to walk, the way one does with a baby; and while they were walking, the creature's feathers opened and closed in a code Fra Giovanni understood, and asked him: "What's this?" And he answered: "This is earth, this is *the* earth." And then, walking along the path through the garden, he explained that the earth was made of earth, and clods of soil, and that plants grew in the soil, such as tomatoes, courgettes and onions, for example.

When they reached the arches of the cloister, the creature stopped. He dug in his heels, stiffened and said he wouldn't go any farther. Fra Giovanni put him down on the granite bench against the wall and told him to wait; and the creature stayed there, leaning up against the wall, staring dreamily at the sky.

"He doesn't want to be inside," explained Fra Giovanni to the father superior, "he's never been inside; he says he's afraid of being in an enclosed space, he can't conceive of space if it's not open, he doesn't know what geometry is." And he explained that only he, Fra Giovanni, could see the creature, no one else. Well, because that's how it was. The father superior, though only because he was a friend of Fra Giovanni's, might be able to hear the rustling of his wings, if he paid attention. And he asked: "Can you hear?" And then he added that the creature was lost, had arrived from another dimension, wandering about; there'd been three of them and they'd got lost, a small band of creatures cast adrift, they had roamed aimlessly through skies, through secret dimensions, until this one had fallen into the pear tree. And he added that they would have to shelter him for the night under something that prevented him from floating up again, since when darkness came the creature suffered from the force of ascension, something he was subject to, and if there was nothing to hold him down he would float off to wander about in the ether again like a splinter cast adrift, and they couldn't allow that to happen, they must offer the creature hospitality in the monastery, because in his way this creature was a pilgrim.

The father superior agreed and they tried to think what would be the best sort of shelter: something that was, yes, out in the open, but that would prevent any forced ascension. And so they took the garden netting that protected the vegetables from hedgehogs and moles; a net of hemp strings woven by the basket weavers of Fiesole, who were very clever with wicker and yarn. They stretched the net over four poles, which they set up at the bottom of the vegetable garden against the perimeter wall, so as to form a sort of open shed; and on the clods of earth, which the bird creature found so strange, they placed a layer of dry straw, and laid the creature on top of it. After rearranging his little body a few times, he found the position he wanted on his side. He sank down with intense pleasure and, surrendering to the tiredness he must have dragged after him across the skies, immediately fell asleep. Upon which the monks likewise went to bed.

The other two creatures arrived the following morning at dawn while Fra Giovanni was going out to check the guest's chicken run and see if he had slept well. Against the pink glow of the dawning day he saw them approaching in a low, slanting flight, as if desperately trying, and failing, to maintain height, veering in fearful zigzags, so that at first he thought they were going to crash against the perimeter wall. But they cleared it by a hair's breadth and then, unexpectedly, regained height. One hovered in the air like a dragonfly, then landed with legs wide apart on the wall. He sat there a moment, astride the wall, as if undecided whether to fall down on this side or the other, until at last he crashed down headfirst into the rosemary bushes in the flower bed. The second creature meanwhile turned in two spiraling loops, an acrobat's pirouette almost, like a strange ball, because he was a rolypoly sort of being without a lower part to his body, just a chubby bust ending in a greenish brushlike tail with thick, abundant plumage that must serve both as driving force and rudder. And like a ball he came down among the rows of lettuce, bouncing two or three times, so that what with his shape and greenish color you would have thought he was a head of lettuce a bit bigger than the others off larking about thanks to some trick of nature.

For a moment Fra Giovanni was undecided as to whom he should go and help first. Then he chose the big dragonfly, because he seemed more in need, miserably caught as he was head down in the rosemary bushes, one leg sticking out and flailing about as if calling for help. When he went to pull him out he really did look like a big dragonfly, or at least that was the impression he gave; or rather, a large cricket, yes, that's what he looked like, so long and thin, and all gangly, with frail slender limbs you were afraid to touch in case they broke, almost translucent, pale green, like stems of unripe corn. And his chest was like a grasshopper's too, a wedge-shaped chest, pointed, without a scrap of flesh, just skin and bones: though there was the plumage, so sheer it almost seemed fur; golden; and the long shining hairs that sprouted from his skull were golden too, almost like hair, but not quite, and given the position of his body, head down, they were hiding his face.

Fearfully, Fra Giovanni stretched out an arm and pushed back the hair from the creature's face: first he saw two big eyes, so pale they looked like water, gazing in amazement, then a thin, handsome face with white skin and red cheeks. A woman's face, because the features were feminine, albeit on a strange insectlike body. "You look like Nerina," Fra Giovanni said, "a girl I once knew called Nerina." And he began to free the creature from the rosemary needles, carefully, because he was afraid of breaking the thing; and because he was afraid he might snap her wings, which looked exactly like a dragonfly's, but large and streamlined, transparent, bluish pink and gold with a very fine latticing, like a sail. He took the creature in his arms. She was fairly light, no heavier than a bundle of straw, and walking across the garden Fra Giovanni repeated what he had said the day before to the other creature; that this was the earth and that the earth was made of earth and of clods of soil and that in the soil grew plants, such as tomatoes, courgettes, and onions, for example.

He laid the bird creature in the cage next to the guest already there, and then hurried to fetch the other little creature, the rolypoly one that had wound up in the lettuces. Though it now turned out that he wasn't as rounded as he had seemed, his body having in the meantime as it were unrolled, to show that he had the shape of a loop, or of a figure eight, though cut in half, since he was really no more than a bust terminating in a beautiful tail, and no bigger than a baby. Fra Giovanni picked him up and, repeating his explanations about the earth and the clods, took him to the cage, and when the others saw him coming they began to wriggle with excitement; Fra Giovanni put the little ball on the straw and watched with amazement as the creatures exchanged affectionate looks, patted each other's feet, and brushed each other's feathers, talking and even laughing with their wings at the joy of being reunited.

Meanwhile dawn had passed, it was daytime, the sun was already hot, and afraid that the heat might bother their strange skins, Fra Giovanni sheltered one side of the cage with twigs; then, after asking if they needed anything else and telling them if they did to please be sure to call him with their rustling noise, he went off to dig up the onions he needed to make the soup for lunch.

That night the dragonfly came to visit him. Fra Giovanni was asleep, he saw the creature sitting on the stool of his cell and had the impression of waking with a start, whereas in fact he was already awake. There was a full moon, and bright moonlight projected the square of the window onto the brick floor. Fra Giovanni caught an intense odor of basil, so strong it gave him a sort of heady feeling. He sat on his bed and said: "Is it you that smells of basil?" The creature laid one of her incredibly long fingers on her mouth as if to silence him and then came to him and embraced him. At which Fra Giovanni, confused by the night, by the smell of basil and by that pale face with the long hair, said: "Nerina, it's you, I'm dreaming." The creature smiled, and before leaving said with a rustle of wings: "Tomorrow you must paint us, that's why we came."

Fra Giovanni woke at dawn, as he always did, and straight after first prayers went out to the cage where the bird creatures were and chose the first model. A few days before, assisted by some of his brother monks, he had painted, in the twenty-third cell in the monastery, the crucifixion of Christ. He had asked his helpers to paint the background *verdaccio*, a mixture of ochre, black, and vermilion, since he wanted this to be the color of Mary's desperation as she points, petrified, at her crucified son. But now that he had this little round creature here, tail elusive as a flame, he thought that to lighten the virgin's grief and have her understand how her son's suffering was God's will, he would paint some divine beings who, as instruments of the heavenly plan, consented to bang the nails into Christ's hands and feet. He thus took the creature into the cell, set him down on a stool, on his stomach so that he looked as though he were in flight, and painted him like that at the corners of the cross, placing a hammer in his right hand to drive in the nails: and the monks who had frescoed the cell with him looked on in astonishment as with incredible rapidity his brush conjured up this strange creature from the shadows of the crucifixion, and with one voice they said: "Oh!"

So the week passed with Fra Giovanni painting so much he even forgot to eat. He added another figure to an already completed fresco, the one in cell thirty-four, where he had already painted Christ praying in the Garden. The painting looked finished, as if there were no more space to fill; but he found a little corner above the trees to the right and there he painted the dragonfly with Nerina's face and the translucent golden wings. And in her hand he placed a chalice, so that she could offer it to Christ.

Then, last of all, he painted the bird creature who had arrived first. He chose the wall in the corridor on the first floor, because he wanted a wide wall that could be seen from a good distance. First he painted a portico, with Corinthian columns and capitals, and then a glimpse of garden ending in a palisade. Finally he arranged the creature in a genuflecting pose, leaning him against a bench to prevent him from falling over; he had him cross his hands on his breast in a gesture of reverence and said to him: "I'll cover you with a pink tunic, because your body is too ugly. I'll draw the Virgin tomorrow. You hang on this afternoon and then you can all go. I'm doing an Annunciation."

By evening he had finished. Night was falling and he felt a little tired, and melancholy too, that melancholy that comes when something is finished and there is nothing left to do and the moment has passed. He went to the cage and found it empty. Just four or five feathers had got caught in the net and were twitching in the fresh wind coming down from the Fiesole hills. Fra Giovanni thought he could smell an intense odor of basil, but there was no basil in the garden. There were the onions that had been waiting to be picked for a week now and perhaps were already going off, soon they wouldn't be good enough for making soup anymore. So he set to pick them before they went rotten.

Translated by Tim Parks

Against Time

It'd gone like this:

The man had boarded at an Italian airport, because everything began in Italy, and whether it was Milan or Rome was secondary, what matters is that it was an Italian airport where you could take a direct flight to Athens, and from there, after a brief stopover, a connecting flight to Crete on Aegean Airlines, because this he was sure of, that the man had traveled on Aegean Airlines, so in Italy he'd taken a flight that let him connect in Athens for Crete at around two in the afternoon, he'd seen it on the Greek company's schedule, which meant this man had arrived in Crete at around three, three thirty in the afternoon. The airport of departure is not so important, though, in the story of the person who'd lived that story, it's the morning of any day at the end of April of 2008, a splendid day, almost like summer. Which is not an insignificant detail, because the man taking the flight, meticulous as he was, gave considerable importance to the weather and would watch a satellite channel dedicated to meteorology around the world, and the weather in Crete, he'd seen, was really splendid: twenty-nine degrees Celsius during the day, clear sky, humidity within normal limits, good seaside weather, ideal for lying on one of those white beaches described in his guide, for bathing in the blue sea and enjoying a well-deserved vacation. Because this was also the reason for the journey of that man who was going to live that story: a vacation. And in fact that's what he thought, sitting in the waiting lounge for international flights at Rome-Fiumicino, waiting for the boarding call for Athens.

And here he is finally on the plane, comfortably installed in business class – it's a paid trip, as will be seen later – reassured by the courtesies of the flight attendants. His age is difficult to determine, even for the person who knew the story that the man was living: let's say he was between fifty and sixty years old, lean, robust, healthy looking, salt-and-pepper hair, fine blond mustache, plastic glasses for farsightedness hung from his neck. His work. On this point too the person who knew his story was somewhat uncertain. He could be a manager of a multinational, one of those anonymous businessmen who spend their lives in an office and whose merit is one day acknowledged by headquarters. But he could also be a marine biologist, one of those researchers who observe seaweed and microorganisms under a microscope, without leaving their laboratory, and so can assert that the Mediterranean will become a tropical sea, as perhaps it was millions of years ago. Yet this hypothesis also struck him as not very satisfying, biologists who study the sea don't always remain shut up in their laboratory, they wander beaches and rocks, perhaps they dive, they perform their own surveys, and that passenger dozing in his business-class seat on a flight to Athens didn't actually look like a marine biologist, maybe on weekends he went to the gym to keep fit, nothing else. But if he really did go to the gym, then why did he go? To what end did he maintain his body, stay so young looking? There really was no reason: it'd been over for quite a while with the woman he'd considered his life companion, he didn't have another companion or lover, he lived alone, stayed away from serious commitments, apart from some rare adventures that can happen to everybody. Perhaps the most credible hypothesis was that he was a naturalist, a modern follower of Linnaeus, and he was going to a convention in Crete along with other experts on medicinal herbs and plants, abundant in Crete. Because one thing was certain, he was going to a convention of fellow researchers, his was a journey that rewarded a lifetime of work and commitment, the convention was taking place in the city of Retimno, he'd be in a hotel made of bungalows a few kilometers from Retimno, and a car service would shuttle him in the afternoons, but he'd have mornings to himself.

The man woke up, pulled out the guide from his carry-on, and looked for his hotel. What he found was reassuring: two restaurants, a pool, room service, the hotel had closed for the winter and had only reopened in mid-April, and this meant very few tourists would be there, the usual clients, the Northern Europeans thirsty for sunlight as the guide described them, were still in their little boreal houses. The pleasant voice from the loudspeaker asked everyone to buckle their seat belts, they'd begun the descent to Athens and would land in about twenty minutes. The man closed the folding tray table and put his seat upright, replaced the guide in his carry-on, and from the pocket of the seat in front of him pulled out the newspaper that the flight attendant had distributed, to which he'd paid no attention. It was a newspaper with many full-color supplements, the usual weekend ones, the economics-financial supplement, the sports supplement, the interior-design supplement, and the weekend magazine. He skipped all the supplements and opened the magazine. On the cover, in black-and-white, was the picture of the atomic bomb's mushroom cloud, with the title: THE GREAT IMAGES OF OUR TIME. He began leafing through, somewhat reluctantly. First came an ad by two fashion designers showing a young man naked to the waist, which at first he thought was a great image of our time, but then there was the first true image of our time: the stone façade of a house in Hiroshima where the heat from the atomic bomb had liquefied a man, leaving only the imprint of his shadow. He'd never seen this image and was astonished by it, feeling a kind of remorse: that thing had happened more than sixty years before, how was it possible he'd never seen it? The shadow on the stone was a silhouette, and in this profile he thought he could see his friend Ferruccio, who for no apparent reason, on New Year's Eve of 1999, shortly before midnight, had thrown himself from the tenth floor of a building onto Via Cavour. Was it possible that the profile of Ferruccio, squashed into the soil on the thirty-first of December in 1999, looked like the profile absorbed by stone in a Japanese city in 1945? The idea was absurd, yet that's what passed through his mind in all its absurdity. He kept riffling the magazine, and meanwhile his heart began beating erratically, one-two-pause, three-one-pause, two-three-one, pause-pause-two-three, the so-called extrasystole, nothing pathological, the cardiologist had reassured him after an entire day of testing, only a matter of anxiety. But why now? It couldn't be those images provoking his emotions, they were faraway things. That naked girl, arms raised, who was running toward the camera in an apocalyptic land-scape: he'd seen this image more than once and it hadn't made such a violent impression, and yet now it produced in him an intense turmoil. He turned the page. There was a man on his knees, palms together, at the edge of a pit, a kid sadistically pointing a gun at his temple. Khmer Rouge, said the caption. To reassure himself he made himself think that these things were also from faraway places and distant times. But the thought wasn't enough, a strange form of emotion, almost a thought, was telling him the opposite, that the atrocity had happened yesterday, it'd happened just that morning, while he was on this flight, and by sorcery had been imprinted on the page he was looking at. The voice over the loudspeaker stated that the landing would be delayed by fifteen minutes due to air traffic, and meanwhile the passengers should enjoy the view. The plane traced a wide curve, banking to the right, from the little window opposite he could glimpse the blue of the sea while in his own, the white city of Athens was framed, with a green spot in the middle, no doubt a park, and then the Acropolis, he could see the Acropolis perfectly, and the Parthenon, his palms were damp with sweat, he asked himself if it weren't a sort of panic provoked by the plane going round in circles, and meanwhile he looked at the photo of a stadium where policemen in riot gear pointed submachine guns at a bunch of barefooted men, under it was written: Santiago de Chile, 1973. And on the opposite page was a photo that seemed a montage, surely retouched, it couldn't be real, he'd never seen it: on the balcony of a nineteenth-century palazzo was Pope John Paul II next to a general in uniform. The pope was without doubt the pope, and the general was without doubt Pinochet, with that hair full of brilliantine, that chubby face, that little mustache, and the Ray-Ban sunglasses. The caption said: His Holiness the Pope on his official visit to Chile, April 1987. He began quickly leafing through the magazine, as though anxious to get to the end, barely looking at the photographs, but he had to stop at one of them, it showed a kid with his back turned to a police van, his arms raised as though his beloved soccer team had scored a goal, but looking closer you could see he was falling backwards, something stronger than he was had struck him. On it was written: Genoa, July 2001, meeting of the eight richest countries in the world. The eight richest countries in the world: the phrase provoked in him a strange sensation, like something that is at once understandable and absurd, because it was understandable and yet absurd. Every photo was on a silvery page as though it were Christmas, with the date in big letters. He'd arrived at 2004, but he hesitated, he wasn't sure he wanted to see the next picture, was it possible the plane was still going around in circles? He turned the page, it showed a naked body collapsed on the ground, a man apparently, though in the photo they'd blurred the pubic area, a soldier in camouflage extended a leg toward the body as though he were kicking a garbage can, the dog he held on a leash was trying to bite a leg, the muscles of the animal were as taut as the cord that held it, in the other hand the soldier held a cigarette. The caption read: Abu Ghraib prison, Iraq, 2004. After that, he arrived at the year he found himself in now, the year of our Lord 2008, that is he found himself in sync, that's what he thought even if he didn't know with what, but in sync. He couldn't tell what image he was in sync with, but he didn't turn the page, and meanwhile the plane was finally landing, the landing strip was running beneath him with the intermittent white bands blurring to a single band. He'd arrived.

Venizelos Airport looked brand new, surely they'd built it for the Olympic Games. He was happy with himself for being able to reach the boarding gate for Crete without reading the signs in English, the Greek he'd learned at school was still useful, curiously. When he landed at the Hania airport at first he didn't realize he'd reached his destination: during the brief flight from Athens to Crete, a little less than an hour, he'd fallen fast asleep, forgetting everything, it seemed, even himself. To such a degree that when he came down the airplane's staircase into that African light, he asked himself where he was, and why he was there, and even who he was, and in that amazement at nothing he even felt happy. His suitcase wasn't long in arriving on the conveyor belt, just beyond the boarding gates were the car rental offices, he couldn't remember the instructions, Hertz or Avis? It was one or the other, fortunately he guessed right, along with the car keys, they gave him a road map of Crete, a copy of the program of the convention, his hotel reservation, and the route to the tourist village where the convention goers were lodged. Which by now he knew by heart, because he'd studied and restudied it in his guide, nicely furnished with road maps: from the airport you went straight down to the coast, you had to go that way unless you wanted to reach the Marathi beaches, then you turned left, otherwise you wound up west and he was going east, toward Iraklion, you passed in front of the Hotel Doma, went along Venizelos, and followed the green signs that meant highway though it was actually a coastal freeway, you exited shortly after Georgopolis, a tourist spot to avoid, and followed the directions for the hotel, Beach Resort, it was easy.

The car, a black Volkswagen parked in the sun, was boiling, but he let it cool down a little by leaving the doors open, entered it as though he were late for an appointment, but he wasn't late and he didn't have any appointments, it was four o'clock in the afternoon, he'd get to the hotel in a little more than an hour, the convention wouldn't start till the evening of the following day, with an official banquet, he had more than twenty-four hours of freedom, what was the hurry? No hurry. After a few kilometers a tourist sign indicated the grave of Venizelos, a few hundred meters from the main road. He decided to take a short break to freshen up before the drive. Next to the entrance to the monument was an ice-cream shop with a large open terrace overlooking the little town. He settled himself at a table, ordered a Turkish coffee and a lemon sorbet. The town he saw had been Venetian and then Turkish, it was nice, and of an almost blinding white. Now he was feeling really good, with an unusual energy, the disquiet he'd felt on the plane had completely vanished. He checked the road map: to get to the freeway to Iraklion he could pass through the town or go around the gulf of Souda, a few kilometers more. He chose the second route, the gulf from up above was beautiful and the sea intensely azure. The descent from the hill to Souda was pleasant, beyond the low vegetation and the rooftops of some houses he could see little coves of white sand, a strong urge to swim came over him, he turned off the air-conditioning and lowered the window to feel the warm air smelling of the sea on his face. He passed the little industrial port and the residential zone and arrived at the intersection where, turning to the left, the road merged with the coastal highway to Iraklion. He put on his left blinker and stopped. A car behind him beeped for him to go: there was no oncoming traffic. He didn't move, just let the car pass him, then signaled right and went in the opposite direction, where a sign said Mourniès.

And now we're following him, the unknown character who arrived in Crete to reach a pleasant seaside locale and who at a certain moment, abruptly, for a reason also unknown, took a road toward the mountains. The man proceeded till Mourniès, drove through the village without knowing where he was going, though as if he did. Actually he wasn't thinking, just driving, he knew he was headed south: the sun, still high, was already behind him. Since he'd changed direction, that sensation of lightness had returned, which he'd briefly felt at the table in the ice-cream shop, looking down on the broad horizon: an unusual lightness, and with it an energy he no longer recalled, as though he were young again, a sort of light euphoria, almost a happiness. He arrived at a village called Fournès, drove through the town confidently as though he already knew the way, stopped at a crossroads, the main road went to the right, he took the secondary road with a sign that said: Lefka Ori, the white mountains. He drove on calmly, the sensation of well-being was turning into a sort of cheerfulness, a Mozart aria came to mind and he felt he could reproduce its notes, he began whistling them with amazing ease, but then went hopelessly out of tune in a couple of passages, which made him laugh. The road slipped into the rugged canyons of a mountain. They were beautiful and wild places, the car went along a narrow asphalt road bordering the bed of a dry creek, at a certain point the creek bed disappeared among the rocks and the asphalt ended in a dirt road, in a barren plain among inhospitable mountains, meanwhile the light was fading, but he kept going as though he already knew the way, like someone obeying an old memory or an order received in a dream, and at a certain point he saw a crooked tin sign riddled with holes as if from gunshots or from time, and the sign said: Monastiri.

He followed it as though he'd been expecting it all along, until he came to a tiny monastery, its roof in ruins. He realized he'd arrived. Went down. The dilapidated door of those ruins sagged inward. He figured no one was there any longer, a beehive under the little portico seemed the only housekeeper. He went down and waited as if he had an appointment. It was almost dark. Then at the door a monk appeared, he was very old and moved with difficulty, he had the look of an anchorite, with his hair down to his shoulders and a yellowish beard, what do you want? he asked in Greek. Do you know Italian? answered the traveler. The old man nodded. A little, he murmured. I've come to change places with you, said the man.

So it'd been like this, and no other conclusion was possible, because that story didn't call for any other possible conclusions, but the person who knew this story was aware that he couldn't let it conclude in this way, and at this point he made a leap in time. And thanks to one of those leaps in time that are possible only in the imagination, things landed in the future with regard to that month of April 2008. How many years ahead no one knows, and the person who knew the story remained vague, twenty years, for instance, which in the lifetime of a man is a lot, because if in 2008 a man of sixty still has all his energy, in 2028 he'll be an old man, his body worn out by time.

And so the person who knew this story imagined it continued like this, and so let's accept that we're in 2028, as the person who knew the story had wanted and had imagined it would continue.

And at this point, the person who imagined how the story would continue saw two young people, a guy and a girl wearing leather shorts and trekking boots, who were hiking in the mountains of Crete. The girl said to her companion: I think that old guide you found in your father's library doesn't make any sense, by now the monastery will be a pile of stones full of lizards, why don't we head toward the sea? And the guy responded: I think you're right. But just as he said this she replied: no, let's keep on for a bit, you never know. And in fact it was enough to walk around the rugged red-stone hill that cut through the countryside and there it was, the monastery, or rather ruins of the monastery, and the two of them approached, a wind blew in from the canyons raising the dust, the monastery's door had collapsed, wasps' nests defended that empty cave, the two of them had already turned their backs on that gloom when they heard a voice. In the empty space of the door stood a man. He was very old, looked dreadful, with a long white beard to his chest and hair down to his shoulders. Oooh, called the voice. Nothing else. The couple stood still. The man asked: do you understand Italian? They didn't respond. What happened in 2008? asked the old man. The two young people looked at each other, they didn't have the courage to exchange a word. Do you have photographs? asked the old man, what happened in 2008? Then he gestured for them to go away, though perhaps he was brushing away the wasps that whirled under the portico, and he returned to the dark of his cave.

The man who knew this story was aware that it couldn't finish in any other way. Before writing his stories, he loved telling them to himself. And he'd tell them to himself so perfectly, in such detail, word by word, that one might say they were written in his memory. He'd tell them to himself preferably late in the evening, in the solitude of that big empty house, or on those nights when he couldn't sleep, those nights in which insomnia yielded nothing but imagination, not much, yet imagination gave him a reality so alive that it seemed more real than the reality he was living. But the most difficult thing wasn't telling to himself his stories, that was the easy part, it was as though he'd see the words of the stories he told himself written on the dark screen of his room, when fantasy would keep his eyes wide open. And that one story, which he'd told himself in this way so many times, seemed to him an already printed book, one that was very easy to express mentally but very difficult to write with the letters of the alphabet necessary for thought to be made concrete and visible. It was as if he were lacking the principle of reality to write his story, and in order to live the effective reality of what was real within him yet unable to become truly real, he'd chosen this place.

His trip was planned in fine detail. He landed at the Hania airport, got his luggage, went into the Hertz office, picked up the car keys. Three days? the clerk asked, astonished. What's so strange about it? he said. No one comes to Crete on vacation for three days, the clerk replied, smiling. I have a long weekend, he responded, it's enough for what I have to do.

The light in Crete was beautiful. It wasn't Mediterranean but African; he'd reach the Beach Resort in an hour and a half, at most two, even going slowly, he'd arrive there around six, a shower and he'd start writing imme-diately, the hotel restaurant was open till eleven, it was Thursday evening, he counted: all of Friday, Saturday, and Sunday, three full days. They'd be enough: in his head everything was already written.

Why he turned left at that light he couldn't say. The pylons of the free-way were clearly visible, another four or five hundred meters and he'd be at the coastal freeway to Iraklion. But instead he turned left, where a little blue sign indicated an unknown place. He thought he'd already been there, for in a moment he saw everything: a tree-lined street with a few houses, a plain square with an ugly monument, a ledge of rocks, a mountain. It was a flash of lightning. That strange thing which medical science can't explain, he told himself, they call it déjà vu, already-seen, it'd never happened to me before. But the explanation he gave himself didn't reassure him, because the already-seen endured, it was stronger than what he was seeing, like a membrane enveloping the surrounding reality, the trees, the mountains, the evening shadows, even the air he was breathing. He felt overcome by vertigo and was afraid of being sucked into it, but only for a moment, because as it expanded that sensation went through a strange metamorphosis, like a glove turning inside out and bringing forth the hand it covered. Everything changed perspective, in a flash he felt the euphoria of discovery, a subtle nausea, a mortal melancholy. But also a sense of infinite liberation, as when we finally understand something we'd known all along and didn't want to know: it wasn't the already-seen that was swallowing him in a never-lived past, he instead was capturing it in a future yet to be lived. As he drove among the olive trees on that little road taking him toward the mountains, he knew that at a certain point he'd find an old rusty sign full of holes on which was written: Monastiri. And that he'd follow it. Now everything was clear.

Translated by Martha Cooley and Antonio Romani

Little Gatsby

"*I hope it's beautiful and a fool – a beautiful little fool.*"
– Zelda Fitzgerald

The evenings were slow, lingering, bloodstained with magnificent sunsets. Hot languid nights came after, punctuated by the green sob of the lighthouse across the gulf. That's how you'd like my story to begin, right? You were always so fond of convention. Beneath your quiet, discreet sophistication – your *charme* – there hid a veneer of bad taste that was yours alone. And yet how you hated "bad taste!" It disgusted you. And the banal, the everyday: these were monstrous things. All right, then, here's how my story can begin. Of course I loved the villa. The evenings were slow, lingering, bloodstained with magnificent sunsets. Hot, languid nights came after, punctuated by the green sob of the lighthouse across the gulf. I stood at the window. I always slept very little – you never realized. I'd get up and stand by the window, behind the curtains. Around two, sometimes a light breeze would rise and ripple the surface of the water. It slipped over the extremely hot tiles of the portico and, reaching my face, was tepid, almost comforting. There were always a few ships gliding into the frame of the window, mainly freighters, I think, guided by the call of the lighthouse. In the background, on the left, the harbor teemed with lights. It seemed to be waiting. For what? Was I waiting for something? The minutes slowly passed, the breeze filled the curtains. A restlessness flowed through my blood. I barely managed to control it, leaning on the windowsill, facing the sea. The coast was a promise, lights glittering like a holiday. I repeated to myself that my story was inside me and that one day, I'd write it. I'd sit down at the table as in a dream, not even looking at the sheet of white paper in front of me, and the story would gush forth like water from a spring: and then I'd write, as if by magic, the words would arrange themselves on the page, as if enchanted, drawn by a magnet called inspiration. Would you expect me to think this way, leaning on the window? Naturally, I didn't. It never crossed my mind – I'd never write another line.

There was something else far more urgent. I murmured the opening lines of a novel: *Yes, of course, if it's fine tomorrow, said Mrs. Ramsay. But you'll have to be up with the lark*; the wind shifted the curtains, you slept on, the lighthouse sobbed, the night was peaceful, almost tropical; but I'd arrive at my lighthouse soon, I could feel that it was near, that I only had to wait in the night for it to send me a signal of light, and I wouldn't let this opportunity escape (this, *my one and only* opportunity), I wouldn't spend my old age regretting a missed trip to the lighthouse. And meanwhile, I was growing old, I realized. Yet I was still young, still a "good-looking man" – when I stepped onto the terrace I was aware of the furtive, appreciative glances from your girlfriends – but the age I felt had nothing to do with any registry office, it was suffocating, like a curtain drawn around my face. I studied my hands on the windowsill: they were long, strong, supple. And they were old. Not you. The old age you feared was something else. You tried overcoming it with creams and lotions, afraid of those little spots appearing on the backs of your hands; your worst enemy was the midday sun, and when you smiled, two small menacing lines marked the corners of your mouth. You were jealous watching your guests bask in the sun, plunge into the swimming pool, stroll down to the beach, indifferent to the salt. Such a fool – all your suffering for nothing. You were *truly* young, that's not old age, you should've understood back then, you understand this now; you had a splendid body, I'd stare at your legs, the only part of your body you dared expose to the sun, your long, smooth legs. It was a Mediterranean midday. Gino wandered around the veranda serving Calvados, Bacardi, and Mazagrán. Someone lazily rose: "We're going down to the beach, Martine. We'll wait for you there . . ." You half-opened your eyes, the faintest smile marked the corners of your mouth. I was the only one who noticed because

I knew those two little lines; you didn't move, you just sat back on your deck chair, immersed in a pool of shadow, just your legs glowing in the sun, the fringe of the beach umbrella shifting in the breeze.

Of course I loved the villa. I liked the two mansards with their tiled crowns high on the rooftop, the portico with its bell tower like a monastery, the white shutters freshened up every summer. Early in the morning, while you slept, the palm grove was full of seagulls that came for the night and left traces of their wanderings in the sand. The afternoons were sultry, so Mediterranean, smelling of pine, of myrtle; I sat in my wicker chair in the colonnade, by the small granite stairway covered in vines, waiting for Scottie to wake up. Around four she arrived, barefoot, with pillow marks on her flushed face and dragging a doll by one leg.

"Do you prefer being called Scottie or Barbara?"

"Scottie."

"But Scottie's not your real name."

"It's what Miss Bishop calls me – she says you came up with it."

"Not me."

"Well, a friend of yours, anyway, the one who's a writer, and when I grow up, I'll be a little fool."

"Did Miss Bishop say that, too?"

"Yes, because she says there's no escaping the fate of the babyushka."

"The what?"

"The little girl. But Miss Bishop calls them babyushkas because that's what a lady named Zelda said, too."

In the evening we talked about Fitzgerald and listened to Tony Bennett singing *Tender Is the Night*. The truth is, nobody liked the movie, not even Mr. Deluxe, who really wasn't all that difficult to please. But Tony Bennett had a voice that was "all-consuming, like the novel"; listening to him provided atmosphere, and Gino had to keep playing that record over and over, who knows how many times. Inevitably, they asked me for the opening lines of the book, everyone found it *delightful* that I had all the opening lines to Fitzgerald's novels memorized – just the openings – it was one of my passions. Mr. Deluxe, serious as always, asked those present to be quiet, I tried getting out of it, but there was no refusing, the Tony Bennett record was playing softly, Gino had served the Bacardi, I stared at you, and you knew those lines were dedicated to you, almost as if I'd written them myself, and you lit a cigarette and slipped it into your holder, and that was a part of the performance, too, you were playing the flapper, but there was nothing of the flapper about you, you didn't have the hair for it or the rayon stockings, and certainly not the soul: you belonged to a different category, to a Drieu or Pérez Galdós novel maybe; you had a tragic sense of life, like you were condemned, your insurmountable egoism, maybe. Then, with the others growing impatient, I began, and Gino stopped serving drinks so as not to disturb anyone, there was only the voice of Tony Bennett and the lapping of the Mediterranean: *On the pleasant shore of the French Riviera, about half way between Marseilles and the Italian border, stands a large, proud, rose-colored hotel. Deferential palms cool its flushed façade, and before it stretches a short dazzling beach. Lately it has become a summer resort of notable and fashionable people; a decade ago it was almost deserted after its English clientele went north in April...*

As usual, Bishop went to change the record. The sickly sweet tones of Cole Porter swept over us – Bishop was crazy about him, thought Cole Porter was perfect for Fitzgerald; or maybe she put on Nat King Cole singing *Quiáz, quiáz, quiáz.* Anyway, I liked the King Cole song, too, it seemed to be about me somehow and made me slightly wistful, *Siempre que te pregunto, que cómo dónde y quándo* ... I tried to go on, you were all looking past me, to the sea and the lights of the coast, *In the early morning the distant image of Cannes, the pink and cream of old fortifications, the purple Alp that bounded Italy, were cast across the water and lay quavering in the ripples and rings sent up by sea plants through the clear shallows* ... but something hindered me, I could hear it in my voice, an uncertainty. Why was it painful to go on? Was it perhaps the evening? The lights of the coast? Nat King Cole? I stared at you in the shadows, *y así pasan los días, y yo, desesperado* ... you might have nodded at least, but no, you calmly looked at me like the others, like you didn't know that *all that* concerned me: I'm okay for the night, right, Martine? I was telling you with my eyes, good for a few nocturnal moments, but then you fall asleep, and sleep, sleep, sleep, the wind fills the curtains, and there are lights down the coast . . . but in daylight – what's your Perri in daylight – a character in some little game, a figurine in some story.

Enough. I didn't feel like reciting anymore, and the others didn't feel like sitting and listening anymore, either; the game had opened up, that beginning was enough for openers, now Bishop felt like Rosemary Hoyt absorbed in a slow, very sentimental dance; okay, she wasn't eighteen anymore and she couldn't manage Rosemary's "choppy little four-beat crawl" in the water, but so what? Everything was so mixed up: Rosemary Hoyt was dancing with Tom Barban, who should be dancing with you, but that would happen tomorrow night, maybe; that night, the roles had been assigned, and Mr. Deluxe was perfect for the adventurous, dissatisfied ex-aviator, not bad at all, well, maybe a bit too distinguished, too well fed for a legionnaire. As for the other two, it didn't take much imagination to place them. They were so irrelevant, so interchangeable, the handsome Brady and his little blonde. And as for you, yes, you made a splendid Nicole, you were doing her perfectly, you looked like Lauren Bacall, our Tom Barban was saying, that's what I heard him whisper to you. So annoying. And his clumsy efforts, pulling at his jacket, trying to hide his erection under his linen pants? Unbearable. But he was Tom Barban, the legionnaire: legionnaires are quite virile, you know, while dancing with a lady who looks like Lauren Bacall . . .

And I, who was I? I wasn't Dick even if did have his role – in real life, I mean. And, no, I wasn't Abe North, either, in spite of my old novel, and while everyone pretended otherwise, I'd never know how to write another, much less the story of our painful story. The only thing I knew how to do was memorize the openings of other people's novels, I belonged to a similar story, was a character who'd migrated from another novel, stylized on a smaller scale, without the grandeur, the tragedy; at least my model had his own sort of gangster grandeur; but my part didn't foresee madness, had no dream to sacrifice life for, not even a lost Daisy – worse yet – my Daisy was you, but you were Nicole. I was a game in our game: I was your dear little Gatsby.

The night advanced in small steps. You'd like this to be a line in my story, wouldn't you? I'll indulge you: the night advanced in small steps. No – the tender night advanced in small steps. Now the phonograph was playing Charlie Parker's "Easy to Love," I'm the one who bought that record, beneath poor Bird's sobbing horn came Stan Freeman's chattering piano, almost happy, choked-on chuckles, a brief phrasing of happiness. I'd have preferred Jelly Roll Morton, but Rosemary thought he was a bore – you couldn't dance to Jelly Roll Morton. Okay, then, what's there to do at that hour of the tender night advancing in small steps? St. Raphaël or l'Hôtel du Cap? St. Raphaël was better, what's there to do at the Cap once you've had your Negronis? You'll die of boredom; and the handsome Brady (but what was the handsome Brady's name in real life?) would agree to any program as long as he could moon over you, his stupid little blonde would follow him anywhere, "*c'est cocassse*," she'd chirp, "*c'est cocasse*," everything was *cocasse*. Even Deluxe's old Benz was *cocasse*, with its beige fenders and its glass partition; it was once owned by a Parisian taxi driver, Deluxe liked to brag about getting it for peanuts, "but it breaks my heart that he wanted to keep the meter – people get so attached to silly things!" and he laughed with all those extremely white teeth. He had too many teeth: de luxe teeth. Or was that too easy?

But who was this Mr. Deluxe – a sophisticated musicologist? Come on – that name of his! I think he was a little *cocasse* himself, like his Benz, "I so loved your novel for its musicality," he told me. What a twit. "But in your next novel – because you are writing another, aren't you? – in your next novel you must have the courage to express your love for music. Don't be afraid to include citations, cram it with names, with titles – once they're added, a novel becomes magical, add Coltrane's name, Alban Berg's, I know you love Coltrane and Alban Berg, and I completely agree." He talked about loving Alban Berg, that he wished he had "more time to discuss this," but then he didn't go beyond Gershwin. But how could he understand death, with that big, beautiful smile of his? You couldn't understand death, either. It was beyond your grasp, for the moment. You could understand the dead, but death and the cadaver are two different things. *Death is the curve in the road, to die is simply not to be seen*, do you remember these lines? I said them one evening, but I deceived you all, they weren't from Fitzgerald, like everyone thought; it was a fake quotation, and deep down, I enjoyed the ruse. We were driving along the coast, I think near Villefranche, I recited this and said: Fitzgerald, *This Side of Paradise*. Deluxe braked a bit sharply. He murmured, "Sublime, sublime," or some stupid nonsense, and he wanted us to go down to the beach, we had to take off our shoes and walk right up to the water's edge, one man, one woman, a chain, it was absolutely urgent to do *something lustral*, his words, an homage to being, to being there, to being on the straightaway of life: so, screw the curves – that was the basic idea.

Your mother, yes, she understood death. Right when I met her I understood that she was a woman who understood death. And she understood this about me as well. That my horrible novel included a bit of this, and that's why she worked so hard for it to become a book, she kept me from Menton, freed me from the state of the "poor, aspiring young writer, the immigrants' son, returning to his native land with a manuscript in his pocket." Did you think my love for Fitzgerald was so vast that it drove me on a pilgrimage over his route, that my descriptions of his Baltimore hotel were the result of fanatical passion? Not really. Let's just say I'm a reporter. And that hotel's where I spent my childhood. I'd rather skip the details. For twenty-nine years, my father was a waiter there, and yes, he knew Fitzgerald, had some books inscribed by him, often talked to me about him, and about Zelda too, who'd loved him, was fond of him because he made her such generous drinks, she even put him in *Save Me the Last Waltz*, under a different name. Then over the years the hotel went into decline, the clientele grew worse, my father and I were given a room in the back wing, after my mama died he didn't know anyone he could leave me with, at least I was safe there, or so he thought; he spent his final years serving dinner to old fur-wrapped whores, to refined morphine addicts, to quarrelsome pederasts . . . So that's him, my Fitzgerald. Your mother understood a great deal about me. And I about her. Would you like to know what our relationship was exactly? It's not something described in a few lines. I loved her very much – that's enough, I think.

Everybody wanted St. Raphaël, but the evening dragged on at l'Hôtel du Cap instead. Maybe the Negronis were a little strong. Plus there was lots of Gershwin, for Mr. Deluxe. And then there were the Arrigos installed on the terrace, who could resist those two, a pair of perfect McKiscos, bickering and bitter, too *cocasse*, totally revved up by ten o'clock, like they'd just stepped out of *Tender Is the Night*, and it was impossible to shake them, to go to St. Raphaël. Poor things never knew they were the McKiscos, maybe never even heard of Fitzgerald. "And your novel, Perri, how far are you in your novel?" Mrs. McKisco would always ask the same question, she was polite, apologetic, wore very elegant scarves and a pearl shamrock on the collar of her white jacket. You never saw her without that white jacket. I said it wasn't going badly, yeah, it really wasn't going too badly, I was at a good place, you see, the story already had everything, meaning, the drama, but also a touch of frivolity, frivolity is good for drama: two destinies that don't meet, a life full of mistakes, two lives full of mistakes . . . Despair? sure, but only in moderation. A death, maybe. His or hers, I couldn't say, or maybe, I don't know, some huge betrayal. But mainly, an inadequacy to life, like nothing's ever enough, and a sense of dissipation, along with something like non-reason, and depraved egoism. Mrs. McKisco gave me an understanding sigh, as if to say: but when does anyone find that life is enough? Her voluminous bosom rose, the pearl shamrock sparkled, Mr. McKisco watched her grimly, like he might sink his teeth into her, she looked sad, ill at ease, her unhappiness was touchingly simplistic; off with you, Mrs. McKisco, I wish I could console you, rest your generous bosom on my shoulder and let it out, sob away: true, your life's a waste, your husband's an orangutan filled up with Pernod, you have too much money and now you're asking yourself what good is money, what's the point of paper mills, but the hell with it all, right Mrs. McKisco? You'd have liked children, and instead you find yourself here, trying to staunch old age and solitude, you'd like to convince yourself that children aren't everything, and you stare at the lights of Cannes and feel a strong urge to cry. Come over to the railing with me, let's stare out to sea, and I'll tell you about a frivolous, desperate novel, and we'll laugh like crazy, all very Fitzgeraldesque, he's the writer of a single book, he had a decayed childhood that aches now and then, sharp waves of pain, his methods for coping with life haven't been exactly clean, you might say he's a bit debauched but basically kind – you want to hear the beginning? – it could begin like this, for instance: *In 1959, when this story's protagonist was thirty-five, it had already been two years since irony – today's Holy Spirit – had, at least theoretically, descended upon him. Irony was the last polishing swipe to his shoes, the last dab of the clothes-brush, an intellectual "There you go!": and yet, on the brink of this story, he still hasn't gone beyond the stage of consciousness* ... The truth is, it's not my beginning, dear Mrs. McKisco, only the dates are mine, but it hardly matters.

Around midnight, Mr. McKisco collapsed on the table and had to be physically raised. Bishop was fairly drunk, too, and kept giggling, a happy drunk, she felt in top shape now to pop over to St. Raphaël's – and we're off – a race to eat a couple of shrimp – I broke away then, I preferred waiting for you at home: you'd be back in an hour or so. You want to know why I didn't come back that night of August twelfth? I never wondered why you didn't, and I don't want to know – I don't care. But I want to tell you why I didn't come back – it's really funny. Because it was San Macario Day. My father was named Macario, and I wanted to remember him on my own, un-interrupted, away from your place. And I had Scottie's picture in my pocket.

I've got it here in front of me now. Taken when she was four years old. She's in a flowered dress, white socks, her braids bleached by the sun. She's holding onto a stuffed toy, a sad-eyed basset hound, she's got it dangling by one ear, named Socrates – do you remember Socrates? – I bought him. There's a hole in the picture: that's you. And there in the background, that's the villa, taken from the west side, the stairs covered in fox grape vine leading up to Scottie's rooms, the white door with the lead-glass window, English-style. So I had Scottie's picture in my pocket, and I sat down in a café. I felt pretty good. My plan was perfect, and in various spots toward Menton you could see fireworks, it had to be a patron saint festival, a good omen, I thought. For a month and half, every Saturday night, I'd drive my car across the border. There was a customs agent who started his shift at ten o'clock on the dot, a boy from Benevento, who was used to seeing me by now, I'd go to Italy for an espresso, and at ten thirty I'd cross the border again – "homesick for Italian coffee, sir?" – he'd greet me, hand to his visor, and I'd respond to his salute, sometimes stop and chat a little, to him I was some rich guy obsessed with Italian coffee, he'd never dream to look in my car. Asleep under a plaid blanket, Scottie could easily get through.

I loitered for a little while along the promenade, watching the fireworks toward Menton. They'd be for tomorrow evening. It was the San Macario festival, a beautiful night, I thought about my father dead in a stinking Baltimore hotel; I stopped at the "Racé" to pick up some money, I was involved in some dealings there, but this would be the last time: I needed the money to set up an honest business in Italy – not that I was short on money, but the more I had the better – those first days wouldn't be easy. There was a jam session going on at the "Racé," and this incredible musician was doing a perfect imitation of Rex Stewart, Ellington's cornet player in the thirties, he was happy, playing "Trumpet in Space" and "Kissing my Baby Goodnight," imagine that, and I was happy too, I stayed a bit, then left, went for a long walk because I wanted some fresh air. There you go. The slightest thing, and a whole life can change. Or stay the same.

Time is treacherous – it makes us believe it never passes, and when we look back, it's passed too quickly. You'd enjoy a line like that in my story, wouldn't you, Martine? Granted. Time is treacherous – I look back, and it's passed too quickly, and how slow it's been to pass! Almost twenty years have passed, and Scottie's still four years old, to us. But in the end, I'm also the same age as then, to you. Because I'm unattainable, in a way eternal, here, where I find myself. I'm beyond the curve in the road, do you understand this idea? Twenty years should be enough to understand this sort of idea. But you, no, you've kept to the straightaway, exposed. You've aged, Martine, that's normal. You'll finally be unafraid when old age comes: it has already. Bishop's left no trace behind – she disappeared into England. But I know what happened to her: she's half-nun, never married, lives in a convent in Sussex, teaches American culture to girls from good homes. By God, even

Deluxe has aged, has lost his aviator looks. He's visited you a few times but can't resume the game, he gets nothing from it now. He's a portly gentleman with a blue Citroën, a business consultant in the suburbs: so long, Tom Barban. And the villa – how it's aged. I went by recently and imagined going in. On the outside wall, by the gate, is a blue-tiled panel of a brigantine with blowing sails. We bought that in Èze Village, remember? The white paint's peeling off the wrought-iron gate. It's bubbled up from the salt and sun, large swellings that crumble to the touch, revealing, below, a fine, very yellow rust. You must have to push hard on those double wings, otherwise, with their stiff hinges, they won't open. Impatient, you give the gate a shake, and at last it opens, letting out a quiet, prolonged creaking, like a far-off groan that's finally reached us. Once, I happened to glance up, searching for the source of that cry, and then I saw the sky-blue of the sea. Past the gate and to the right, beneath a palm tree, is the gatekeeper's lodge, painted yellow, a little room like a miniature house. The caretaker used to keep his tools there, but I can imagine what's there now: a baby carriage with one of those folding hoods, like you see in photos from the thirties; a cordless toy xylophone; some old, scratched-up records. Unbearable things, impossible to look at, impossible to throw away: you need to find some little room. But why am I describing things that you know better than me? To create a note of longing in my story, a sense of dissipation? You always preferred desperate, futile lives: Francis and Zelda, Bessie Smith, Isadora . . . I do what I can – it depends what we have at our disposal. Ah, yes, the villa's really looking rundown, it needs a good makeover: the façade, windows, garden, grillwork . . . but money's scarce; they don't have Perri's discreet little business dealings, so questionable and so lucrative – you can't eat tradition for dinner. If you'd just consider making use of everything. It's an unusually elegant location, the rooms are magnificent, so delightfully art nouveau; you could retire to Scottie's rooms, so you'd be even closer to the memory of her – and two rooms are enough for you now – turn the rest into a hotel. A small, elitist hotel: ten rooms, dining room on the main floor, lamps with green shades on the tables, a pianist on the terrace for after dinner, lots of Gershwin, moonlight and Bacardi. The rich, middle-aged Swiss adore that sort of place. Find the right name, sophisticated and clever: "Au petit Gatsby," say. And then you could face a quiet old age, spend your days in blessed peace staring at the coast and thinking about the future *that year by year recedes before us. It eluded us then, but that's no matter – tomorrow we will run faster, stretch out our arms farther . . . And one fine morning . . .* It's a Fitzgerald finale, of course.

Translated by Janice M. Thresher

Cinema

The small station was almost deserted. It was the station of a town on the Riviera, with palms and agaves growing near the wooden benches. At one end, behind a wrought-iron gate, a street led to the center of the town; at the other a stone stairway went down to the shore.

The stationmaster came out of the small glass control room and walked under the overhanging roof to the tracks. He was a short, stout man with a mustache. He lit a cigarette, looked doubtfully at the cloudy sky, stuck out a hand beyond the roof to see if it was raining, then wheeled around and with a thoughtful air put his hands in his pockets. The two workmen waiting for the train on a bench under the sign bearing the station's name greeted him briefly and he nodded in reply. On the other bench there was an old woman, dressed in black, with a suitcase fastened with a rope. The stationmaster peered up and down the tracks then, as the bell announcing a train's arrival began to ring, went back into his small room.

At this moment the girl came through the gate. She was wearing a polka-dotted dress, shoes laced at the ankles, and a pale blue sweater. She was walking quickly, as if she were cold, and a mass of blond hair floated under the scarf tied around her head. She was carrying a small suitcase and a straw handbag. One of the workmen followed her with his eyes and elbowed his apparently distracted companion. The girl stared indifferently at the ground, then went into the waiting room, closing the door behind her. The room was empty. There was a large cast-iron stove in one corner and she moved toward it, perhaps in the hope that it was lit. She touched it, disappointed, and then laid her straw handbag on top. Then she sat down on a bench and shivered slightly, holding her face between her hands. For a long time she remained in this position, as if she were crying. She was good-looking, with delicate features and slender ankles. She took off her scarf and rearranged her hair by shaking her head. Her gaze wandered over the walls of the room as if she were looking for something. There were threatening signs on the walls addressed to the citizenry by the Occupation Forces and notices of "wanted" persons, displaying their photographs. She looked around in confusion, then took the handbag she had left on the stove and laid it at her feet as if to shield it with her legs. She hunched her shoulders and raised her jacket collar. Her hands were restless; she was obviously nervous.

The door flew open and a man came in. He was tall and thin, wearing a belted tan trenchcoat and a felt hat pulled down over his forehead. The girl leaped to her feet and shouted, with a gurgle in her throat: "Eddie!" He held a finger to his lips, walked toward her, and, smiling, took her into his arms. She hugged him, leaning her head on his chest. "Oh, Eddie!" she murmured finally, drawing back, "Eddie!"

He made her sit down and went back to the door, looking furtively outside. Then he sat down beside her and drew some folded papers from his pocket.

"You're to deliver them directly to the English major," he said. "Later I'll tell you how, more exactly."

She took the papers and slipped them into the opening of her sweater. She seemed fearful, and there were tears in her eyes. "And what about you?" she asked.

He made a gesture signifying annoyance. Just then there was a rumbling sound and a freight train was visible through the door's glass panel. He pulled his hat farther down and buried his head in a newspaper. "Go and see what's up."

The girl went to the door and peered out. "A freight train," she said. "The two workmen sitting on the bench climbed aboard."

"Any Germans?"

"No."

The stationmaster blew his whistle and the train pulled away. The girl went back to the man and took his hands into hers. "What about you?" she repeated.

The man folded the newspaper and stuffed it into his pocket. "This is no time to think about me," he said. "Now tell me, what's your company's schedule?"

"Tomorrow we'll be in Nice, for three evening performances. Saturday and Sunday we play in Marseille, then Montpellier and Narbonne, one day each, in short, all along the coast." "On Sunday you'll be in Marseille," said the man. "After the show you'll receive admirers in your dressing room. Let them in one at a time. Many of them will bring flowers; some will be German spies, no doubt, but others will be our people. Be sure to read the card that comes with the flowers, in the visitor's presence, every time, because I can't tell you what the contact will look like."

She listened attentively; the man lit a cigarette and went on: "On one of the cards you'll read: *Fleurs pour une fleur*. Hand over the papers to that man. He'll be the major."

The bell began to ring again, and the girl looked at her watch. "Our train will be here in a minute. Eddie, please. . ."

He wouldn't let her finish. "Tell me about the show. On Sunday night I'll try to imagine it."

"It's done by all the girls in the company," she said unenthusiastically.

"Each one of us plays an actress of today or of the past. That's all there is to it."

"What's the title?" he asked, smiling.

"Cinemà Cinemà."

"Sounds promising."

"It's a disaster," she said emphatically. "The choreography is by Savinio, just imagine that, and I play Francesca Bertini, dancing in a dress so long that I trip on it."

"Watch out!" he joked. "Great tragic actresses simply mustn't fall."

Again she hid her face in her arms and started to cry. She was prettier than ever with tears on her cheeks. "Come away, Eddie, please, come away," she murmured.

He wiped her tears away gently enough, but his voice hardened, as if in an effort to disguise his feelings. "Don't, Elsa," he said. "Try to understand." And, in a playful tone, he added: "How should I get through? Dressed like a dancer, perhaps, with a blond wig?"

The bell had stopped ringing and the incoming train could be heard in the distance. The man got up and put his hands in his pockets. "I'll walk with you," he said.

"No," she said, shaking her head resolutely. "You mustn't do that; it's dangerous."

"I'm doing it anyhow."

"Please!"

"One last thing," he said; "I know the major's a ladies' man. Don't smile at him too much."

She looked at him supplicatingly. "Oh, Eddie!" she exclaimed with emotion, offering him her lips.

He seemed nonplussed for a moment, as if in embarrassment or because he didn't have the courage to kiss her. Finally he deposited a fatherly kiss on her cheek.

"Stop!" called out the clapperboy. "A break!"

"Not like that!" The director's voice roared through the megaphone. "The last bit has to be done again."

He was a bearded young man with a long scarf wound around his neck. Now he got down from the seat on the boom next to the camera and came to meet them. "Not like that," he snorted with disappointment. "It must be a passionate kiss, old-fashioned, the way it was in the original film." He threw an arm around the actress's waist, bending her backward. "Lean over her and put some passion into it," he said to the actor. Then looking around him, he added, "Take a break!"

2

The actors invaded the station's shabby café, jostling one another in the direction of the bar. She lingered at the door, uncertain what to do, while he disappeared in the crowd. Soon he came back, balancing two caffè lattes, and beckoned to her with his head to join him outside. Behind the café there was a rocky courtyard, under a vine-covered arbor, which served also for storage. Besides cases of empty bottles, there were some misshapen chairs, and on two of these they sat down, using a third one as a table.

"We're winding up," he said.

"He insisted on doing the last scene last," she answered. "I don't know why."

"That's *modern*," he said emphatically. "Straight out of the *Cahiers du Cinema* . . . look out, that cappuccino's boiling hot."

"I still don't know why."

"Do they do things differently in America?" he asked.

"They certainly do!" she said. "They're less pretentious, less . . . intellectual."

"This fellow's good, though."

"It's only that, once upon a time, things weren't handled this way."

They were silent, drinking their coffee. It was eleven in the morning, and the sea was sparkling, visible through a privet hedge around the courtyard.

The vine leaves of the pergola were flaming red and the sun made shifting puddles of light on the gravel.

"A gorgeous autumn," he said, looking up at the leaves. And he added, half to himself. "'Once upon a time' . . . Hearing you say those words had an effect on me."

She did not answer, but hugged her knees, which she had drawn up against her chest. She, too, seemed distracted, as if she had only just thought about the meaning of what she had said. "Why did you agree to play in this film?" she asked.

"Why did *you?*"

"I don't know, but I asked you first."

"Because of an illusion," he said; "the idea of re-living . . . something like that, I suppose. I don't really know. And you?"

"I don't really know, either. The same, I suppose."

The director emerged from the path that ran around the café in good spirits and carrying a tankard of beer. "So here are my stars!" he exclaimed, sinking into one of the misshapen chairs, with a satisfied sigh.

"Please spare us your speech on the beauties of direct takes," she said. "You've lectured us quite enough."

The director did not take offense at this remark and fell into casual conversation. He spoke of the film, of the importance of this new version, of why he had taken on the same actors so many years later and why he was underlining the fact that it was a remake. Things he had said many times before, as was clear indifference of the other two. But he enjoyed the repetition, it was almost as if he were talking to himself. He finished his beer and got up. "Here's hoping it rains," he said as he left. "It would be too bad to shoot the last scenes with pumps." And, before turning the corner, he threw back: "Half an hour before we start shooting again."

She looked questioningly at her companion, who shook his head and shrugged.

"It did pour during the last scene," he said, "and I was left standing in the rain."

She laughed and laid a hand on his shoulder as if to signify that she remembered.

"Do they still show it in America?" he asked with a stolid expression on his face.

"Hasn't the director projected it for our benefit exactly eleven times?" she countered, laughing. "Anyhow, in America it's shown to film clubs and other groups from time to time."

"It's the same thing here," he said. And then, abruptly: "How's the major?"

She looked at him questioningly.

"I mean Howard," he specified. "I told you not to smile at him too much, but obviously you didn't follow my advice, even if the scene isn't included in the film." And, after a moment of reflection: "I still don't understand why you married him."

"Neither do I," she said in a childlike manner. "I was very young." Her expression relaxed, as if she had put mistrust aside and given up lying. "I wanted to get even with you," she said calmly. "That was the real reason, although perhaps I wasn't aware of it. And then I wanted to go to America."

"What about Howard?" he insisted.

"Our marriage didn't last long. He wasn't right for me, really, and I wasn't cut out to be an actress."

"You disappeared completely. Why did you give up acting?"

"I couldn't get anywhere with it. After all, I'd been in just one hit, and that was thanks to winning an audition. In America they're real pros. Once I made a series of films for television, but they were a disaster. They cast me as a disagreeable rich woman, not exactly my type, was it?"

"I think not. You look like a happy woman. Are you happy?"

"No," she said, smiling. "But I have a lot going for me."

"For instance?"

"For instance a daughter. A delightful girl, in her third year at college, and we're very close."

He stared at her incredulously.

"Twenty years have gone by," she reminded him. "Nearly a lifetime."

"You're still so beautiful."

"That's makeup. I have wrinkles. I'm practically a grandmother."

For some time they were silent. Voices from the café drifted out to them, and someone started up the jukebox. He looked as if he were going to speak, but stared at the ground, seemingly at a loss for words. "I want you to tell me about your life," he said at last. "All through the filming I've wanted to ask you, but I've got around to it only now."

"Sure," she said, spiritedly. "And I'd like to hear you talk about yours."

At this juncture, Mrs. Ferraretti, the production secretary, appeared in the doorway, a thin, homely, plaintive young woman with her hair in a ponytail and a pair of round glasses on her nose.

"Makeup time, Madam!" she called out. "We start shooting in ten minutes."

3

The bell stopped ringing and the incoming train could be heard in the distance. The man got up and put his hands in his pockets.

"I'll walk with you," he said.

"No," she said, shaking her head resolutely. "You mustn't do that, it's dangerous."

"I'm doing it anyhow."

"Please!"

"One last thing," he said, "I know the major's a ladies' man. Don't smile at him too much."

She looked at him supplicatingly. "Oh, Eddie!" she exclaimed with emotion, offering him her lips.

He put his arm around her waist, bending her backward. Looking into her eyes, he slowly brought his mouth toward her and gave her a passionate kiss, a long intense kiss, which aroused an approving murmur, and some catcalls.

"Stop!" called the clapperboy. "End of scene."

"Lunchtime," the director announced through the megaphone. "Back at four o'clock."

The actors dispersed in various directions, some to the café, others to trailers parked in front of the station. He took off his trenchcoat and hung it over his arm. They were the last to arrive on the street, where they set out toward the sea. A blade of sunlight struck the row of pink houses along the harbor, and the sea was a celestial, almost diaphanous blue. A woman with a basin under her arm appeared on a balcony and began to hang up clothes to dry. She carefully hung a pair of pants and some boys' t-shirts. Then she grasped a pulley and the clothes slid along a line from one house to another, fluttering like flags. The houses formed the arches of a portico and underneath there were stalls, covered during the midday break with oilcloth. Some bore painted blue anchors and a sign saying FRESH FISH.

"Back then, there was a pizzeria here," he said, "I remember it perfectly, it was called *Da Pezzi*."

She looked down and did not speak.

"You *must* remember," he continued. "There was a sign 'Pizza to take out,' and I said to you: 'Let's take out a pizza from Pezzi,' and you laughed."

They went down the steps of a narrow alley with windows joined by an arch above them. The echo of their footsteps on the shiny paving stones conveyed a feeling of winter, with the crackling tone that sounds acquire in cold air. Actually there was a warm breeze and the fragrance of mock-orange. The shops on the waterfront were closed and café chairs were stacked up around empty tables.

"We're out of season," she observed.

He shot her a surreptitious look, wondering if the remark had a double meaning, then let it go. "There's a restaurant that's open," he said, gesturing with his head. "What do you say?"

The restaurant was called *L'Arsella*; it was a wood and glass construction resting on piles set into the beach next to the blue bathhouses. Two gently rocking boats were tied to the piles. Some windows had blinds drawn over them; lamps were lit on the tables in spite of the bright daylight.

There were few customers: a couple of silent, middle-aged Germans, two intellectual-looking young men, a blond woman with a dog, the last summer vacationers. They sat down at a corner table, far from the others. Perhaps the waiter recognized them; he came quickly but with an embarrassed and would-be confidential air. They ordered broiled sole and champagne and looked out at the horizon, which was slowly changing color as the wind pushed the clouds. Now there was a hint of indigo on the line separating sea and sky, and the promontory that closed the bay was silvery green like a block of ice.

"Incredible," she said after a minute or two, "only three weeks to shoot a film, ridiculous, I call it. We've done some scenes only once."

"That's avant-garde," he said, smiling. "Realism, *cinéma-vérité* – only fake. Today's production costs are high, so they do everything in a hurry." He was making bread crumbs into little balls and lining them up in front of his plate. "Anghelopoulos," he said ironically. "He'd like to do a film like *O Thiassos*, a play within a play, with us acting ourselves. Period songs and accessories and transitional sequences, all very well, but what's to take the place of myth and tragedy?"

The waiter brought on the champagne and uncorked the bottle. She raised her glass to make a toast. Her eyes were malicious and shiny, full of reflections.

"Melodrama," she said, "Melodrama, that's what." She took short sips and broke into a smile. "That's why he wanted the acting overdone. We had to be caricatures of ourselves."

He raised his glass in return. "Then hurrah for melodrama!" he said. "Sophocles, Shakespeare, Racine, it's all melodrama. That's what I've been up to myself all these years."

"Tell me about yourself," she said.

"Do you mean it?"

"I do."

"I have a farm in Provence, and I go there when I can. The countryside is just hilly enough, people are welcoming, I'm comfortable, and I like the horses."

He made more bread-crumb balls, two circles of them around a glass, and then he moved one behind the other as if he were playing solitaire.

"That's not what I meant," she said.

He called the waiter and ordered another bottle of champagne.

"I teach at the Academy of Dramatic Arts," he said. "My life's made up of Creon, Macbeth, Henry VIII." He gave a guilty smile. "That's my specialty: hard-hearted men."

She looked at him intently, with a concentrated, almost anxious air. "What about films?" she asked.

"Five years ago I was in a mystery story. I played an American private detective, just three scenes, and then they bumped me off in an elevator. But in the titles they ran my name in capital letters . . . 'With the participation of . . .'"

"You're a myth," she said emphatically.

"A leftover," he demurred. "I'm this butt between my lips, see . . ." He put on a hard, desperate expression and let the smoke from the cigarette hanging between his lips cover his face.

"Don't play Eddie!" she said, laughing.

"But I *am* Eddie," he muttered, pulling an imaginary hat over his eyes. He refilled the glasses and raised his.

"To cinema!"

"If we go on like this we'll be drunk when we go back to the set, *Eddie*." There was a malicious glint in her eyes.

He took off the imaginary hat and laid it over his heart. "Better that way. We'll be more melodramatic."

For dessert they had ordered gelato with hot fudge sauce. The waiter arrived with a triumphal air, bearing a tray with ice creams in one hand and the steaming chocolate sauce in the other. While serving them he asked, timidly but coyly, if they would honor him with their autographs on a menu and shot them a gratified smile when they assented.

The gelato was in the shape of a flower, with deep red cherries at the center of the corolla. He picked one of these up and popped it into his mouth.

"Listen," he said. "Let's change the ending."

She looked at him, somewhat perplexed, but perhaps her look signified that she knew what he was driving at and was merely awaiting confirmation.

"Don't go," he said. "Stay here with me."

She lowered her eyes to her plate as if embarrassed. "Please," she said, "please."

"You're talking the way you do in the film," he said. "That's the exact line."

"We're not in a film now," she said, almost resentfully. "Stop playing your part; you're overdoing it."

He made a gesture as if he wanted to drop the whole thing. "But I love you," he said in a low voice.

"Sure, you do," she teased, slightly condescending, "in the film."

"Same thing," he said. "It's all a film."

"What is?"

"Everything." He stretched his hand across the table and squeezed hers. "Let's run the film backwards and go back to the beginning."

She looked at him as if she didn't have the courage to reply. She let him stroke her hand and stroked his in return. "You've forgotten the title of the film," she said, trying for a quick retort. "*Point of No Return.*"

The waiter arrived, beaming and waving the menus for them to autograph.

4

"You're crazy!" she said laughing, but letting him pull her along. "They'll be furious."

He pulled her onto the pier and quickened his steps. "Let them be furious," he said. "Let that cock-of-the-walk wait. Waiting makes for inspiration."

There were no more than a dozen people on the boat, scattered on the benches in the cabin and on the iron seats, at the stern. Their dress and casual behavior marked them as local people, used to this crossing. Three women were carrying plastic bags bearing the name of a well-known shop. Plainly they had come from villages on the perimeter of the bay to make purchases in the town. The employee who punched the tickets was wearing blue trousers and a white shirt with the company seal sewed onto the pocket. The actor asked how long it would take to make the round trip. The ticket collector made a sweeping gesture toward the bay and enumerated the villages where they would be stopping. He was a young man with a blond mustache and a strong local accent. "About an hour and a half," he said, "but if you're in a hurry, there's a larger boat that returns to the mainland from our first stop, just after we arrive, and will bring you back in forty minutes." He pointed to the first village on the right side of the bay, a cluster of ten houses, lit by the sun.

She still seemed undecided, torn between doubt and temptation. "They'll be furious," she repeated. "They wanted to wrap it up by evening."

He shrugged and threw up his hands. "If we don't finish today we'll finish tomorrow," he countered. "We're paid for the job, not by the hour, so we can surely take an extra day."

"I have a plane for New York tomorrow," she said. "I made a reservation, and my daughter will be waiting for me."

"Please make up your mind, Ma'am," said the ticket collector. "We have to push off."

A whistle blew twice and a sailor started to release the mooring rope. The ticket collector pulled out his pad and tore off two tickets. "You'll be better off at the bow," he remarked. "There's a bit of breeze, but you won't feel the rolling."

The white iron seats were all free, but they leaned on the low railing and looked at the scene around them. The boat drew away from the pier and gathered speed. From a slight distance the town revealed its exact lay-out, with the old houses falling into an unexpected and graceful geometrical pattern. "It's more beautiful viewed from the sea," she observed. She held down her windblown hair with one hand, and red spots had appeared on her cheekbones.

"You're the beauty," he said, "at sea, on land, anywhere."

She laughed and searched her bag, perhaps for a scarf. "You've turned very gallant," she said. "Back then you weren't like that at all."

"Back then I was stupid, stupid and childish."

"Actually, you seem more childish to me now. Forgive me for saying so, but that's what I think."

"You're wrong, though. I'm older, that's all." He shot her a worried glance. "Now don't tell me I'm old."

"No, you're not old. But that's not the only thing that matters."

She took a tortoiseshell case out of her bag and extracted a cigarette. He cupped his hands around hers to protect the match from the wind. The sky was very blue, although there was a black streak on the horizon and the sea had darkened. The first village was rapidly approaching. There was a pink bell tower and a bulging spire as white as meringue. A flight of pigeons rose up from the houses and took off, a wide curving line by the sea.

"Life must be wonderful there," he said, "and very simple."

She nodded and smiled. "Perhaps because it's not ours."

The boat they were to meet was tied up at the pier, an old boat looking like a tug. For the benefit of the new arrival it whistled three times in greeting. Several people were standing on the pier, perhaps waiting to go aboard. A little girl in a yellow dress, holding a woman's hand, was jumping up and down like a bird.

"That's what I'd like," he said. "To live a life other than ours." From her expression he saw that his meaning was not clear and corrected himself. "I mean a happy life rather than ours, like the one we imagine they lead in this village." He grasped her hands and made her meet his eyes, looking at her very hard.

She gently freed herself, giving him a rapid kiss. "Eddie," she said tenderly, "dear Eddie." Slipping her arm into his she pulled him toward the gangplank. "You're a great actor," she said, "a truly great actor." She was happy and brimming over with life.

"But it's what I feel," he protested feebly, letting her pull him along.

"Of course," she said, "like a true actor."

5

The train came to a sudden stop, with the wheels screeching and puffs of smoke. A window opened and five girls stuck out their heads. Some of them were peroxide blondes, with curls falling over their shoulders and on their foreheads. They started to laugh and chat, calling out: "Elsa! Elsa!" A showy redhead, wearing a green ribbon in her hair, shouted to the others: "There she is!" and leaned even farther out to wave in greeting. Elsa quickened her step and came close to the window, touching the gaily outstretched hands. "Corinna!" she exclaimed, looking at the redhead, "What's this get up?"

"Saverio says it's attractive," Corinna called back, winking and pointing her head toward the inside of the compartment.

"Come on aboard," she added in a falsetto voice; "you don't want to be stuck in a place like this, do you?" Then, suddenly, she screamed: "Look girls, there's a Rudolph Valentino!"

The girls waved madly to catch the man's attention. Eddie had come out from behind the arrivals and departures board; he advanced slowly along the platform, with his hat pulled over his eyes. At that same moment, two German soldiers came through the gate and went toward the stationmaster's office. After a few moments the stationmaster came out with his red flag under his arm and walked toward the engine, with rapid steps, which accentuated the awkwardness of his chubby body. The soldiers stood in front of the office door, as if they were on guard. The girls fell silent and watched the scene looking worried. Elsa set down her suitcase and looked confusedly at Eddie, who motioned with his head that she should go on. Then he sat down on a bench under a tourist poster, took the newspaper out of his pocket, and buried his face in it.

Corinna seemed to understand what was up. "Come on, honey!" she shouted. "Come aboard!" With one hand she waved at the two staring soldiers and gave them a dazzling smile. Meanwhile the stationmaster was coming back with the flag now rolled up under his arm.

Corinna asked him what was going on.

"Don't ask me," he answered, shrugging. "It seems we have to wait for a quarter of an hour. It's orders, that's all I know."

"Then we can get out and stretch our legs, girls," Corinna chirped, and she quickly got off followed by the others. "Climb aboard," she whispered as she passed Elsa. "We'll take care of them."

The little group moved in the direction opposite to where Eddie was seated, passing in front of the soldiers. "Isn't there anywhere to eat in this station?" Corinna asked in a loud voice, looking around. She was superb at drawing attention to herself, swinging her hips and also the bag she had taken off her shoulder. She had on a clinging flowered dress and sandals with cork soles. "The sea, girls!" she shouted. "Look at that sea and tell me if it isn't divine!" She leaned theatrically against the first lamppost and raised her hand to her mouth, putting on a childish manner. "If I had my bathing suit with me, I'd dive in, never mind the autumn weather," she said, tossing her head and causing her red curls to ripple over her shoulders. The two soldiers were stunned and couldn't take their eyes off her. Then she had a stroke of genius, due to the lamppost, perhaps, or to the necessity of resolving an impossible situation. She let her blouse slip down off her shoulders, leaned against the lamppost, stretched out her arms, purse swinging, and addressed an imaginary public, winking as if the whole scene were in cahoots with her. "It's a song they sing the world over," she shouted, "even our enemies!" And, turning to the other girls, she clapped her hands. It must have been part of the show, because they fell into line, raising their legs in marching time but without moving an inch, hand to their forehead in a military salute. Corinna clung to the lamppost with one hand and, using it as a pivot, wheeled gracefully around it. Her skirt fluttered, showing her legs.

> *"Vor der Kaserne vor dem grossen Tor,*
> *Stand eine Laterne, und steht sie noch davor . . .*
> *So wollen wir uns da wiedersehen,*
> *Bei der Laterne wollen wir stehen,*
> *Wie einst Lili Marlene, wie einst Lili Marlene."*

The girls applauded, a soldier whistled. Corinna thanked them with a mock bow and went to the fountain near the hedge. She passed a wet finger over her temples while looking down at the street below; then, trailed by the other girls, she started to reboard the train. "*Auf wiedersehen*, darlings!" she called to the soldiers as she climbed on, "now we must retreat – *la tournée* awaits."

Elsa was waiting in the corridor and threw her arms around her. "It's okay, Corinna," she said, giving her a kiss.

"Think nothing of it," said Corinna, starting to cry like a baby.

The two soldiers had come close to the waiting train; they looked up at the girls and tried to exchange a few words; one of them knew some Italian.

Just then there was the sound of a motor, and a black car came through the gate and traveled the length of the platform until it stopped at the front of the train, just behind the engine. The girls tried to fathom what was happening, but there was a curve in the tracks and they couldn't see very well around it. Eddie hadn't moved from the bench. Apparently he was immersed in the newspaper that shielded his face. "What's up, girls?" asked Elsa, trying to seem indifferent as she stowed her things in the luggage net.

"Nothing," one of the girls answered. "It must be a big shot who arrived in the car. But he's in civilian clothes and traveling first-class."

"Is he alone?" Elsa asked.

"Looks like it. The soldiers are standing at attention and not boarding the train."

Elsa peered out the window. The soldiers by the train did an about-face and were walking toward the road leading into the town. The stationmaster came back, dragging the red flag behind him and looking down at his shoes. "The train's leaving," he said in a philosophical, knowing manner, and waved the flag. The train whistled. The girls returned to their seats, only Elsa stayed at the window. She had combed her hair off her forehead and her eyes were still gleaming. At this moment Eddie came up and stood directly under the window.

"Goodbye, Eddie," Elsa murmured, stretching out her hand.

"Shall we meet in another film?" he asked.

"What the hell is he saying?" shouted the director from behind him. "What the hell?"

"Shall I hold?" asked the cameraman.

"No," said the director. "It's going to be dubbed anyhow." And he shouted into the megaphone, "Walk, man, the train's moving, move faster, follow it along the platform, hold her hand."

The train had, indeed, started to move, and Eddie obeyed, quickening his pace and keeping up as long as he could. The train picked up speed and went around the curve and through a switch on the other side. Eddie wheeled about and took a few steps before stopping to light a cigarette, then walked slowly on into camera. The director made gestures to regulate his pace, as if he were manipulating him with strings.

"Insert a heart attack," said Eddie imploringly.

"What?" the director shouted

"A heart attack," Eddie repeated. "Here, on the bench. I'll look exhausted, sink onto the bench and lay my hand on my heart like Dr. Zhivago. Make me die."

The clapperboy looked at the director, waiting for instructions. The director moved his fingers like scissors to signify that he'd cut later, but meanwhile the shooting must go on.

"What do you mean by a heart attack?" he said to Eddie. "Do you think you look like a man about to have a heart attack? Pull your hat over your eyes, like a good Eddie, don't make me start all over." And he signaled to the crew to put the pumps into action. "Come on, move! It's starting to rain. You're Eddie, remember, not a poor lovesick creature . . . Put your hands in your pockets, shrug now, that's it, good boy, come toward us . . . your cigarette hanging from your lips . . . perfect! . . . eyes on the ground."

He turned to the cameraman and shouted: "Pull back – tracking shot; pull back!"

Translated by Frances Frenaye

Small Blue Whales
Strolling about the Azores

Fragment of a Story

She owes me everything, said the man heatedly, everything: her money, her success. I did it for her, I shaped her with my own hands, that's what. And as he spoke he looked at his hands, clenching and unclenching his fingers in a strange gesture, as if trying to grasp a shadow.

The small ferry began to change direction and a gust of wind ruffled the woman's hair. Don't talk like that, Marcel, please, she muttered, looking at her shoes. Keep your voice down, people are watching us. She was blond and wore big sunglasses with delicately tinted lenses. The man's head jerked a little to one side, a sign of annoyance. Who cares, they don't understand, he answered. He tossed the stub of his cigarette into the sea and touched the tip of his nose as if to squash an insect. Lady Macbeth, he said with irony, the great tragic actress. You know the name of the place I found her in? It was called 'La Baguette', and as it happens she wasn't playing Lady Macbeth, you know what she was doing? The woman took off her glasses and wiped them nervously on her T-shirt. Please, Marcel, she said. She was showing off her arse to a bunch of dirty old men, that's what our great tragic actress was doing. Once again he squashed the invisible insect on the tip of his nose. And I still have photographs, he said.

The sailor going round checking tickets stopped in front of them and the woman rummaged in her bag. Ask him how much longer it'll be, said the man. I feel ill, this old bathtub is turning my stomach. The woman did her best to formulate the question in that strange language, and the sailor answered with a smile. About an hour and a half, she translated. The boat stops for two hours and then goes back. She put her glasses on again and adjusted her headscarf. Things aren't always what they seem, she said. What things? he asked. She smiled vaguely. Things, she said. And then went on: I was thinking of Albertine. The man grimaced, apparently impatient. You know what our great tragedian was called when she was at the Baguette? She was called Carole, Carole Don-Don. Nice, eh? He turned toward the sea, a wounded expression on his face, then came out with a small shout: look! He pointed southward. The woman turned and looked with him. On the horizon you could see the green cone of the island rising in sharp out-line from the water. We're getting near, the man said, pleased now, I don't think it'll take an hour and a half. Then he narrowed his eyes and leaned on the railings. There are rocks too, he added. He moved his arm to the left and pointed to two deep-blue outcrops, like two hats laid on the water. What nasty rocks, he said, they look like cushions. I can't see them, said the woman. There, said Marcel, a little bit more to the left, right in line with my finger, see? He slipped his right arm around the woman's shoulder, keeping his hand pointing in front. Right in the direction of my finger, he repeated.

The ticket collector had sat down on a bench near the railing. He had finished making his rounds and was watching their movements. Maybe he guessed what they were saying, because he went over to them, smiling, and spoke to the woman with an amused expression. She listened attentively, then exclaimed: noooo! and she brought a hand to her mouth with a mis-chievous, childish look, as though suppressing a laugh. What's he say? the man asked, with the slightly stolid expression of someone who can't follow a conversation. The woman gave the ticket collector a look of complicity. Her eyes were laughing and she was very attractive. He says they're not rocks, she said, deliberately holding back what she had learned. The man looked at her, questioning and perhaps a little annoyed. They're small blue whales stroll-ing about the Azores, she exclaimed, those are the exact words he used. And she at last let out the laugh she'd been holding back, a small, quick, ringing laugh. Suddenly her expression changed and she pushed back the hair the wind had blown across her face. You know at the airport I mistook someone else for you? she said, candidly revealing her association of ideas. He didn't even have the same build as you and he was wearing an extraordinary shirt you'd never put on, not even for Carnival, isn't it odd? The man made a gesture with his hand, butting in: I stayed behind in the hotel, you know, the deadline's getting closer and the script still needs going over. But the woman wouldn't let him interrupt. It must be because I've been thinking about you so much, she went on, and about these islands, the sun. She was speaking in what was almost a whisper now, as if to herself. I've done nothing all this time but think of you. It never stopped raining. I imagined you sitting on a beach. It's been too long, I think. The man took her hand. For me too, he said, but I haven't been to the beach much, the main thing I've been looking at is my typewriter. And then it rains here too, oh yes, you wouldn't believe the rain, how heavy it is. The woman smiled. I haven't even asked you if you managed to do it, and to think, if ideas were worth anything, I'd have written ten plays with trying to imagine yours: tell me what it's like, I'm dying to know. Oh, let's say it's a reworking of Ibsen in a light vein, he said, without disguising a certain enthusiasm – light, but a little bitter too, the way my stuff is, and seen from her point of view. How do you mean? asked the woman. Oh, the man said with conviction, you know the way things are going these days, I thought it would be wise to present it from her point of view, if I want people to take notice, even if that's not why I wrote it, of course. The story's banal in the end, a relationship breaking up, but all stories are banal, what matters is the point of view, and I rescue the woman, she is the real protagonist, he is selfish and mediocre, he doesn't even realize what he's losing, do you get me?

The woman nodded. I think so, she said, I'm not sure. In any case I've been writing some other stuff as well, he went on, these islands are a crushing bore, there's nothing to do to pass the time but write. And then I wanted to try my hand at a different genre. I've been writing fiction all my life. It seems nobler to me, the woman said, or at least more gratuitous, and hence, how can I put it, lighter ... Oh right, laughed the man, delicacy: *par délicatesse j'ai perdu ma vie*. But there comes a time when you have to have the courage to try your hand at reality, at least the reality of our own lives. And then, listen, people can't get enough of real-life experience, they're tired of the imaginings of novelists of no imagination. Very softly the woman asked: Are they memoirs? Her subdued voice quivered slightly with anxiety. Kind of, he said, but there's no elaboration of interpretation or memory; the bare facts and nothing more: that's what counts. It'll stir things up, said the woman. Let's say people will take notice, he corrected. The woman was silent for a moment, thoughtful. Do you already have a title? she asked. Maybe *Le regard sans école*, he said, what do you think? Sounds witty, she said.

Steering around in a wide curve, the boat began to sail along the coast of the island. Puffs of black smoke with a strong smell of diesel flew out of the funnel and the engine settled into a calm chug, as if enjoying itself. That's why it takes so long, the man said, the landing stage must be on the other side of the island.

You know, Marcel, the woman resumed, as if pursuing an idea of her own, I saw a lot of Albertine this winter. The boat proceeded in small lurches, as if the engine were jamming. They sailed by a little church right on the waterfront and they were so near they could almost make out the faces of the people going in. The bells summoning the faithful to Mass had a jarring sound, as though dragging their feet.

What?! The man chased the invisible insect from the tip of his nose. What on earth do you mean? he said. His face took on an expression of amazement and great disappointment. We kept each other company, she explained. A lot. It's important to keep each other company in life, don't you think? The man stood up and leaned on the railing, then sat on his seat again. But what do you mean, he repeated, have you gone mad? He seemed extremely restless, his legs couldn't keep still. She's an unhappy woman, and a generous one, the woman said, still following her own reasoning, I think she loved you a great deal. The man stretched out his arms in a disconsolate gesture and muttered something incomprehensible. Listen, forget it, he finally said with an effort, anyway, look, we've arrived.

The boat was preparing to dock. At the stern two men in T-shirts were unrolling the mooring cable and shouting to a third man standing on the landing stage watching them with his hands on his hips. A small crowd of relatives had gathered to greet the passengers and were waving. In the front row were two old women with black headscarves and a girl dressed up as though for her first communion hopping on one foot.

And what about the play, the woman suddenly inquired, as if all at once remembering something she had meant to ask, do you have a title for the play? You didn't tell me. Her companion was sorting out some newspapers and a small camera in a bag that bore the logo of an airline company. I've thought of hundreds and rubbished them all, he said, still bending down over his bag, not one that's really right, you need a witty title for a thing like this but something that sounds really good too. He stood up and a vague expression of hope lit up in his eyes. Why? he asked. Oh nothing, she said, just asking; I was thinking of a possible title, but maybe it's too frivolous, it wouldn't sound right on a serious poster, and then it's got nothing to do with your subject matter, it would sound completely incongruous. Oh come on, he begged, at least you can satisfy my curiosity, maybe it's brilliant. Silly, she said, completely off target.

The passengers crowded around the gangway and Marcel was sucked into the crush. The woman stood apart, holding on to the cable of the railing. I'll wait for you on the wharf, he shouted, without turning, I've got to move with the crowd! He raised an arm above the gaggle of heads, waving his hand. She leaned on the railing and began to gaze at the sea.

Translated by Tim Parks

Yo me enamoré
del aire

The taxi stopped in front of a wrought-iron gate painted green. The botanical garden is here, said the driver. He paid and got out. Do you know from which side you might be able to see a building from the twenties? he asked the driver. The man didn't seem to understand. It has some Art Nouveau friezes on the façade, he explained, it was certainly a building with some architectural value, I doubt they demolished it. The taxi driver shook his head and left. It must have been nearly 11:00 a.m. and he was starting to feel the strain – the trip had been long. The gate was wide open and a sign informed visitors that on Sundays admission was free and the doors closed at 2:00 p.m. He didn't have much time, then. He started down a driveway lined with tall, thin palm trees topped with meager tufts of green. He thought: so are these the Buritì? At home they always talked of the Buritì palms. At the end of the driveway the garden began, with a paved clearing from which little paths departed for the four cardinal points. A compass rose was designed in the paving stones. He stopped, not sure which direction to take: the botanical garden was large and he'd never find what he was seeking by closing time. He chose south. In his life he'd always looked south, and now that he'd arrived in this southern city he thought it fitting to continue in the same direction. Yet, within, he felt a *tramontana* breeze. He thought of the winds in life, because there are winds that accompany life: the soft zephyr, the warm wind of youth that later the mistral takes upon itself to cool down, certain southwesterly winds, the sirocco that weakens you, the icy mistral. Air, he thought, life is made of air, a breath and that's it, and after all we too are nothing but a puff, a breath, then one day the machine stops and that breath ends. He stopped too because he was panting. You're really short of breath, he told himself. The path climbed steeply toward the terraced land he could just make out beyond the shadows of some enormous magnolias. He sat on a bench and pulled a little notebook from his pocket. He jotted down the names of the countries of origin of the plants around him: the Azores, the Canary Islands, Brazil, Angola. With his pencil he drew some leaves and flowers, then, using the two pages at the center of the notebook, he drew the flower of a tree with a very strange name, which came from Canary-Azores. It was a magnificent giant with long lanceolate leaves and huge swollen flowers shaped like ears of corn, which seemed like fruit. The age of that giant was quite remarkable, he worked it out: at the time of the Paris Commune it must have already been full grown.

He'd caught his breath now, and he took off at a brisk pace down the path. The sun hit him straight on, blinding him. It was hot, yet the breeze from the ocean was fresh. The southern part of the botanical garden ended in that huge terrace that provided a complete panorama of the city: the valley and the old districts with their dense grid of roads and alleys, the buildings mostly white, yellow, and blue. From up there you could embrace the whole horizon, and far off to the right, beyond the port with its cranes, lay the open sea. The terrace was bordered by a low wall, only chest-high, on which the city was depicted in a mosaic of yellow and blue azulejos. He began deciphering the topography, trying to orient himself with that primitive map: the triumphal arch of the lower city from which the three main arteries departed, that Enlightenment architectural style owing to re- construction after the earthquake; the center, with the two large squares side by side, to the left the rotunda with the huge bronze monument, then the newer zone toward the north, its architecture typical of the fifties and sixties. Why did you come here? he asked himself, what are you looking for? It's all vanished, everybody evaporated, poof. He realized he'd spoken aloud and laughed at himself. He waved at the city, as if it were a person. In the distance, a bell rang three times. He checked his watch, it was a quarter to noon, he decided to visit a different part of the garden and headed back to another path. At that moment a voice reached him. A woman was singing, but he didn't know where. He stopped, trying to locate that sound. He went back, leaned over the wall, and looked down. Only then did he realize that to the left, just by the garden's steep embankment, there was a building. It was old, one side to the botanical garden, but its façade was fully visible, and he could see it was a building from the beginning of the twentieth century, at least judging by the stone cornices and the stucco friezes representing theatrical masks laced with laurel wreaths. On the building's flat roof was a huge terrace with chimneys jutting up and laundry cords running across it. The woman had her back to him, from behind she seemed a girl, she was hanging sheets but had to stand on tiptoe to reach the cords, her arms raised like a dancer. She was wearing a cotton print dress that outlined her slender body, and was barefoot. The breeze swelled the sheet toward her like a sail, and it seemed she was embracing it. Now she'd stopped singing, she bent over a wicker basket on a stool and pulled out colored garments, shirts it seemed to him, as though trying to decide which to hang first. He realized he was sweating a little. The voice he'd heard and no longer heard wasn't gone, he could still hear it in his head, as if it had left a continuing echo, and at the same time he felt a strange yearning, a truly curious sensation, as though his body had lost all weight and was now fleeing into the distance, who knows where. Sing again, he murmured, please, sing again. The girl had put on a head scarf, had taken the basket off the stool, and now was sitting on it, trying to find shelter from the sun in the little bit of shade created by the sheets. Her back was to him so she couldn't see him, but he stared at her,

mesmerized, unable to avert his gaze. Sing again, he whispered. He lit a cigarette and realized his hand was trembling. He thought he'd had an auditory
hallucination, sometimes we think we hear what we'd like to hear, nobody
would sing that song anymore, those who once sang it were all dead, and
then what song was it, from what era? It was quite old, from the sixteenth
century or earlier, who could say, was it a ballad, a chivalrous song, a song of
love, a song of farewell? He'd known it in another time, but that time was
no longer his. He searched his memory, and in an instant, as if an instant
could swallow up years, he returned to the time when somebody used to call
him Migalha. *Migalha* means crumb, he said to himself, back then you were
a crumb. Suddenly there came a strong gust of wind, the sheets snapped
in the wind, the woman stood and began to hang colored shirts and a pair
of short pants. Sing again, he whispered, please. At that moment the bells
of the church nearby began pealing the midday hour and, as though summoned by the sound, a boy leaned out of the little rooftop dormer, where
surely there was a set of stairs leading to the terrace, and ran toward her. He
must have been four or five, curly-haired, his sandals with two semicircular
openings at the toes and his shorts held up by suspenders. The girl put the
basket on the ground, crouched down, cried out: Samuele! and opened her
arms wide, and the boy dived into them, the girl stood and began spinning
around, hugging the boy, they were both spinning like a merry-go-round,

the boy's legs were outstretched, and she was singing, *Yo me enamoré del aire, del aire de una mujer, como la mujer era aire, con el aire me quedé.*

He let himself slide to the ground, his back against the wall, and he gazed upward. The blue of the sky was a color that painted a wide-open space. He opened his mouth to breathe that blue, to swallow it, and then he embraced it, hugging it to his chest. He was saying: *Aire que lleva el aire, aire que el aire la lleva, como tiene tanto rumbo no he podido hablar con ella, como lleva polisón el aire la bambolea.**

Translated by Martha Cooley and Antonio Romani

*A free translation of the two stanzas: "I was in love with the air, / With the air of a woman, / Because the woman was air, / I was left with a handful of air, / Air that car-ries off the air, / Air that the air carries off, / Because she went so quickly, / I couldn't talk with her, / As if it were lifting a skirt / The air swayed her."

Voices

for my friend M.I., who once entrusted me with a secret.

The first call came from a girl who'd phoned for the third time in three days and kept saying over and over that she just couldn't take it anymore. You have to be careful in these cases, as there's the risk of psycho-dependence. You have to be kind but cautious; the person calling needs to hear a friend on the other end of the line, not some deus-ex-machina that her life depends upon. But the main rule is that the caller shouldn't become attached to one particular voice: this can create difficulties. Depressed people slip into this quite easily, they need a confidant, aren't satisfied with an anonymous voice; it has to be *that* voice that they desperately cling to. But with a certain kind of depression, for those with a fixed idea they use to wall themselves off, the situation grows even more complicated. Their calls are chilling, and you rarely make a connection. This time, though, it went well, because I was fortunate enough to discover something of interest to her.

Another rule that's valid in a good number of cases: steer the conversation toward a topic of interest to the caller, because deep down, even the most desperate of callers have one thing that interests them, even those callers who are the most cut off from reality. Often it's a matter of our good will, you might need to resort to little tricks, to ploys; at times I've managed to clear up some seemingly impossible situations with a little game involving a glass, establishing some form of communication. Let's say the phone rings, you answer with the usual stock phrase, or something of the sort, and on the other end, nothing, absolute silence, not even someone breathing. So you insist, trying to be tactful, that you know someone's listening, so please say something, whatever you want, whatever comes to mind: an absurdity, a curse, a scream, a syllable. Nothing, complete silence. Yet if someone's called, there is a reason, but you can't know what that reason is – you don't know anything – the caller might be foreign, mute, anything. So I pick up a glass and a pencil and say: listen to me, in this world there are millions and millions of us, and yet we two have met, true, it's only on the phone, we haven't actually met or seen each other, but we have met, let's not throw away this meeting, it must mean something – listen to me – let's play a game, I have a glass here, I'll tap my pencil on it – *ting* – do you hear me? If you hear me, do the same, tap twice, or if there's nothing in front of you, tap the receiver with your nail, like this, *tick tick*, do you hear me? If so, then please answer, listen to me, I'll try and name a few things, what comes to mind, and you tell me if you like them, the sea, for instance, do you like the sea? For yes, tap twice, and once means no.

But it's hard to understand what interests a girl who dials a number, stays quiet for nearly two minutes, then starts in with: I just can't take it anymore, I just can't take it anymore, I just can't take it anymore, I just can't take it anymore. Like that: over and over. It was just pure luck, because I'd put on a record earlier, thinking that on August 15, the start of *Ferragosto*, it wouldn't be busy; and in fact my shift had been going for over two hours with no calls. It was incredibly hot out, the small fan I'd brought provided no relief, the city seemed dead, everyone gone, off on vacation, and I'd settled into an armchair and started to read, but the book dropped onto my chest, I don't like falling asleep on my watch, my reflexes are slow, and if someone calls, I'm startled for a few seconds, and sometimes it's these first seconds that count, because the person might hang up and might not have the courage to call again. So I put on Mozart's "Turkish March," the volume down, it's cheerful, stimulating, it keeps up your morale. She phoned while the record was playing and was quiet a long while, then started saying she just couldn't take it anymore, and I let her say it, because in these cases it's best to let the caller express herself, say anything she wants and as often as she wants; when I only heard her troubled breathing over the phone, I said: just a minute, all right? and I took off the record, and she said: no, leave it on. Of course, I said, I'd be happy to leave it on, so you like Brahms? I don't know how I'd sensed the music could provide a possible opening, the trick just came to me, sometimes a small untruth is providential; as for Brahms, probably the suggestion of the title by Sagan had played in my subconscious, a title always lying dormant in one's memory. That's not Brahms, she said, it's Mozart. What do you mean, Mozart? I said. Of course it's Mozart, she said quickly, it's the "Turkish March" by Mozart. And thanks to this she started talking about the conservatory where she'd studied before something happened to her, and everything went very well.

Time, then, passed slowly. I heard the bell of San Domenico's strike seven, and I went to the window, a light haze of heat over the city, a few cars going by on the street. I touched up my mascara, I sometimes feel pretty, and stretched out on the couch by the record player, and I thought about things, about people, life. The phone rang again at seven thirty. I said the usual stock phrase, maybe somewhat tiredly, on the other end came a moment of hesitation, then a voice said: my name is Fernando, but that doesn't make me an Italian gerund. It's always best to appreciate a caller's jokes – they show the desire to make contact – and I laughed. I answered that my grandfather's name was Andrei, but that didn't make him an Italian conditional, just Russian, and he laughed a little, too. And then he said that he did have something in common with verbs, though, a particular quality of verbs. He was intransitive. All verbs are useful in the construction of a sentence, I said. It felt like the conversation allowed for a certain allusiveness, plus you always needed to go along with a caller's chosen register. But I'm deponent, he said. Deponent in what sense, I asked. In the sense that I lay down, he said, I lay down my arms. Perhaps the mistake was thinking that arms shouldn't be laid down, wasn't that true? Perhaps we were taught bad grammar, it was better for belligerent people to arm themselves, so many people were unarmed, he certainly would be in good company. He said: could be, and I said our conversation sounded like a verb-conjugation table, and now it was his turn to laugh, a gruff chuckle. And then he asked me if I knew the sound of time. No, I said, I don't. Well, he said, all you have to do is sit on your bed, at night, when people can't sleep, just sit there with your eyes open in the dark, and after a little while you'll hear it, like a distant roar, like the sound of an animal breathing while it devours people. Why not tell me about those nights, there was all the time in the world, I had nothing better to do but sit and listen. But he was already off someplace else, he'd skipped over some crucial connection for me to follow his story; he didn't need this part, or perhaps wanted to avoid it. I just let him talk – there's never a reason for interrupting – but I didn't like his voice, it was a bit shrill, and then at times a whisper. The house is very large, he said, an old house, with furniture that belonged to my ancestors, awful, Empire-style, claw-foot furniture; and threadbare rugs, and paintings of gruff men and proud, unhappy women with slightly drooping lower lips. And why that curious shape to their mouths? – because the bitterness of an entire life outlines a lower lip and makes it droop, these women had spent sleepless nights beside stupid husbands incapable of affection, and these women, they too would lie in the dark, their eyes open and their resentment growing. There are still some of her things in the dressing room off my bedroom, things she left: some withered underclothes on a footstool, a simple gold chain she wore around her wrist, a tortoiseshell barrette. The letter sits on the bureau, beneath the glass bell that once protected a humongous alarm clock from Basel, the alarm clock I broke when I was a boy, one day, when I was sick, and no one came up to see me; I remember like it was yesterday, I got up and took the clock out from under that protective glass, the tick-tock was so scary, and I removed the bottom and methodically took the clock apart until there were tiny gears strewn across the sheet. I can read it to you if you want, the letter, I mean – no – I can recite it from memory, I read it every night: Fernando, if only you knew how much I've hated you all these years ... that's how it starts, the rest you can gather on your own, that glass bell guards a massive, repressed hatred.

And then he skipped over another part, but this time I think I understood the connection, and he said: and little Giacomo? How do you suppose he turned out? He's a man, somewhere, out in the world. And then I asked if that letter was from August fifteenth – I'd sensed it was – and he said yes, it was the exact anniversary, and he'd celebrate it accordingly, he had his instrument for celebrating all ready to go, it was there, on the table, by the phone.

He was silent, and I waited for him to go on, but he didn't speak. Then I said: wait another anniversary, Fernando, try to wait one more year. Right away I knew how ridiculous that sounded, but nothing else came to mind, I was talking just to talk, and in the end it's the idea that mattered. I've listened to all sorts of phone calls, to all sorts of people, in the most absurd of situations, and yet this was perhaps the time my normal bravura wavered, and I felt lost as well, like I needed someone else to sit and listen and tell me a few kind words. It was only for a moment, he didn't answer, and I pulled myself together, now I knew what to say, I could talk about micro-visions, and I talked about micro-perspectives. Because in life there are all kinds of perspectives, so-called broad perspectives that everyone thinks of as fundamental, and those I call micro-perspectives, that I admit are probably insignificant, but if everything is relative, if nature allows for both ants and eagles to exist, then I wonder why can't we live like ants, through micro-perspectives. Yes, micro-perspectives, I insisted, and he found my definition entertaining, but what do these micro-perspectives consist of, he asked, and I was determined to explain. The micro-perspective is a *modus vivendi*, let's say it is, anyway, a means to focus our attention, *all* our attention, on one small detail of life, the daily grind, as if this detail were the most important thing in the world – but ironically – knowing it's not even slightly the most important thing in the world, and that everything is relative. Making lists helps, jotting down appointments, following strict schedules, not compromising. The micro-perspective is a concrete way to stick to concrete things.

He didn't seem particularly convinced, but my objective wasn't to try and convince him. I knew perfectly well I wasn't revealing the secret of the philosopher's stone; but just that he felt someone might be interested in his problems had to help. It was all I could do. He asked if he could call me at home. Sorry, I didn't have a phone. And here? Sure, here, whenever he liked, no, unfortunately, not tomorrow, but he could leave me a message of course, no, he had to, a friend would be here in my place who would pass it on to me, I'd be happy to hear about the micro-perspective of his day.

He said goodbye politely, sounding somewhat sorry. It was a hot night, but I hadn't noticed – sometimes talking takes a crazy level of concentration. From the window I watched Gulliver crossing the street, coming to relieve me, Gulliver, visible from the top of a skyscraper – we don't call him Gulliver for nothing – I gathered up my things. Only then did I notice it was already ten to nine, damn it, I'd promised Paco I'd be home by nine sharp, but even if I hurried now, I wouldn't make it by nine thirty. Not to mention public transportation – a disaster most days, much less August fifteenth. Maybe it would be better to walk. I darted past Gulliver, didn't even give him the chance to say hello, he called after me, joking, I answered from the stairs that I had a date, so please be on time in the future; I left him the fan though he didn't deserve it. At the front door, just by luck, I saw the 32 rounding the corner, it wouldn't get me home but would save me a good distance, so I jumped on; it was completely empty, which was unsettling, considering what it was like most evenings. The driver was going so slowly, I felt like saying something, but let it pass – he seemed so resigned, his eyes so dull. Well, I thought, if Paco's annoyed, too bad – it's not like I can fly; I got off at the stop by the department stores, and I did hurry, but it was already nine twenty-five, so no point in running only to be late anyway but sweaty and gasping like a crazy person. I slipped in the key, trying to be quiet. The house was dark and silent, unsettling, for some reason, I thought of something unpleasant, and anxiety washed over me. I said: Paco, Paco, it's me, I'm back. Briefly, I felt consumed by despair. I laid my books and purse on the stool in the entranceway and then approached the living room door. Paco, Paco, I felt like saying. At times, silence is an awful thing. I know what I would've like to tell him, if he were there: please, Paco, I'd say, it's not my fault, I had an endless call, and transportation's on a reduced schedule, it's August fifteenth. I went to close the door to the back balcony, because the mosquitos in the garden swarm inside when a light goes on. I recalled there were still tins of caviar and paté in the refrigerator that could be opened, and a bottle of Moselle wine. I laid a yellow linen placemat on the table, and a red candle. My kitchen furniture is of light wood, and the candlelight gives the room a soothing feel. While I was making my preparations, I called again, faintly: Paco. I took a spoon and just tapped a glass, *ting*, then tapped harder, *ting!*, the sound lingered all through the apartment. And then I had an inspiration. Opposite my plate I set a placemat, a plate, silverware, and a glass. I filled both glasses, then went into the bathroom to freshen up. And if he really did return, what then? Sometimes reality surpasses the imagination. He'd hit the buzzer twice, two short bursts, the way he always did, and I'd open the door a crack, like an accomplice: I set the table for two, I'd say, I was expecting you, I don't know why, but I was expecting you. Who knows what sort of face he'd make.

Translated by Janice M. Thresher

Postscript

A Whale's View of Man

Always so feverish, and with those long limbs waving about. Not rounded at all, so they don't have the majesty of complete, rounded shapes sufficient unto themselves, but little moving heads where all their strange life seems to be concentrated. They arrive sliding across the sea, but not swimming, as if they were birds almost, and they bring death with frailty and graceful ferocity. They're silent for long periods, but then shout at each other with unexpected fury, a tangle of sounds that hardly vary and don't have the perfection of our basic cries: the call, the love cry, the death lament. And how pitiful their lovemaking must be: and bristly, brusque almost, immediate, without a soft covering of fat, made easy by their threadlike shape, which excludes the heroic difficulties of union and the magnificent and tender efforts to achieve it.

They don't like water, they're afraid of it, and it's hard to understand why they bother with it. Like us they travel in herds, but they don't bring their females, one imagines they must be elsewhere, but always invisible.

Sometimes they sing, but only for themselves, and their song isn't a call to others, but a sort of longing lament. They soon get tired and when evening falls they lie down on the little islands that take them about and perhaps fall asleep or watch the moon. They slide silently by and you realize they are sad.

Translated by Tim Parks

THE ENGLISH TRANSLATIONS of Dino Campana's verses are taken from *Canti Orfici / Orphic Songs* (Bordighera Press, 2003), Translation, Introduction and Notes by Luigi Bonaffini. The specific lines quoted are from "Prison Dream" (p. 167), "To a Whore with Steel-Gray Eyes" (p. 277), "La petite promenade du poète" (p. 97), "Carnival Night" (p. 95), "Arabesco Olimpia" (p. 245), "Genoese Woman" (p. 277), and "A Trolley Ride to America and Back" (p. 195). Dr. Carlo Pariani was the psychiatrist who treated the poet at the hospital in Castel Pulci, Florence, where he was admitted in 1918 and where he remained until his death in 1932.

"**L**etter from casablanca," "Little Gatsby," "Voices," and "The Reversal Game" are translated by Janice M. Thresher and appeared in *Letter from Casablanca* (New Directions, 1986); "Little Misunderstandings of No Importance," "Islands," "The Trains That Go to Madras," and "Cinema" are translated by Frances Frenaye and appeared in *Little Misunderstandings of No Importance* (New Directions, 1987); "Wanderlust" and "The Cheshire Cat" are translated by Anne Milano Appel and appear in *Il gioco del rovescio* (Feltrinelli, 1991); "The Flying Creatures of Fra Angelico," "Message from the Shadows," "The phrase that follows this is false: the phrase that precedes this is true," and "The Translation" from *The Flying Creatures of Fra Angelico* (Archipelago Books, 2012) and "Small Blue Whales Strolling about the Azores," "The Woman of Porto Pim," and "Postscript" from *The Woman of Porto Pim* (Archipelago, 2013) are translated by Tim Parks; "Drip, Drop, Drippity-Drop," "Clouds," "Yo me enamoré aire," "Bucharest Hasn't Changed a Bit," and "Against Time" are translated by Martha Cooley and Antonio Romani, and appeared in *Time Ages in a Hurry* (Archipelago, 2015); "Night, Sea, or Distance" first appeared in *L'angelo nero* (Feltrinelli, 1991) is translated by Elizabeth Harris.

archipelago books
is a not-for-profit literary press devoted to
promoting cross-cultural exchange through innovative
classic and contemporary international literature
www.archipelagobooks.org